LONE STAR NOIR

LONE STAR NOIR

EDITED BY BOBBY BYRD & JOHNNY BYRD

AKASHIC BOOKS

This collection is comprised of works of fiction. All names, characters, places, and incidents are the product of the authors' imaginations. Any resemblance to real events or persons, living or dead, is entirely coincidental.

Published by Akashic Books
©2010 Akashic Books

Series concept by Tim McLoughlin and Johnny Temple
Texas map by Aaron Petrovich

ISBN-13: 978-1-936070-64-0
Library of Congress Control Number: 2010922717

First printing

Akashic Books
PO Box 1456
New York, NY 10009
info@akashicbooks.com
www.akashicbooks.com

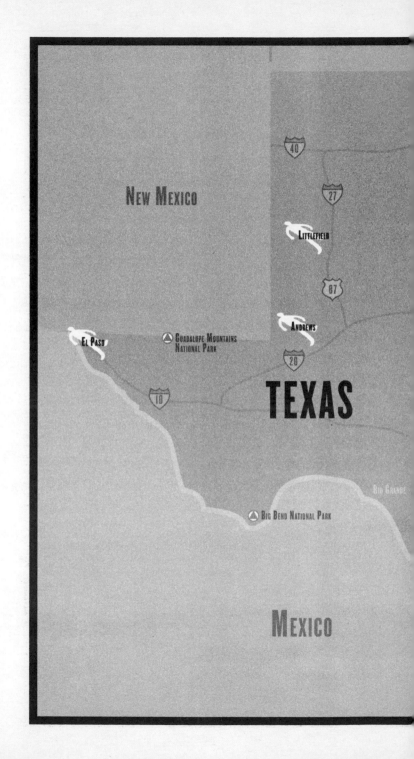

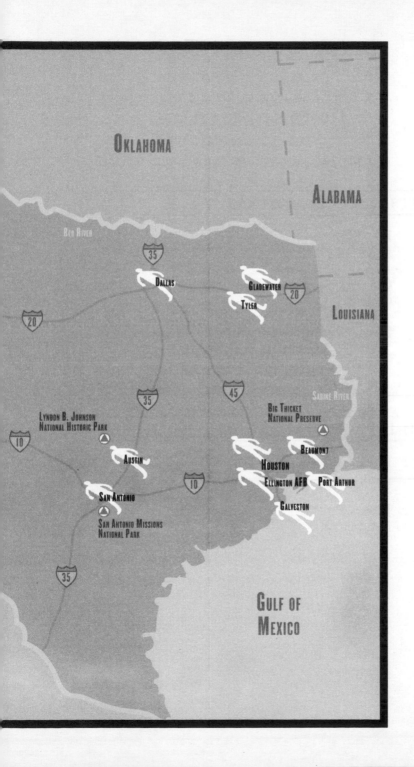

TABLE OF CONTENTS

PART III: BIG CITY TEXAS

INTRODUCTION
WHAT THE HELL IS TEXAS, ANYWAY?

I dearly love the state of Texas,
but I consider that a harmless perversion on my part,
and discuss it only with consenting adults.
—Molly Ivins

Forgive me, but I am a poet by trade. I don't come to noir fiction on the morning train in the bright sunlight. I come obliquely through the back roads of my poetics and love for the American idiom. I'm a member of the second generation of those notorious "New American Poets" anthologized by Donald Allen in 1960. Folks like Robert Creeley, Paul Blackburn, Philip Whalen, Jack Spicer, Ed Dorn, Gary Snyder, and, yes, Ginsberg and Jack Kerouac—radical workers of the language back in their day. Because of these roots, and like so many of my fellow travelers, I have always been drawn to noir fiction. Especially as it's practiced in America. My heroes from the beginning were Dashiell Hammett and Raymond Chandler, and later in the 1990s Elmore Leonard came along to feed my imagination when my writing needed an injection of hard-boiled storytelling and cutthroat dialogue.

But Texas? That was another journey. Growing up in Memphis and living for years in Arizona, Colorado, and New Mexico, I never would have guessed that I would move to Texas. Yet, here I am, a longtime Texan.

When my family and I moved south from Albuquerque thirty-something years ago, we asked our friends (the worse sort—writers, intellectuals, ex-hippies) from the so-called "land of enchantment" where we should move: Las Cruces, New Mexico, or El Paso. "Las Cruces," they all said without blinking. They sneered at anything Texas. That's common in New Mexico. Colorado too. Texans are the Ugly Americans of the American Southwest. That's the stereotype. Loud and arrogant. They buy a piece of land in the mountains, wanting to flee the flatlands and horrendous weather of Texas, and they bring Texas along with them.

So, taking our friends' advice, we moved to Las Cruces. It was a mistake of the first order. After a couple of years we got bored. We started sniffing around El Paso forty-five miles down the road. Life was different there, somehow weird, a taste of dark mystery even in the bright Chihuahuan desert sunlight—Spanish in the streets, goddamned real-life cowboys, Mennonites and Mormons from Mexico, a whole herd of Lebanese immigrants, the red-light district of Juárez a stone's throw from downtown, regular people who transformed themselves into strange gory tales in the newspaper, the hot dog vendor on the street with his little stash of cheap dope to pay the bills, the bloody smell of the 1910 Mexican Revolution still hanging in the air. The place actually echoes loudly in the American psyche. It pops up all over American literature—Ambrose Bierce, Jack Kerouac, Oscar Zeta Acosta, Carlos Fuentes, Dagoberto Gilb, Benjamin Alire Sáenz, James Crumley, Abraham Verghese, Cormac McCarthy, and so many more. The place felt like home.

So I got my feet Texas wet in El Paso. Why we didn't move here in the first place, I'll never know. But people in El Paso will tell you they don't live in Texas anyway. They live in El Paso.

Huh?

Seems like everybody who lives in Texas has a snotty attitude about the place where they live. Even if they hate it. Like the bumper sticker from the 1980s, *Lucky me, I'm from Lubbock.* That was popular the year after Lubbock almost got wiped off the map by a series of God's worst tornados. But what you learn from living in this state is that most of Texas is not Texas. It's not the stereotype that the rest of the nation carries around in the collective consciousness. During the 2008 Obama-versus-Hillary Democratic primary madness, the national press complained that Texas did not fit into the Red State cookie cutter they expected. Beaumont was nothing like Austin which was nothing like Odessa which was nothing like Houston. And Marfa, how did that happen? The talking heads were confused. One guy I saw on TV said, "Texas is not like any other state. It's huge, it's insanely diverse, it's more like a country."

Bingo!

I got a hunch the talking heads never got close to Chicken Shit Bingo. In Austin you can go play Chicken Shit Bingo. The rooster walks around a big board with all the numbers on it. And wherever the rooster takes a shit, that's the number that gets called out. That's Texas.

Chicken Shit Bingo is the Texas of *Lone Star Noir.*

But really, for the world at large, Texas is not so much a state or a country. It's popular legend pumped up on steroids to become mythos.

Back in the '70s and '80s, the American media gave us two hunks of the Texas legend. One was the prime-time soap opera *Dallas.* Millions of men and women from around the country—indeed, from around the world—scheduled their lives so they wouldn't miss *Dallas.* At its center was J.R. Ewing, the epitome of Texas cynicism and greed played ever so shrewdly by Larry Hagman. He wore his $5,000 suits, his top-dollar Stetson, and his elegant chocolate crocodile-hide cowboy boots. When was J.R. ever going to have to pay up for his sins and his silk underwear? The guy had enough money and power to buy Houston, but he'd screw his best friend to get more. And after lunch he'd screw the guy's wife. J.R. enjoyed those sins of his, and he very much enjoyed being a Texan. Indeed, he flaunted Texas. Big and rich Texas. And his public hated him and loved him at the same time.

The cowboy side of that Texas coin was embodied in Larry McMurtry's *Lonesome Dove*. The novel became a hugely popular television miniseries starring Robert Duvall and Tommy Lee Jones as ex–Texas Rangers Woodrow Call and Gus Mc-Crae. The story is simple. Those old boys get tired of living the ranching life down on the Rio Grande so they go steal a herd of longhorns from the "Meskins," killing a few in the bargain. The series follows the heroes and their herd up through Texas to Wyoming with enough adventures and fights and evil to satisfy Ulysses fresh from the killing fields of Troy. McMurtry is a scholar about cowboy life and the great cattle drives of the nineteenth century, and so the book and the miniseries are rich with the lifestyle and paraphernalia of cowboy legend. The stuff of Texas lore. Neither the book nor the TV series, it should be noted, was kind to Mexicans, blacks, Indians, or women. But, as a matter of fact, the Texas Rangers and the state of Texas weren't exactly kind to these citizens either. It's like a Texas disease.

Still, you can drive around Texas for a long time and never meet J.R. Ewing or Woodrow Call. The real Texas hides out in towns and cities like you'll find in *Lone Star Noir*, and in that very Texas reality, among the everyday good folks of Texas, you'll find the hard-boiled understanding of guns and dope and blood money and greed and hatred and delusion that makes these fourteen stories come alive on the page. Sure, you might catch a glimpse of J.R. and old Woodrow Call, like a shadow at the edge of your sight, feel their heat at your back, catch a whiff of the dead flowers which are their Texas dreams. This is basic foodstuff for a Texas writer telling a story, but the story must always stay true to its place and the people who live there. That's the strength of these stories in *Lone Star Noir*—the particular place they come from, the language that the characters speak. Yes, they are pieces of the larger puzzle that is Texas, but they are more true to the pieces of ground they reveal.

Texas, in all its many places, bleeds noir fiction.

In putting together the collection, we had to decide how to group the stories. Texas is not easily divided. It's not a pie chart. But like most things literary, the stories themselves told us how to do the job. People think of Texas, they think cowboys and dirt farming. They think "Back Roads Texas." But Texas has changed. Lee Harvey Oswald and Jack Ruby made sure we got that message. "Big City Texas"—Houston, Dallas, San Antonio, Austin, El Paso—is now the face of the state. But we also had these strange and dark stories from the Gulf Coast, so different than tales from the cities and back roads. Those stories made a place for themselves. And luckily for us, the only two carpetbaggers in the collection—Luis Alberto Urrea and David Corbett—collaborated on a road journey across Texas. That story's heart is in the Cajun world of the Gulf Coast, but it wanders upstream on Interstate 10 through San Antonio and careens toward El Paso, finally to disappear in the darkness that is now Juárez, 2010. It reminds us that all these stories are tied together by the Texas that is right now.

Speaking of luck, nothing could have been better karma than having an unpublished story from James Crumley

(1939–2008). Jim's widow Martha Elizabeth in Missoula, a wonderful lady and a true keeper of Jim's flame, was delighted to work with us and she found nestled in one of his files the story "Luck." Now being hailed as "the patron saint of the post-Vietnam private eye novel," Jim was born in Three Rivers and raised in South Texas. He was one of those writers who could hate Texas and love Texas in the same sentence. He understood Texas, his own piece of Texas—its language, its machismo, its fears and loves—even if he fled the place. His busted-up heroes Milo Milodragovitch and C.W. Sughrue don't exist without Texas.

Many people have aided and abetted this anthology, and Johnny Byrd and I thank them, especially David Thompson of Murder by the Book in Houston, Clay Smith of the Texas Book Festival, Susan Post of BookWoman in Austin, Milton T. Burton, and Bill Cunningham. Props go out to publisher Johnny Temple (a.k.a. Johnny Akashic)—friend and colleague. The guy has patience, the guy has smarts. Thanks and kudos especially to the writers, all of whom came up with such excellent stories, some like Joe R. Lansdale and Jessica Powers at very short notice.

And finally, on a very personal note, I want to say that it's been an honor to work with my coeditor and son Johnny Byrd. He brings a wise and steady hand to the sometimes erratic whims of his old man.

It's been such a pleasure.

And now it's done. I hope there will be more. One *Lone Star Noir* won't do the job.

Bobby Byrd
El Paso, TX
August 2010

PART I

GULF COAST TEXAS

Well, you better walk right, you better not stagger,
and you better not fight . . .
—Leadbelly

PHELAN'S FIRST CASE

BY LISA SANDLIN

Beaumont

Five past eight. Phelan sat tipped back in his desk chair, appreciating the power of the *Beaumont Enterprise*. They'd centered the ad announcing his new business, boxed it in black, and spelled his name right. The other ad in the classifieds had brought in two girls yesterday. He figured to choose the brunette with the coral nails and the middle-C voice. But just then he got a call from his old high school bud Joe Ford, now a parole officer, and Joe was hard-selling.

"Typing, dictation, whatcha need? She learned it in the big house. Paid her debt to society. What say you talk to her?"

"Find some other sucker. Since when are you Acme Employment?"

"Since when are you a private eye?"

"Since workers' comp paid me enough bread to swing a lease."

"For a measly finger? Thought you liked the rigs."

"Still got nine fingers left. Aim to keep 'em."

"Just see this girl, Tommy. She knows her stuff."

"Why you pushing her?"

"Hell, phones don't answer themselves, do they?"

"Didn't they invent a machine that—"

Joe blew scorn through the phone. "Communist rumor. Lemme send her over. She can get down there in two shakes."

"No."

"I'm gonna say this one time. Who had your back the night you stepped outside with Narlan Pugh and all his cousins stepped outside behind him?"

"One time, shit. I heard it three. Time you realized gratitude comes to a natural end, same as a sack of donuts."

Joe bided.

Phelan stewed.

"Goddamnit, no promises."

"Naw! Course not. Make it or break it on her own. Thanks for the chance, it'll buck her up."

Phelan asked about the girl's rap sheet but the dial tone was noncommittal.

Drumming his fingers, he glanced out his window toward the Mobil refinery's methane flare, Beaumont's own Star of Bethlehem. Far below ran a pewter channel of the Neches, sunlight coating the dimples of the water. Black-hulled tankers were anchored in the port, white topsides, striped flags riffling against the drift of spring clouds.

Or that's the view he'd have once his business took off—San Jacinto Building, seventh floor. Mahogany paneling, brass-trimmed elevator. Now he looked out on the New Rosemont, *$1 and Up*, where a ceiling fan once fell on the proprietress. The secretary's office had a window too, where sunlight and humidity pried off the paint on the Rosemont's fire escape.

8:32. Footsteps were sounding on the stairs to his second-story walk-up.

Wasn't skipping up here, was she? Measured tread. The knock on the door lately lettered *Thomas Phelan, Investigations* wasn't fast, wasn't slow. Not loud, not soft.

Phelan opened up. Well. Not a girl. Couple crows had

stepped lightly at the corners of her eyes; a faint crease of bitter slanted from the left side of her barely tinted lips. Ash-brown hair, jaw-length, roomy white blouse, navy skirt. Jailhouse tan. Eyes gray-blue, a little clouded, distant, like a storm rolling in from out in the gulf. This one wouldn't sit behind the desk blowing on her polish. The hand he was shaking had naked nails cut to the quick.

"Tom Phelan."

"Delpha Wade." Her voice was low and dry.

Delpha Wade. His brain ratcheted a picture toward him but not far enough, like when a Mars bar gets hung up partway out the vending machine.

They sat down in his office, him in a gimpy swivel behind a large metal desk, both included in the rent. Her in one of the proud new clients' chairs, padded leather with regally tall backs.

"Gotta be honest with you, Miss Wade. Think I already found a secretary."

No disappointment in those blue eyes, no hope either. She just passed a certificate with a gold seal across the desk. The paper said she typed seventy words a minute, spoke shorthand, could do double entry. The brunette with the coral nails claimed all that too, but she'd backed it up with a giggle, not a diploma from Gatesville.

"Your first choice of a job a P.I.'s office?"

"My first choice is a job."

Touché. "What number interview would this be for you?"

"Number one."

"I'm flattered. Get off the bus, you come here."

The blue eyes let in a smidgen of light. "Course that doesn't count the dozen applications I wrote out 'fore they showed me the door."

No wonder Joe was pushing her. "Had your druthers . . . where'd you work, Miss Wade?"

"Library. I like libraries. It's what I did *there*."

There being Gatesville. Now that she'd brought it up. "How many you do?"

"Fourteen."

Phelan quelled the whistle welling up. That let out check-kiting, forgery, embezzling from the till, and probably dope. He was about to ask her the delicate when she handed it to him on a foil tray. "Voluntary manslaughter."

"And you did fourteen?"

"He was very dead, Mr. Phelan."

His brain shoved: the picture fell into the slot. Phelan'd been a teenager, jazzed by blood-slinging, and reporters had loved the story. Waitress in a bayou dive, waiting for the owner to collect the take. Alone. Two guys thrown out earlier came back—beat her, raped her, cut her. Father and son, that was the kicker. That, and they went for the girl before the cash register. But surprise. Somehow the knife had changed hands. The father'd got punctured and son sliced. When the owner's headlights showed, dear old Dad ran for their heap and peeled. Delpha Wade had not let nature take its course. She finished off Junior in the oyster-shell parking lot.

The Gatesville certificate was being fit into a faded black leather clutch, years out of date. She gathered her feet under her. But didn't stand up. Those eyes got to him. No hope, no despair. Just a storm cloud back on the blue horizon.

The outer door tapped. A hesitant tap, like a mouse was out there. "'Scuse me," Phelan said and stood. His chair flopped its wooden seat upward like its next occupant would arrive in it via the ceiling. He wrenched it up; the seat surrendered again. "Gotta fix that," he muttered.

When he looked up, he saw Delpha Wade's straight back, walking out. Funny, he'd had the impression she wouldn't fold so easy.

"Forgot your purse, Miss Wade."

"No, I didn't." She shut the door between their offices—or rather, the door between his office and whoever got the secretary job's office—soundlessly. He heard, "Good morning, ma'am. Do you have an appointment to see Mr. Phelan?" Her dry voice was smooth as a Yale lock.

Phelan smiled. *I'll be damned.* He tipped the chair's seat into loading position and sat in it, like the boss should.

Mumbling.

"May I ask what your visit is in reference to?"

More mumbling, a lot of it. Then—Phelan hated this sound—sobbing. Not that he hadn't prepared for it. He'd bought a box of Kleenex at the dime store for the broken-hearted wives. Stashed it in the desk's bottom drawer next to the husbands' fifth of Kentucky. Had his .38 license in his wallet, P.I. license on the wall, newly minted business cards on the desk. An ex-con impersonating a secretary.

Delpha Wade entered, closing the door behind her. "Can you see a client now, Mr. Phelan?"

"Bring her on." He was rooting for a cheated-on society matron in crocodile pumps, her very own checkbook snapped inside a croc bag.

"You can go in now, Mrs. Toups."

A bone-thin woman in yesterday's makeup and rumpled shirtwaist took the doorway. Leatherette purse in her fists, little gold nameplate like a cashier's pinned over her left breast. The two slashes between her eyebrows tightened. "You're kinda young. I was looking for—"

"An old retired cop?" Delpha Wade said. On *cop* her neutral voice bunched. "Mr. Phelan has a fresh point of view."

What Mr. Phelan had was a fresh legal pad. He wielded a ballpoint over it. "Please, sit down, Mrs. Toups. Tell me what I can do for you."

Delpha Wade scooped an elbow, tucked her into the client chair, at the same time saying, "Can I get you some coffee? Cream and sugar?"

Phelan furrowed his own brow, trying to grow some wrinkles. *Coffee*, he thought. *What coffee?*

"Take a Coke, if you got one."

The inner door closed behind Delpha Wade, and he heard the outer door shut too. His first client stammered into her story; Phelan's ballpoint despoiled the virginal legal pad. The Kleenex stayed in their drawer. Caroleen Toups had her own hankie.

By the time his nonsecretary returned with a dewy bottle of Coke, Phelan had the story. The Toups's lived over on the north side, not far off Concord, nothing that could be called a neighborhood, more like one of a string of old wooden houses individually hacked out of the woods. Her boy Richard was into something and she didn't like it. He'd been skipping school. Running around all hours. Then last night Richard had not come home.

Gently, Phelan asked, "Report that to the police?"

"Seven o'clock this morning. They said boys run off all the time. Said been a bunch of boys running off lately. Four or five. Like it's a club."

Phelan silently agreed, **having** once woken up with two or three friends on a New Orleans sidewalk, littered, lacquered, and convinced somebody'd driven rebar through his forehead. "What does your husband think?"

"He passed last fall. Took a virus in his heart." Her reddened eyes offered to share that grief with him, but Phelan bowed his head and went on.

"Does Richard have a favorite item of clothing?"

"Some silly shoes that make him taller. And a Johnny Winter T-shirt he bought at a concert over in Port Arthur."

"Would you know if those are gone from his room?"

"I would . . . Mr. Phelan." Having managed to bestow on T. Phelan's callow mug that title of respect, Mrs. Toups looked at him hopefully. "They're not."

"Have a piggy bank?"

She snapped the purse open and took out a roll, Andrew Jackson on top. "Till about midnight," she said, "I read the *Enterprise*. That's where I saw your ad. After midnight I searched my son's room with a fine-tooth comb. This was in a cigar box under his bed. Along with some baseball cards and twisty cigarettes. There's $410 here. Ricky's in tenth grade, Mr. Phelan. He don't have a job."

The phone rang in the outer office, followed by the light click of the reconditioned Selectric. "You wouldn't a brought a picture of him?"

Mrs. Toups dug into the leatherette, handed over a school photo. Fair and baby-faced, long-haired like a lot of kids these days. Grinning like he was saddled on a Christmas pony. Ricky Toups when he still had a daddy.

The mother's tired eyes held a rising rim of water. "Why I wanted you to look old and tough—you find Ricky, scare him good. I cain't take any more a this."

Phelan was jolted by a gut feeling, a pact connecting him to that haggard mother. He hadn't expected it. "Okay," he said quickly. While Mrs. Toups sipped her Coke, he scrawled her address and phone number, then jotted an inventory of

Ricky's friends. Make that friend, a neighbor girl, Georgia Watson. School? French High, Phelan's own alma mater, an orange-brick sprawl with a patchy football field. The legal pad was broken in now.

He wrote her name on a standard contract and slid it toward her. He'd practiced the next part so he could spit it out without blinking. "Fee is seventy-five a day. Plus expenses."

Nobody was blinking here. Mrs. Toups peeled off five Jacksons. "Could you start now?"

"First day's crucial on a missing-child case," Phelan said, like he knew. "You're at the top of the schedule."

He guided Mrs. Toups through the outer office to the door. To his right, Delpha Wade sat behind the secretary's desk, receiver tucked into her neck, typing. Typing what? And where had she got the paper?

"A Mrs. Lloyd Elliott would like to speak with you about a confidential matter. Says her husband's an attorney." Delpha Wade's dry voice was hushed, and she rubbed her thumb and fingers together in the universal sign for money.

She got that right. According to the *Enterprise*, Lloyd Elliott had just won some court case that paid him 30 percent of yippee-I-never-have-to-work-again.

Mrs. Toups stuck her reddened face back in the door, a last plea on it. But at the sight of Phelan taking the phone, she ducked her head and left.

"Tom Phelan," he said. Crisply, without one *um* or *you know*, the woman on the phone told him she wanted her husband followed, where to, and why. She'd bring by a retainer. Cash.

"That'll work. Get back to you soon. Please leave any relevant details with my . . . with Miss Wade. You can trust her."

And don't I hope that's true, he thought, clattering down the stairs.

The band was playing when Phelan pulled up to French High School. God, did he remember this parking lot: clubhouse, theater, and smoking lounge. He lit up for nostalgia's sake.

A little shitkicker perched on the trunk of a Mustang pushed back his Resistol. He had his boots on the bumper, one knee jackhammering hard enough to shiver the car. Phelan offered him a smoke.

Haughtily, the kid produced some Bull and rolled his own. "Take a light."

Phelan obliged. "You know Georgia Watson?"

"Out there. Georgia's in Belles." The boy lofted his chin toward the field that joined the parking lot.

"What about Ricky Toups?"

The kid tugged down the hat, blew out smoke. "Kinda old to be into weed, ain't ya?"

"That why people come looking for Ricky?"

Marlboro-Man-in-training doused the homemade, stashed it behind his ear. Slid off the trunk and booked.

Phelan turned toward the field, where the band played a lazy version of "Grazing in the Grass." The Buffalo Belles were high-kicking, locked shoulder to shoulder. Line of smiling faces, white, black, and café au lait, bouncing hair and breasts, 120 teenage legs, kicked up high. Fondly remembering a pair of those white boots hooked over his shoulders postgame, he strolled toward the rousing sight.

After their routine, the girls milled sideline while the band marched patterns. Phelan asked for Georgia and found her, said he wanted to talk.

This is who Ricky Toups thought hung the moon? Georgia

Watson had an overloaded bra, all right, and cutoffs so short the hems of white pockets poked out like underwear. But she was a dish-faced girl with frizzled hair and cagey brown eyes. Braided gold chain tucked into the neck of a white T-shirt washed thin.

She steered him away from the knots of babbling girls. Her smile threw a murky light into the brown eyes. Black smudges beneath them from her gobbed eyelashes.

He introduced himself with a business card. "Ricky Toups's mother asked me to check up on him. He got any new friends you know about?"

She jettisoned the smile, shrugged.

"C'mon, Georgia. Ricky thinks you're his friend."

She made a production of whispering, "Ricky was helping this guy with something, but I think that's all over."

"Something."

"Something," she hissed. She angled toward some girls staring frankly at them and fluttered her fingers in a wave. Nobody waved back.

"This guy. Why's Ricky not helping him anymore?"

Georgia shook her head, looking over Phelan's shoulder like she was refusing somebody who wasn't there. "Fun at first, then he turned scary. Ricky's gonna quit hanging out with him, even though that means—" Her trap shut.

"Giving up the green," Phelan finished. His little finger flicked out the braided chain around the girl's neck. Fancy G in twenty-four carat. "How long y'all had this scary friend?"

The head shaking continued, like a tic now.

Phelan violated her personal space. "Name. And where the guy lives."

The girl backed up. "I don't know, some D name, Don or Darrell or something. Gotta go now."

Phelan caught her arm. "Ricky didn't come home last night."

White showed around the brown eyes. She spit out a sentence, included her phone number when pressed, then jerked her arm away and ran back to the other girls on the sideline. They practiced dance steps in bunches, laughed, horsed around. Georgia stood apart biting her bottom lip, the little white square of his business card pinched in her fingers.

11:22. He drove back to the office, took the stairs two at a time. Delpha handed him Mrs. Lloyd Elliott's details neatly typed on the back of a sheet of paper. Phelan read it and whistled. "Soon's she brings that retainer, Lloyd better dig himself a foxhole."

He flipped the sheet over. Delpha Wade's discharge from Gatesville: *April 7, 1973. Five foot six, 120 pounds. Hair brown, eyes blue. Thirty-four. Voluntary manslaughter.*

"Only paper around," she said.

Phelan laid a ten on the desk. "Get some. Then see what's up in the Toups's neighborhood, say, the last three months. Thought this was a kid pushing weed for pocket money, but could be dirtier water." He told her what Georgia Watson had given him: the D name, Don or Darrell, and that Ricky brought other boys over to the guy's house to party. "I'm guessing Georgia might've pitched in with that."

Delpha met his eyes for a second. Then, without comment, she flipped through the phone book while he went to his office, got the .38 out of a drawer, and loaded it. Glanced out the window. New Rosemont's ancient proprietress, the one the fan had gonged, rag in hand, smearing dirty circles on a window.

When he came out, Delpha had the phone book open to

the city map section. "Got a cross directory?" she asked.

Phelan went back and got it from his office. "Run through the—"

"Newspaper's police blotter."

"Right. Down at the—"

"Library," she said. She left, both books hugged to her chest.

Just another girl off to school.

The parole office nudged up to the courthouse. His buddy Joe Ford was in, but busy. Phelan helped himself to a couple donuts from an open box. Early lunch. Joe read from a manila file to two guys Phelan knew. One took notes on a little spiral pad. Phelan, toting the long legal pad, realized he should have one of those. Neater, slipped in a jacket pocket. More professional. Joe closed the folder and kept on talking. One guy gave a low whistle; the other laughed.

Joe stood up, did a double take. "Hey, speak of the devil. Tommy, come on down."

Phelan shook hands with Fred Abels, detective. Stuck his hand out to the other, but the man bear-hugged him. "Hey, Uncle Louie," Phelan said. Louie Reaud, a jowly olive-skinned man with silvered temples, married to Phelan's aunt. Louie boomed, "*Bougre, t'es fou ouais toi! T'as engage un prisonnier.*" Which meant Phelan was crazy for hiring himself a convict.

Who said he'd hired anybody?

Abels, sporting a Burt Reynolds 'stache and burns, only not sexy, studied Phelan like he was a mud tire track lifted from a scene.

Phelan zeroed in on Joe, who raised his eyebrows, pulled down his lips, shook his head to indicate the purity permeating his soul.

"Okay." Phelan set hands on his hips and broadened his stance. "All right. So my friend here appeals to my famous heart of gold. So I interview his girl. So she stuck some bad-doer. So what."

"Minced that one, yeah. I worked that case." Louie wagged a finger. "I'm gonna tell you, *cher*, lock up the letter opener." He punched his nephew's arm, nodded at Joe, and he and Abels ambled off, chortling.

"Loudmouth bastard," Phelan said to Joe. "Give me the dopers and perverts north side of town." Commandeering Joe's chair, Phelan reeled off some street names.

"That's confidential."

"Could have my secretary call you."

"Hand full a 'Gimme' and a mouth full a 'Much obliged'— that's you." Joe squinted, put-upon. "Not my territory, but old Parker lives in the can." Joe stalked over to his coworker Parker's vacant desk, the one next to his, and rambled through its file drawers.

Phelan phoned Tyrrell Public Library. Formerly a church— thus the arches and stained glass—it was a downtown stand-out, a sand castle dripped from medieval gray stone. He asked the librarian to get a Miss Wade, who'd be in the reference section, going through newspapers.

"This is not the bus station, sir. We don't page people."

Seems like, Phelan thought while locating his desperately-polite-but-hurting voice, *one bad crab always jumps in the gumbo.*

"I'm just as sorry as I can be, ma'am. But couldn't you find my sister? We're down at the funeral home, and our daddy's lost his mind."

Clunk. Receiver on desk. Joe was still pulling files.

Footsteps, then Delpha came on. "Hey, Bubba," she said.

Phelan grinned.

She told him she'd call him back from a pay phone. "Call Joe's," he said.

In three minutes Joe's phone rang, and Delpha read out what she had so far. "Check this one from last night." A Marvin Carter, eighteen, wandering down Delaware Street, apparent assault victim, transported to a hospital. Then, outside of husband-wife slugfests, thefts, one complaint of tap-dancing on the roof of a Dodge Duster, she'd found seven dope busts and two missing-boy reports. She gave him names and addresses, phone numbers from the cross directory.

Joe dumped files on his desk, said, "Vacate my chair, son." Phelan ignored him, boring in on each mug shot as he scribbled names on his unprofessional legal pad.

One of the names was a Don Henry. Liberated from Huntsville two months back.

Some D name, Don or Darrell.

There you go. Cake.

No mud, no grease, no 500-pound pipe, no lost body parts. Man, he should have split the rigs while he still had ten fingers.

2:01. He drove back to the office and hit the phone. Got a child at the Henry number, asked for its mother.

"She went the store. Git away, Dwight, I'm on the phone." A wail from the background.

"Honey, your daddy there?"

The child scolded Dwight. Dwight was supposed to shut up while the child had dibs on the telephone. But little Dwight wasn't lying down; he was pitching a fit.

"Honey? Hey, kid!" Phelan hollered into the phone.

"Shut up, Dwight! I cain't hear myself talk. They took Daddy back Satiddy."

"Saturday? Back where, honey?"

"Where he *was*. Is this Uncle Merle?" The child yelped. Now two wails mingled on the other end of the line.

A woman's harsh voice barked into the phone, "Low-down, Merle, pumping the kids. They pulled Don's paper, okay? You happy now? Gonna say 'I told you so'? You and Ma can kiss my ass." The phone crashed down.

Saturday was six days ago. Frowning, Phelan X'd Don Henry. Next, mindful of the gray-haired volunteers in pink smocks on the end of the line, he called Baptist Hospital and inquired feelingly for his cousin Marvin Carter. Strike one. Next was Saint Elizabeth, long wait, transfer, and strike two. Finally Hotel Dieu and a single to first.

He parked in a doctor's space in front of the redbrick hospital by the port. Eau de Pinesol and polished tile. A nun gave him the room number.

The face on the pillow was white-whiskered, toothless, and snoring. A pyramid of a woman in a red-flowered muu-muu sat bedside. Phelan checked the room number. "Marvin Carter?"

The woman sighed. "My husband's name is Mar-tin. Cain't y'all get nothing right?"

Phelan loped back to the desk and stood in line behind a sturdy black woman and a teenage boy with a transistor radio broadcasting the day's body count in a jungle on the other side of the globe. The boy's face was lopsided, the wide bottom out of kilter with a narrow forehead. He nudged the dial and a song blared out. "Kung Fu Fighting." The woman slapped shut a checkbook, snatched the transistor, and dialed back to the tinny announcer spewing numbers and Asian place names.

"Jus' keep listenin'. 'Cause you keep runnin' nights, thas where you gonna be, in that war don't never end, you hear me, Marvin? What *you* lookin at?" She scowled at Phelan.

The boy turned so that Phelan verified the lopsidedness as swelling. He ventured, "Marvin Carter?"

The woman's eyes slitted as she asked who he was. Phelan told her, emphasizing that he was not a policeman. He told her that he was looking for Ricky Toups, kept his eyes on the boy.

The boy flinched. Bingo.

"Les' go." The woman pushed the teenager toward the glass doors.

Phelan dogged them. "Did that to you, Marvin, what's he gonna do to Ricky, huh? Want that on your slate? Could be a lot worse than the dope."

The boy tried the deadeye on Phelan. Couldn't hold it.

"We talking *dope* now?" The woman's voice dropped below freezing. "You done lied to me, Marvin Carter." Her slapping hand stopped short of the swollen jaw.

Marvin grunted something that was probably "Don't, Mama," enough so Phelan understood his jaw was wired.

"Ricky got you there promising dope," Phelan said, "but that wasn't all you got, was it?"

The boy squeezed his eyes shut.

"Wasn't white kids did this to you? Was some grown man?" Marvin's mother took hold of his skinny waist.

"Listen," Phelan leaned in, "if he said he'd hurt your mama here, I'll take care of that. It's just a line. But Ricky's real. You know him, and he's wherever you were last night. Help me find him, Marvin."

"Avy," the boy said.

"Avie? The street near the LNVA canal?"

Shake from Marvin said no. And he mumbled again, "Avy."

"Davy? That's his name?"

A shudder ran through the teenager.

Phelan scanned his list of parolees. Didn't have to be one of them, but he had a feeling. "Dave Deeterman? Concord Street?"

Shake from Marvin said yes. "Kakerd." Marvin muttered directions, minus lots of consonants. The mother glared Phelan away, and Marvin bent down and shook against her neck.

Phelan dashed back to the hospital's two pay phones, called Delpha, told her where he was heading, and if she didn't hear from him within the hour, to call Louis Reaud down at the station. "That's R-E—"

"Know how to spell it," she said. "Guess your second client brought over your retainer. Somebody left a wrapped-up box at the door."

"Hot damn. Why didn't she hand it to you?"

"Don't know. Just heard her on the stairs. Want me to unwrap the box?"

"No time. 'Less it's ticking, just hold on to it."

"Got time for one question, Mr. Phelan?"

"Shoot."

Throat clearing. "You think you might hire me?"

"Miss Wade, you were hired when you called me Bubba." He hung up the silent phone and jogged for the doors.

3:15. The house with the orange mailbox, painfully described by Marvin, was a dingy white ranch. It was set deep in the lot, backed up to tall pines and oak and magnolia, pockets of brush. Rusty-brown pine needles and dried magnolia leaves, big brown tongues, littered the ground. With oil shot up to twelve dollars a barrel, somebody'd be out here soon, hammering up pasteboard apartments, but for now wildlife was renting this leftover patch of the Big Thicket.

No car, but ruts in the grass where one had parked.

Phelan knocked on the door. Waited. Tried the knob, no dice. He went around the back to a screen porch that looked to be an add-on. Or it had been a screen porch before plywood was nailed over its large windows. A two-by-four had been pounded across the door; the hammer lying there in the dirt suggested that Dave Deeterman might be recently away from his desk. Maybe. Phelan could hear something. He beat on the door. "Ricky. Ricky Toups, you in there?"

He put his ear to the door. Something. Phelan pounded again, louder. "I'm looking for Ricky Toups."

A low creaking. Rhythmic. What *was* that sound? Like a rocking chair with serious rust.

He jogged back to his car, shoved a flashlight into his pocket, and snagged a pry bar. Ripped off the two-by-four. Opened the door. Directly across the porch was the door that led into the house. Phelan stepped over there, .38 drawn, and rattled it: locked. Already he was smelling piss in the hot, dead air. Then herb and cigarettes and some kind of dead-fish bayou stink. That creaky noise came from the far left, high up. He found a switch by the locked door and flipped it. Not a gleam.

He'd got the creaks figured now, and he shined the white circle up and left, to their source.

Christ Almighty.

Phelan's jaw sagged. On the top of metal shelves was a naked gargoyle, perched there. No, clinging. Haunches with a smooth, sheened back folded over them, fingers clawed around the metal, head cut sharply toward Phelan. Blinking eyes protruded from sunken holes; the downturned mouth wheezed.

"Asthma, right?"

An indrawn, "Yeah."

"Deeterman coming back?"

Ricky Toups's head bobbed loosely, flapping sweat-dark hair that had been dishwater-blond in last year's school photo.

"How long's he been gone?"

"Hour or—" The kid flung out a hand, pointing.

Phelan zigzagged the light downward over matted orange shag littered with marijuana debris, the arm of a bamboo couch, beer cans. He pivoted. The shaft of light from the door revealed the round edge of a black pile that blended into the darkness. What? Shit? Most of him failed to make sense of what he saw. But not his skin—it was crawling off his belly, his nuts squeezing north of nutsack.

The pile of shit shifted until only a tip remained. Then the tip disappeared into blackness.

That it was heading toward him told Phelan enough. Most snakes light out for the hills; cottonmouths come at you.

Phelan strode to the shelves and hauled Ricky down, shined the light till it hit the bamboo couch, and dumped the boy on it. "Keep your feet off the floor."

He scanned with the flashlight. Where the fuck was it?

Shag. Spilt ashtray. More shag.

Then the beam caught a section of sinuous black. He moved the light. There it was. Pouring toward him, triangular head outthrust.

Phelan fired.

The black snake convulsed but kept coming, tongue darting.

He fired again. Still the black form writhed in the orange grass. He blew its head off with the third round.

Phelan stepped wide of the quivering snake; wasn't dead enough yet to keep the head from biting. Ears ringing, he tossed the flashlight, looped the boy's arm around his neck, dragged him out of that room.

He saw the blue thumb-sized bruises on the boy's shoulders, a streak of blood on the back of his thigh, as he draped him in his own jacket and a blanket from his trunk. "It's the hospital, Ricky, 'less you got a full inhaler at home."

"Home," the kid panted, then turned the black tunnel of his eyes onto Phelan. "Book."

"What book?"

But the kid folded, struggling for air.

Phelan laid on the horn when they gunned into the Toups's driveway. In two seconds, Caroleen Toups busted out of the house, face lit up like stadium lights.

Phelan smoked in the Toups's pine-paneled living room that opened onto a pine-paneled kitchen. Except for the mention of a book, he had hold of the thing: Deeterman slipped Ricky cash and dope, Ricky steered him boys. Too stupid to know the son of a bitch would turn on him. *How many* ran in a loop through Phelan's brain. *How many you bring him, Ricky?*

After a while, wearing jeans and breathing, Ricky Toups stumbled out into the living room, trailed by his bewildered mother, her hands clasped at chest level. "There's a book," he said. "Told him I didn't have it. He didn't care, said he'd be back for me."

"What kinda book?"

"Like a diary. You gotta help Georgia." He hit his inhaler, and his jaw jittered sideways like his head was trying to screw off.

"She's got the book. Her idea to take it?"

Ricky's bluish chapped lips parted, like he was going to deny this point, but that was back when he had all the answers, before today. "She said we could get big money from him. That's where he went. To her house."

Phelan leapt up. "Call her."

Ricky mumbled into a phone on the kitchen wall then hung his head listening. The receiver fell to his side. "It's okay. He came to her house but she'd already took it to your office."

Phelan's stomach lurched.

Ricky slid down the wall, hunkered. Georgia'd told Deeterman he could go get the book where she'd left it, wrapped up outside this private eye's office. The guy wouldn't be there; he was out looking for Ricky. She'd talked fast, peeking through a latched screen door with Phelan's card taped to the outside of it.

4:55. Phelan burned up I-10's fast lane, swerving around truckers balling for New Orleans, cursing himself for wasting three rounds on a cottonmouth he could have outrun.

He took the stairs soft. Worked the doorknob soundlessly, hoping Deeterman was somewhere ahead of the truckers on I-10, not sitting in Delpha's chair watching the knob turn. Phelan eased into the still office, .38 out.

Delpha Wade's chair snugged to her desk. On top of it, the sheet with info on Client #2, typed on her release form. The door to his office stood ajar. Pressed against the jamb, Phelan pushed, swinging it open.

He stepped into a curtain of bourbon fume and quiet in the air, waves of it, wave on wave, quiet.

Until glass crunched under his shoe.

The client chair drifted around. Delpha said, "I put it away in your bottom drawer. Under the whiskey bottle."

Phelan slid the gun on his desk next to a wad of brown paper, sank down to her.

Her right hand hung behind the chair arm but her left lay on a small, worn ledger in the middle of a shiny darkness on her skirt. Different-sized spots stained her white blouse, spray and spatter, one red channel.

"'Fore I could get that box for him, he pushed me out of the way and grabbed it. He coulda left. I thought he would. But he had to do one of those things they do. Those extras." Her head lowered, shook once. "They just cain't resist."

He'd seen the legs on the floor by now, the rest of the body blocked from view by the big metal desk, and he needed to get Louie here, get an ambulance first, but he couldn't pick up the phone, couldn't get that motion going because he was listening to her, hearing it in the waves of quiet that rolled over him, quiet riding on waves of quiet, waves widening out from a center—the bayou, singing with insects and frogs, the surge-and-retreat, keening whir of it, the stir in muddy water, and her voice low as that chorus, he heard how she was still holding the bottle when the man licked the knife and cut her, and after he licked it again, she broke the bottle on the edge of the desk and shoved it up through his throat. Then she took the book and she sat down.

"You gonna find some boys."

"Delpha," Phelan whispered. The half of her face he could see wore a sheen of sweat. He laced his fingers through the brown hair, soothed it back.

Not a cloud in the gray-blue eyes that met his. The horizon inside them was clear.

CATGIRL

BY CLAUDIA SMITH

Galveston

The girls are waiting for the ferry, dangling their legs out the side of the van, popsicle juice dripping down their chins. Four girls: Trina, Tricia, Grace, and Allie. Tricia and Trina, the blond twins. Grace Hobel, the quiet one, their best friend. And Allie, kicking Grace in the shins gleefully. She wants the twins for her very own. They are beautiful, those two, and Allie wants to enter their twin world, to learn their twinspeak, to braid their matching white-blond hair. The twins' mother is from Sweden. Allie loves her icewater eyes, her high cheekbones. She wears sunglasses and drinks throughout the day, but in a way that makes her seem slightly mussed, and not soused. Allie wants those twins for sleepovers. They smell like Ivory soap, those two. Even on the beach, after days of swimming in the ocean, they smell sweetly of summer. Not Grace. Grace is getting breasts and has already started her period. She has a body odor problem.

So these girls, setting off on their weekend with a mother the other mothers like because she is pretty and rich, know they will run on the beach, build sand castles, and stand around a bonfire with boys. They lick sticky fingers and sing a song about a smashed bumblebee.

At first, they don't notice the man who is behind them, watching, although if they did it would give them a kick; they like it when people watch them, especially together.

Miss Mary Mack, Mack, Mack
All dressed in black, black, black
With silver buttons, buttons, buttons
All down her back, back, back.

She cannot read, read, read
She cannot write, write, write
But she can smoke, smoke, smoke
Her father's pipe, pipe, pipe.

Then Grace sees the man and covers her mouth. She jabs Tricia's ribs.

"He likes your creamy thighs," Allie says, just to see if Grace will hide behind her fingers. She does.

"He looks like Kenny Rogers," Trina says, and he does.

"Maybe he *is* Kenny Rogers," Allie says. It's possible. His snow-white beard is very well groomed. His nose is red and a little bulbous.

They sing "The Gambler" and point and laugh. He squints his eyes. They slam the door. The ferry has arrived.

Melanie, the twins' mother, puts out her cigarette. They are listening to Neil Diamond. Even Neil Diamond has a kind of soulful glamour when Melanie Parks listens to him.

This all happened years ago, in the summer of 1982.

The girls stand on the ferry, throwing day-old bread at the seagulls. Grace stands at the prow, looking down, waiting to be splashed. She turns green yet will not back away. She is prone to seasickness. But she never backs out of a dare. The girls have to admire her for that.

They feed the gulls, then run to the back of the boat when

the birds dive down. Grace tells a story about mean boys who throw Pop Rocks at the gulls.

"That is just so sad," the twins say.

"Did you think of that together?" Allie asks.

"What?" they say together.

"When you talk together like that. Like you have the same thoughts. It's cool," Allie says.

"We are nothing alike," Tricia says.

Grace smiles, a close-lipped smile. Allie wonders if she does that because of her overbite. It's a cute overbite. Allie likes her again. She has velvety hair and she is good at anything school-related, as long as it doesn't involve athletics. Grace and Allie are the A students; the twins, they are B-plus with an occasional A.

"I'm going inside," Tricia says, and this disappoints Allie. She likes it out on the boat. She sniffs the air; it smells briney, with a hint of dirty bathroom. She would like to stay to see if any dolphins follow the ferry, but she won't be separated from her twins. Once inside, they play Go Fish until the boat docks.

The house is on Crystal Beach. The twins have spent their summers here since they were tots, running up and down the stairs in matching T-shirts. There are only a few rules at the beach: take off your flip-flops on the balcony before you go inside, so that you don't track sand in everywhere; and be sure to check in before sundown with Melanie.

Inside, the house is all one big room, with a little harvest-gold kitchenette and a claw-footed bathtub behind the sink. The house is furnished with rattan and wicker, and there are four big beds. But the girls will sleep out on the balcony on cots, facing the sea.

Maybe on Saturday Melanie will take them back on the

ferry to Galveston, where they can eat shrimp in little glass bowls with red cocktail sauce and bottomless glasses of Coke. Melanie is prone to sudden bursts of happiness, and the girls love her for it. Sometimes on these trips she takes them all to get their toenails painted. Or she'll take them to Murdoch's to buy matching sunglasses and netted bags of shells.

At Crystal Beach they can run as far as they want. At night the girls will find older boys. One boy, Murph, drives a Jeep and they all pile in and scream and he speeds through the water, splashing. "Ah, naw," he says, when Tricia kisses the back of his neck. "He tasted like man-sweat," she whispers to them later. They sing him songs. *Say Say my playmate, come out and play with me.* And then the rhymes get dirtier. But it's Grace that whispers the spookiest:

Miss Mary Mack, Mack, Mack
All dressed in black, black, black
She has a knife, knife, knife
Stuck in her back, back, back.

She cannot breathe, breathe, breathe
She cannot cry, cry, cry . . .

There's a teenager at the beach when they get there. Her name is Sylvia, and she is some distant relation to the twins and Melanie. She and Melanie make daiquiris and sleep on the balcony, slathered in coconut oil. The girls agree that Sylvia is not nearly so beautiful as Melanie, although she is sixteen, the age of beauty. The girls—it was Tricia or Trina who came to this conclusion, Allie can't remember which—all agree. Sixteen is the age; the age that it is appropriate to lose your virginity, to have a boyfriend, to wear a miniskirt.

More interesting than the teenager, there is a girl across the dunes. This girl introduces herself on the second day. Her name is Brandy. Her voice is rich and throaty, like a smoker's.

"It's sort of beautiful," Grace says.

"But too old for her body," Allie declares.

She is a pleasant combination of warm golden hues, honey skin and hair, light amber eyes, jeans cut off before her buttocks end. She lives there. She's a townie. Her house is lit up at night, every night, all night. One of the windows is busted.

"Is that her room? How does she sleep at night?" But once Allie thinks about it, she decides she would like to sleep in a room with the ocean right outside, every night, whistling into the hole in her windowpane.

"It's a bullet hole," Grace says.

"Oh, don't be stupid," Allie tells her. "Whoever lives there, her single mom or whatever, can't afford to fix it. That's all."

Tricia glances over at Grace, casting her pale lashes down. She agrees, she agrees with Allie. Grace can be such a child.

Allie's mom is a single mom. She can afford to fix broken windows, but she can't afford add-a-bead necklaces or adoptive Cabbage Patch dolls. Allie's mother often reminds her that there are children who don't have enough money for band instruments or three square meals. There are children who run wild and don't know their times tables because there is nobody looking out for them, aiming for a better quality of life. Allie isn't sure what she means by better quality of life. When Allie visits the twins, Melanie isn't around much. She imagines it would be very lonely to live that way without a twin. The twins have each other though. And there is little doubt, when she watches them in their matching bunny-fur coats and freshly curled wings, singing the winter holiday program or twirling their batons in unison at the football game, that those two have achieved a finer quality of life. Last winter, when the other girls in the program snuck makeup on in the bathroom, Trina and Tricia wore nothing more than Vaseline on their brow bones and bow-shaped lips. When they throw the batons up high, they spin in unison, and there is never any question that they will catch the batons at the exact same moment. Every time they spin down. Every time.

Many years later, one of the girls will be a woman.

She comes here with her husband and her daughter, they take the ferry out to Crystal Beach.

There isn't any parking, and the husband says, "Goddamnit, why didn't you tell me?" when the state trooper tickets them for expired registration.

"Forgot about that," Tricia says. When their child falls asleep in the back, she reaches over. This trip is about him, how he says he feels no love for her anymore. She climbs over the seat, in the daylight, thinking, *This will do it, this has to do it*. Her long pale hair in his face, her mother's blue eyes, the lashes darkened now. "I love you, I love you, I love you," she says, and when his arm fumbles and he pushes her off, she'll think, *Fuck it. You fucker*.

He doesn't push her off, he is soft there, holding his head back from her face.

"There are worse things in life than a job you don't like and a wife who leaves you cold," she says. "You could have a knife in your back."

"I don't want to talk about that. You aren't thinking about it anyway," he says.

And he is right, until she seats herself again and looks back at her daughter.

"Don't make yourself cry for my benefit," he says.

"Man, it's really changed," she says aloud on the drive back. She'd imagined walking along the beach, their girl on his shoulders, her hand inside his. She would point to the dunes, *And there it is, that's it, that's where* . . . and he would put his hand on the small of her back, guiding her away. Or no, he would rest it on the nape of her neck, cradling.

There is a coffee shop with free wi-fi, and they pass gift shops, even a couple of hotels. "It wasn't like this back then. It was just houses and a corner store. We used to go crabbing, did I tell you that? Mom would cook them for us, if we cleaned them and pulled them apart. We did it when they were alive. It didn't bother us. Grace said they had no nerves. One time, I was about to gut one of them and it started eating its brains out. Autocannibalism, Allie said. She was the smart one. We thought it was funny. And we ate mussels too. Trina and I, we brought the traps in every morning, We woke up at the same time. Trina said the same sound woke us, but I don't remember. I don't know. Maybe I never heard the sound."

He is smoking, window down. She would like to think that he is afraid of his own love for her, but the way he's looking at the windshield, she's thinking maybe not. They've been married for eleven years. When she met him, he was a skinny studio art major at a state college. Now he's grown more handsome. And glib.

In the backseat, her baby girl gurgles. Two years old, fingers in her mouth. Her hair is black like her daddy's, cut straight across her cheeks. Her eyes are blue like her mother's, like her grandmother's, like Trina's.

The girls sleep out on the balcony, listening to Judy Collins tapes. She sounds so otherworldly. There is a song with whales calling, and a song about eyes like isinglass windows. The girls don't know what isinglass is, but it sounds like something from old ships or lighthouses. Then Allie puts in Stevie Nicks. Sylvia and Melanie are dancing in the field. They wear black bathing suits and sarongs. Melanie unties her sarong, letting it float up, up, and away. It's a warm and breezy night. Across the way, at that girl's house, men whoop and holler.

"I want to call my mom," Grace says. "Your mom drinks too much."

"Oh, go inside and call her then," Trina says. Allie and Tricia smile.

Grace falls asleep with her glasses on, her arm thrown over her face.

Allie, Tricia, and Trina watch as Melanie and Sylvia walk off past the dunes.

"She'll find a bonfire," Trina says.

"Will she come back?" Allie says, then thinks about how that sounds.

"She always does," the twins say.

Allie whispers, making her voice low, husky. Like the girl's. "I don't think she's a girl," Allie says. "She's a spook. She's a ghost. She's a demon inside a girl's body."

And then she hisses:

Miss Mary Mack, Mack, Mack
All dressed in black, black, black
With silver buttons, buttons, buttons
All down her back, back, back.

She cannot read, read, read
She cannot write, write, write
But she can smoke, smoke, smoke
Her father's pipe, pipe, pipe.

She asked her mother, mother, mother
For fifty cents, cents, cents
To see the elephants, elephants, elephants
Jump over the fence, fence, fence.

They jumped so high, high, high
They reached the sky, sky, sky
And they didn't come back, back, back
Till the Fourth of July, ly, ly!

July can't walk, walk, walk
July can't talk, talk, talk
July can't eat, eat, eat
With a knife and fork, fork, fork!

She went upstairs, stairs, stairs
To say her prayers, prayers, prayers
And bumped her head, head, head
And now she's dead, dead, dead!

In the mornings the twins carry in the crab traps. They wake up at the same moment, and leave Grace and Allie asleep on the balcony. They walk in their pajamas, and wear flip-flops to protect their calloused feet from the sticker burrs.

July Fourth, firecrackers and watermelon. Melanie sips a mint julep from a tall blue glass. The girls sip from the bottom of the tumblers. Their father is there, for this celebration, an arm thrown over his wife's shoulders. They are surprisingly broad for such a petite woman. Allie approves of the exposed freckles, the blood-red stone dipping in between her breasts. The only makeup she wears is dark lipstick, and her toenails match. Her skin is dead-girl white. Tricia and Trina are wearing batiked sarongs like their mother's. Allie would have said, *On the beach a woman should be golden,* but Melanie's skin is right, it's unexpected. Her husband has the kind of muted, rumpled handsomeness that complements a great beauty. Everyone wants to touch her, just for a moment. Tricia and Trina watch her from a distance, that woman they might become. She is drunk, but not slurry drunk. Women lean in toward her; men brush her arm as they walk by. The girls run up to her with plates of oysters and shrimp, offerings. She rests her hand on Allie's shoulder for a moment and says, "This is my girl. These are all my girls."

The girls stay downstairs in the junk room, sipping lukewarm Lone Stars. That's when they see the neighbor girl across the field, dancing with a sparkler. She moves in waves, making ribbons with the sparks. Allie is the one who stands up and calls to her.

"Brandy, Brandy! Come here. We have beer!"

Brandy motions for them to come to her, waving that sparkler around and around.

The way Melanie taught them in the car, it goes like this:

Miss Mary Mack, Mack, Mack
All dressed in black, black, black
She has a knife, knife, knife
Stuck in her back, back, back.

She cannot breathe, breathe, breathe
She cannot cry, cry, cry
That's why she begs, begs, begs
She begs to die, die, die.

They are clapping, laughing. Tricia loves the way her mother takes to the freeways, speeding, passing, changing lanes with ease. She never curses at the other drivers, and she talks her way out of tickets. One trip, she'd blinked her eyes and said, "My little girl is sick." Trina leaned over the seat and shivered. That officer wanted to give them a police escort to the hospital. Later, they'd laughed, and Melanie bought them all—what were they called back then? Blizzards?—at the DQ. She'd dared Grace to finish it, knowing full well she would. The things they got her to do, just to see if she would. It seems wrong, now, looking back on that, a grown woman getting a little girl to guzzle down something so big and sweet it made her puke.

The two weeks they spent on Crystal Beach in the summer of 1982 are broken bits in Tricia's head.

When they get to Galveston, David asks, "Why are there all these motels without windows?"

"Oh," Tricia answers, happy he is talking, "it's because of the storms. It's cheaper."

"Why would you come to a beach and stay in a motel without windows?"

"Well, but you could spend a lot of time outside. And like I said, it's cheaper."

Murdoch's is still there. Audrey is awake, and her father carries her on his shoulders out to the pier and back. They build a castle; well, Audrey and Tricia build it. They search for shells and bits of broken glass. It isn't safe for a three-year-old to carry broken beer bottles but Tricia wants to show her how to make a castle sparkle. "Don't pick up the glass yourself. Just show Mommy when you find one." Tricia's lost track of the years it's been since she's seen a beach, any beach. Everything feels high and bright and washed out. Audrey grows bored with the castles and wants to swim. "Not today," Tricia tells her. She thought that the ocean might frighten Audrey, but as soon as she saw it, her girl wanted to cross it. The ships, bigger than castles, the way the sky seems so much higher than it does at home—it's Tricia that feels small and afraid.

Allie Saenz was a tall, leggy girl. Her neck seemed long for her body, but she might have grown up to become a great beauty. It was always women who had something unexpected—Audrey Hepburn's long neck, for example, or Angelina Jolie's big, soft lips—that were so beautiful they unnerved. Allie would have been an imposing woman. Not like Melanie, who was soft and white, and she could wear anything and seem naked. There was nothing predatory about Melanie's prettiness.

The strange new girl, Brandy, takes them behind the dunes and whispers stories. "Your mother likes to fuck," she says. The way she says *fuck*, it sounds really bad, like something luscious but wrong. "Fuck," she says. Grace gets up and walks away. "You want to see her do it? Wait till her man leaves. That your daddy?"

"Yes," the twins answer together.

"She'll do anything."

"It's a lie," Allie says. Trina is crying. But Grace is very still, alert. When they walk back, Allie whispers, "She's like a cat in the dark, your mother."

And they listen to the Fleetwood Mac song on the boom box, out on the balcony.

> She is like a cat in the dark
> And then she is the darkness

She rules her life like a fine skylark
And when the sky is starless
All your life you've never seen
A woman taken by the wind . . .

The adults are going to be up all night, out by the bon-fire, drinking, dancing. People spill over from the broken house and the girls watch them. These are guys who get their muscles from working, not working out. Brandy is with them, and the way she stands in the firelight, she seems older. Maybe she's a teenager like Sylvia. She is wearing cutoffs and cowgirl boots, her long hair gathered up at her neck in a ba-nana clip.

"Look at her," Grace whispers, "I think she's sixteen."

Brandy and Melanie dance together in the firelight, one shimmery and white, the other all golden, glinting lights. Melanie's small hand rests gently in the curve of the younger woman's—girl's—waist, and for a few moments the laughter is muffled. Everyone is watching.

It's their father who ends it, laughing, calling them all to come inside.

Sunday, the men go back to their jobs, and Sylvia leaves. Melanie makes daiquiris and lies out on the balcony, sleeping, while the girls dig a hole behind the dunes. "Just one thing, girls," she says. "Stay away from that girl."

"You mean Brandy?"

"Yes, that one."

"Why?" Trina asks.

"Well, she's kind of trashy. I know that's not a nice thing to say. But I don't think she even goes to school."

"You were dancing with her," Allie says, and catches her eye.

"Oh, that . . ." Melanie's voice trails off. "Well, I'm a grown-up. You girls have fun."

A few minutes later, the girls all sit with Brandy beneath her shanty house, looking out at the bright water. It's noon, and the sand is a bright white, bright enough to make Allie close her eyes against it. Brandy's house is right up on the beach.

"Don't you worry it'll get destroyed in one of the storms?" Trina asks.

Brandy shrugs. She's back to looking like one of them, a girl.

"Our mother says we shouldn't play with you," Tricia says.

"Why?"

"Well . . . because."

"That don't make sense. She brought Allie here, and Allie's a Mexican, right Alejandra?" She says the *j* with a puff.

"She thinks you're trash," Allie says.

"She don't want to get caught, that's all," Brandy says.

The girls lie on their backs, looking up at the broken beams under the stilts.

"Where's your family?" Tricia asks.

"Oh, my Uncle Cody? He's gone on his errands."

"Was he out there last night?" the girls want to know.

"Cody? I have a lot of uncles. They all like Melanie. Everyone likes Melanie."

Tricia's father died a few summers later. Or was he their father? He worked a lot. When he was home, his soft eyes were on Melanie, always. He was a tall man, gray hair, gray eyes, cuff links. His heart gave out, and when he was gone, the summer after, her mother brought them to Corpus Christi, to a different beach, and her skin was tanned this time, her hair in blond cornrows. There was a different man and a different party.

"Husband?" Tricia says, thinking he will not answer to anything now. Their daughter is sleeping on the king bed beside them, bottom up in the air, legs tucked under.

"I don't want to talk."

"But I want to know. What made you love me? Something, right? Maybe you can just remember that moment and it will help." But he is already turned away. There is sand in the bed. The sheets smell funky, as if they've been sprayed with air freshener but left unwashed. She won't sleep. She walks out onto the balcony. The hotel doesn't face the ocean; it faces a water park. Beyond the water park is the ocean, but she can't see it, not from here.

When it started, maybe the fourth day? Or the fifth. She remembers her mother's warm breath on their faces.

Melanie, they call her, when they are at the beach. "Girls," she whispers, "my girls . . ." Trina turns around, grabbing Tricia's elbow. Grace and Allie are fast asleep.

"Oh, don't bother," Melanie says. "They won't wake up. I took care of that. This is just for you, for my kittens."

And she takes them out to the sea, one pretty daughter on either side, and they seem to glide with her. She whispers to them, and sings, and she tells them what happens at night is different. "We don't talk about what happens at night in the daytime." They walk and walk until they find a bonfire. "Come on, my kittens." Melanie smiles and everyone smiles back, men who aren't teenagers but not really men, college boys mainly, and a few women in shorts and Rockets T-shirts. Trina takes her mother's hand, and Tricia rolls her pajama bottoms up over her calves, walking into the water. She doesn't know where to go, what to do. Her mother was kissing those men last night, and when she glanced over her shoulder, Trina was too. Tricia puts her head under the water, wishing it were colder. When she looks back everything gleams.

Were things really brighter then, or are they just more vivid in childhood?

She remembers moonlit foam, the waves splashing . . . The women were gone, it was only Melanie and Trina who remained, and Melanie was on top of one of the men, leaning back, digging her hands into the sand, smiling upside down. Tricia was too far to see her mother's face, but she knew she was smiling like a little girl hanging from monkey bars. Melanie's body was bobbing back and forth, all her pale hair spilling on the ground. Trina was on another man, kissing.

"You are both cats," their mother tells them, giggling, as they walk back. "Like your momma. Meow, meow."

Tricia is silent, and Trina runs ahead, her arms open wide. Once they're on the cots out on the balcony, she whispers, "I could taste melted marshmallow on his tongue. It was sweet. He sucked on my tongue hard and then he let it go. It almost hurt, but it felt good."

"I don't want to hear. That's slutty," Tricia tells her.

"No. We're cats. In the morning we'll be different people. Like Melanie said."

They wake at sunrise, and Trina touches her elbow, and they walk out into the ocean to bring in the traps, not speaking. Tricia thinks maybe it **was** something like a dream.

At home, they live in a **long ranch** house. Sometimes they turn off the hallway lights **and play** ghost. Their mother takes many naps during the day, but she is more like a mother there than she is on the beach. She pours them Count Chocula cereal in the morning, she talks about report cards, she makes them grilled cheese sandwiches. She even watches television with them sometimes. It's entirely possible, when they come out here, Tricia thinks, that their mother is some sort of cat lady.

Audrey came out with a head full of dark hair. Then her dark hair fell out and was replaced by still darker, plumier hair. From the beginning, she latched without difficulty. Tricia held her whenever she cried. She remained toothless until she was a year old, and then they all came in at once. Audrey was up all night, feverish, and Tricia would stick her index finger over the sore gums as her baby clamped down. "Go ahead," she'd whisper, "bite Mommy. It's okay." Audrey was colicky too; Tricia held her in the steamy bathroom and rubbed her back as her little one cried and gasped. Sometimes it was Tricia's body Audrey wanted, and the baby would touch her mother's face and turn it away as she took the nipple into her mouth. She twirled her fingers, closed her eyes. Tricia misses that sometimes. How just the breast could soothe her daughter into a trance. Nothing seems to have replaced that kind of content.

Tricia called her mother once, during a particularly difficult day of colick.

"Oh, I wouldn't know, sweetheart," Melanie said. "I didn't nurse you two. Why don't you get someone in to help? Where's the little shit?" That's what she calls David, Tricia's husband.

Her mother is not so very far away now. She lives with another husband, in Dallas. But Tricia has not seen her in almost ten years. She hasn't seen her sister either. It wasn't a big deal, they said. They talk about it, about meeting for something, for a holiday. But there are always islands to visit, things to be done.

Her husband is gone; he is here but he is already gone. Tricia is a woman, not a cat. She can't keep him, nor dispose of him. She loves him, or at least she wants him back so that she can try to love him.

There's something, something that may have happened, or maybe didn't. Not at the beach, but at the house on Albans Lane.

It was a late night, some night outside of time; she can't remember her age. And she can't remember if it was before, or after, the summer Allie and Grace disappeared. Tricia woke to a sound, a low hum. She walked into the living room. Candles flickered. The light was warm and bright, unlike any light she had seen before. The table was set with the green glass plates. Everything seemed burnished, as if someone had polished the air. Her mother was there, leaning back in her chair, white shirtsleeves rolled up to her elbows, a bloodstone dangling where the buttons began. And across from her was Trina. Her hair was brushed clean and pulled back off her neck with a black velvet ribbon. She wore a red dress, white lace tights, and patent leather Mary Janes. She nibbled a big slice of white cake and swung her stockinged legs under the table.

They were more beautiful than any two people Tricia had ever seen. She rubbed the crust from her eyes and watched. Melanie was laughing, and Trina kicked the table leg and looked right back at her.

Watching them together was almost like looking into one of those little plastic snow globes her mother put out at Christmastime. Another world, lovelier and smaller than this one. If it could come outside and into this world, it wouldn't be so magical. But you wanted to get inside it just the same.

The night it happened, the moon was murderously bright.

That's what Melanie says when she wakes them: "Wake up, wake up, my girls, The moon is murderously bright!" And this night, she wakes them all, Grace and Allie, Tricia and Trina. "Wipe the sleepy dirt from your eyes. This night is enchanted. It will last for a hundred years."

The air itself feels charged. Allie and Grace stand up, wobbling, rubbing their eyes. They would follow Melanie anywhere.

The house flickers in the distance. That broken house seems to come alive at night and die every morning.

And Tricia remembers, yes—before that summer, it was an empty, abandoned shack, the stilts sinking into the sand, the windows boarded up. Tricia and Trina would go there, find things that had washed up. A glass disc full of colored blue water and pale sand. There were old shoes, baby bottles, fish skeletons. Once, a ring they thought was diamond, but when they brought it to Melanie, she told them it was cubic zirconia. Oh, and a coral necklace. That had been a treat, how they rinsed it and handed it to their mother. It was their greatest find.

But this night, there are men around and inside it. The women who are there are there for the men. There is a woman with stiff breasts and boots that go way up past her knees, walking toward the water. She looks painted onto the landscape. "It's a stripper," Grace whispers, and Trina says, "Be quiet." The girls run beneath the house, looking for something. They whisper, wonder if they've walked into a ghost story. It's very dark beneath, and there's a sliver of light where the stilts rise to their highest, where the light from the windows and the moonlit ocean cut through.

"Do you think Brandy is here tonight?" one of the girls, probably Allie, whispers. Grace is scared. Allie takes her hand.

Upstairs, Melanie's laughter, ice giggling inside a tumbler, war whoops.

A man jumps from the deck to the sand. When he sees them down there he squats, smiles. "Come out, come out, wherever you are."

He's reaching for Grace, and she begins to cry. She's still in her pink pajamas, the ones with daisies all over them. Allie wraps an arm around her and so she feels the bottoms dampen. Grace has wet herself. It's just a party. That's when they hear Melanie say, "Come on, Grace, it's all right. Come on out."

"It's okay," the twins whisper. "It's Melanie."

It's Mother's Day. There are no Mother's Day gifts; David didn't come up with anything and Audrey's too young to have done anything on her own. They sit in the lobby, eating their free continental breakfasts. Tricia peels a bruised orange for Audrey, and then they make waffles. Audrey is fascinated by the waffle maker. She sticks her fingers into the syrupy cherry sauce. "Oh, sorry, Mommy," she says, "not sanitary."

David looks awful. Like his eyes are just holes punched into his face. He hasn't even bothered to shave. "Why would you, for this grand occasion?" she says, and too late she realizes she said it aloud. But he just nods.

And that's when she squints, blurring his features a bit. Men, for her mother, were interchangeable. She liked to have sex with them, and she liked to look at them. She liked them to look at her. But beyond that, they didn't interest her. And so, for Tricia, her father had been a scent, a cigar, cuff links, a nice leather chair. Those men on the beach, they were bar boys or college boys, or working men in soiled shirts and Stetsons. Her father wore boots with his suit. He liked to call them his girls.

She squints at David, and sees him . . . tries to make him flat. Isn't that what he's done to her? She is nothing, he says, it's nothing, it's never been any good, it's no use . . . For a moment, he's a loser with a five o'clock shadow. And then he gets up for more coffee and he's back to being David again.

"Well," she says when he comes back, "can we go out? For crab maybe? I'd like to do that."

When David and Tricia were first married, they lived in Austin, down the street from UT. They walked their dog to the Crown and Anchor once a week for beer and soggy fries, and she liked to sit out on the lawn and listen to the football games. She liked the roar of the crowd, which carried like voices over water down Duval Street. The announcer's voice was masculine, rich, slow and easy, like her father's. After the game, if they'd won, kids would drive down the roads yehawing, whooping. She reminds herself that they were innocent whoops of joy. Or probably. Or most likely. But maybe there was a fine line. Something David said to her, tonelessly, once, as he was throwing out platitudes in that dim voice he used lately, was, "There's a fine line between love and hate."

That wasn't it, though, for Melanie. She didn't hate anyone, really. Some people were beneath her, that's all. She liked fun.

David won't go out, and so it's Audrey and her mommy, facing the seawall. Audrey has pineapple juice and a sunfish bib. Tricia orders king crab, and then another. She can't remember ever feeling so hungry.

"It's all right, it's Melanie," they tell Grace. There's that windchime laugh, and Melanie's voice, saying sweetly, "That one's the plain one." Then the sounds settle, as if something thick has descended on them all. Upstairs there's moaning and sighs, and something warm and rich, a cawing, a mewing. Tricia and Allie crawl under the floorboards of the deck and look up through the slats. Grace is whimpering, and those moans, they seem to come from a creature buried for centuries, but they're coming from Melanie. She's straddling one of the men. Her body moves up and down, riding waves. Brandy's there too. She looks like a boy, standing in the doorway in a man's shirt, a pipe in her mouth. Tricia and Trina climb from under the deck and their mother looks over the man's shoulder and smiles.

Grace is in laps, hands around and inside her, the pink pajamas in a soiled heap, flung across the deck. Tricia chews the back of her hand, then bites her tongue and tries to taste. She turns away, crawls back under. And Trina stays.

Tricia and Allie lie there, thinking. Tricia holds Allie's hand, then puts her head against her chest, listening. Allie is still, but for her heartbeat.

Even now that she's grown, she believes in this, that Allie heard her thoughts.

They know you are here. You have to run.

I'm afraid. We have to do it together.

No. They won't hurt me. I'm her kitten.

They took Allie down though. Tricia's eyes were closed, her hands digging deep, deep into the sand, pushing deeper, to where the sand was damp. So she didn't see it, but she knows Allie fought. She wasn't even looking for Melanie, but Melanie was watching, Tricia knew she was watching. Allie screamed and flailed, fighting with her nails and teeth. The men were different than they were with Grace, they weren't thick and private. They whooped and laughed. What must it have sounded like? There were still people out there, in their vacation homes. But later, in the morning, when the patrol cars came, people said they only heard a party.

Tricia never dreams of that night. Instead, she dreams of a dark room and sounds: a rooster crowing, wind chimes tinkling, men whooping, a woman moaning, giggling, tearing, screaming. Sometimes there are people there with her, in the black. Sometimes an alarm clock interrupts, and sometimes the other sounds overwhelm.

In the morning, her girls stood behind her. Melanie's eyes were red-rimmed, and she pushed her sunglasses up her nose. The policeman spoke to them separately. "No, we were sleeping. They must have dared one another to go exploring," Melanie told the men. "Those girls were always fascinated with that house."

Allie's mother, a nurse at Texas Children's, moved away to somewhere in Virginia, and then to someplace in the Midwest, and then she moved again and again, from hospital to hospital. She felt no anger toward Melanie. She wrote letters, asking again and again what the girls did that day. And Melanie sang her the songs they sang, told her about the virgin daiquiris she made them. "I feel close to you, Melanie," Allie's mother said.

"I know. I do too. I know how lucky I am. I'm surprised you don't hate me, with my two still here."

"I don't have many girlfriends," Melanie said to her twins when she hung up. "I'm glad she feels she can talk to me."

After a while the phone calls stopped. Allie's mom never came back to Texas.

On that drive back, they returned early. The sky was damp and close. It was the kind of muggy Houston weather that felt as wet as rain, but the rain wouldn't come.

"The clouds look like smashed brains," Tricia said.

"It's a hard day, I know, kittens," Melanie said. She turned on the radio and rolled the windows down. She sniffled, wiping her nose with her wrist, and lit a cigarette. In that moment, Tricia believed her mother was as close to sad as she could ever be.

She and Trina weren't really twins, after that.

Someday, when David is gone—and he will be gone, Tricia is sure of that now—she'll bring Audrey back to the beach. They'll buy matching skull shirts on the Strand and have their pictures taken together in a booth. They'll come here in the winter and search for sand dollars, and dip their ankles into the surf. It's not so crowded in the wintertime. Tricia will raise her hand up to the sky and sprinkle the shimmers all over the water, just as her mother used to do. She'll laugh and tickle her black-haired daughter. "I come from a long line of witches," she'll say. "My grandmother was a witch, and her daughter was a witch, and I am a witch, and you!" She'll jab Audrey in the ribs until she giggles. "But not for real. Just for pretend."

"That's right," Tricia will cackle, "we're good witches. And just for pretend."

What she remembers that day as they drive back, David silent as she points out the freighters and the gulls to Audrey, what she remembers on that very bright day is how, after the men had gone away in their trucks, her mother carried the naked bodies out into the sea.

It wasn't ceremonious; it wasn't unkind either. The bodies looked like bodies, not Allie, not Grace. Legs and arms and necks in the moonlight. They were lovely the way a wet, dead fish shining in the dark is lustrous before it splits open and begins to rot.

WHO STOLE MY MONKEY?

BY DAVID CORBETT & LUIS ALBERTO URREA

Port Arthur

> *Can you really make it stink?*
> —Beau Jocque and the Zydeco Hi-Rollers

L ooking back later, Chester could not convince himself he'd heard the sound at all, not at first, for what memory handed up to him was more sensation than sound, the tight sawtooth grind of a key in a lock, opening the door to hell.

They were midway through a cover of "Big Legs, Tight Skirt," Chester caressing the custom Gabbanelli Cajun King he used for the night's first sets. Saturday night at the old Diamond 21, some of the dancers in western getup, down to the Stetsons and hoopskirts, the rest in the usual Gulf Coast duds—muscle shirts, ass-crack jeans, shifts so cellophane-tight a blind man would weep—the cowboy contingent arrayed in three rows for the line dance, the others rocking to their own inner need, women holding the hair off their necks, men combing back damp locks, the band double-clutching but bluesy too, John Lee Hooker meets Rockin' Dopsie with a tip of the hat to Professor Longhair. Yeah—'fess, chile. Midnight in East Texas, the music savage and hip, the band hitting it good, the room steamy, the dance crowd punchy from the beat but craving more, always more.

But the sound. It came from outside, no denying it now,

that distinctive growl, like the sulfurous thunder-chuckle of the devil himself—a rear-mounted diesel, rebuilt Red Diamond in-line six. Chester even caught a scent of the oil-black exhaust and the muffled scattershot of spewed gravel as the bus tore out of the parking lot.

No, he thought, blinking like a man emerging from a silly dream. Two-toned copper and black, a perfect match not just for the gear trailer but his ostrich-skin boots—100 percent personal style, that bus. Last gasp of the days when oil money ran flush, when Chester had a nice little stilt home in Cameron Parish (before the hurricane took it to Belize, that is), when the clubs were paying sweet money and Beau Jocque was still alive and touring the country and a good two-step chanky-chank band could make beaucoup cash dollars. That bus was just about it for the Chester Richard empire, the final signature on a bleak dotted line.

But that wasn't what broke his heart.

Lorena, he thought.

His fingers stopped their flight across the mother-of-pearl buttons as a drop of sweat, fat as a bumblebee, splashed onto the accordion's Honduras rosewood. He wore a tight leather apron-vest, cut and sized in Lafayette so the bellows didn't pinch his nipples. Underneath, his chest was a swamp.

The rest of the band, oblivious, pushed on, the dancers unfazed too, a whirlwind thrall of spins and dips and shuffles. He glanced into the mold-speckled mirror above the stage as though the smile of some last hope might reveal itself. Fog hazed his reflection.

Turning his back to the dance floor, he waved the band to a stop. Geno, his frottoir man, lost the rhythm with his spoons. Skillet, the drummer, faltered when the rubboard did. The tune stumbled and fell apart.

"You didn't hear that?" They stared at him gape-eyed. "Someone just stole the motherfucking Flyer."

Two hours later he sat in a nearby diner, waiting for Geno and Skillet to return with a car, the night pitch-black beyond the screens. One fan hummed in the doorway to keep out the wasps and skeeters, another sat propped on the ancient counter to whip the soupy heat around, the air thick with the smell of sweet crude off the ship channel. The cook was in back puzzling out the walk-in's condenser. A plain bare bulb swam overhead in the breeze, casting a dizzy light.

Chester, craving a pinch, leaned back in his chair, shirt clinging to his skin as he pretended to listen. The woman did go on. If he only had some Red Man. Hell, any chaw at all— he'd take gas station rubbish right now if it had some mint in it. All the other club patrons had trudged on home, demanding their cover charge back, getting half, everybody ripped off one way or the other. But this woman here, she'd elected to stay.

He remembered her from the first set, waltzing with the others in the grand counterclockwise circle, her partner a doodlebugger wearing throwback pomade. Small wonder they'd parted. Coppery freckles dusted her cleavage which, from time to time, she mopped with a white paper napkin. Her hair was the color of bayou amber and she wore it swirled messily atop her head, strands curling down like so many afterthoughts, a pair of chopsticks holding it so. Another time and place, he could imagine himself saying, *I bet you taste just like rice pudding, sha.*

Chester had suffered three marriages, survived as many divorces, more time spent with lawyers, it seemed, than in love. He had a wandering eye and a ravenous crotch and a

Category 5 temper, his love life a tale of wreckage—one judge had nicknamed him Hurricane, given his knack for sheer, mean, indifferent destruction. No woman could endure him for long, but few could resist him, neither. Like fortune tellers staring into a glowing ball, they could sense within him a tragic, beautiful, lonesome soul. Hell, he was the crown prince of lonely; open his heart you'd find a howling wasteland, make West Texas look like Biloxi. And the ladies could not resist that—*I'll soothe you, sugar. Save you.* But no bride, no groupie, no rice-pudding blonde with chopstick hair had ever honored his longing, or yielded to his touch, like Lorena.

"Mr. Richard," she whispered, pronouncing it *richered*, like something that happened when money landed in your lap, "I have been a hopeless fan ever since that night at Slim's Y-Ki-Ki Lounge in Opelousas, that first night I heard you, heard you and your band." Her hand rushed across the table like a hawk toward his. "I've been on my share of tailrides and I've been not just to the Y-Ki-Ki but Harry's Club over in Beaux Bridge and Richards Club in Lawtell, the Labor Day festival in Plaisance . . ."

Chester, cocking an ear for sounds of the car, shook himself from his thoughts. "Let me stop you, darlin' dear."

She clutched his hand as though afraid it might escape, her eyes a pair of low-hanging plums; their skin a telling contrast, hers creamy and white like egg custard, his the shade of caramel.

I must be hungry, he thought.

"I have never," she intoned, "never heard a man play as wild, as free, as hard as you."

He could no longer see her face. His mind's eye conjured Lorena.

She was a custom Gabbanelli, not unlike the one he'd

been playing onstage when the music stopped, but finer, older, one-of-a-kind. Handmade in Castelfidardo sixty-five years ago, during the war, she'd been bought by his granddad for twenty dollars and a pig.

Chester thought he'd seen one of the Cheniers play one just like her at the Acadiana music festival, and the prospect had coiled a skein of fear around his heart. But no, theirs lacked the purple heart accents, the buttons of polished bone, much more. And sure enough, Lorena proved her royalty that day. An accordion war, oh yes, him and Richard LeBoeff at the end, Chester taking the prize with a fiery rendition of an original he'd penned just the night before, titled "Mutt-fish Gumbo." Next day, the local headlines screamed, *The Jimi Hendrix of the Squeezebox*, and there she was, in the picture with Chester: Lorena. Who else was worthy to share his crown? He grinned, in spite of himself. What would Granddad think of that?

He'd been a marksman in the 92nd Infantry, the fabled Buffalo Soldiers, moving up the Italian peninsula in '44 while most white troops got shipped to Normandy for the push to Berlin. He hefted Lorena on his back like a long-lost child as the Mule Pack Battalion marched up alongside Italian black-smiths and resistance volunteers, South Africans, Brazilians, trudging across minefields and treadway bridges, scaling man-made battlements and the Ligurian hills toward von Kessel-ring's Gothic Line.

He endured the march up the Serchio Valley, survived the Christmas slaughter in Gallicano, suffered the withering German 88s and machine-gun fire as the 92nd crawled across the Cinquale Canal. Throughout his boyhood, Chester sat be-side his granddad's rocker and listened to his tales, enthralled, inspired, and each one circled back to guess who? The accordion became his granddad's prize, his lucky talisman, his reason for fighting, and he named her Lorena, same as his girl back home, the one who refused to wait. In time, the beautiful box with all that luck inside became the real Lorena, the one who was true.

And she was a stone beauty—pearl inlays, seasoned mahogany lacquered to the color of pure cane syrup, the grille cut lath by lath from brass with a jeweler's saw, double reeds made from Swedish blue steel for that distinctive tremolo, a deep mournful throbbing tone unmatched by any instrument Chester had ever heard. She had the voice of a sad and beautiful thrush, the tragic bride of a lost soldier. And yes, Granddad had come back from that war lost. The accordion became a kind of compass, guiding him back, at least halfway.

In time, Granddad passed her on to Papa Ray and he in turn handed her over to Chester, the prodigy, the instrument not so much a gift as a dare. *Be unique and stunning and wise*, she seemed to whisper, *like me*. And that was the full shape of the inheritance, not just an instrument but a sorrow wrapped in warrior loneliness. Chester treated her like the dark mystery she was, never bringing her out until the final set of the night, queen of the ball—which was why she'd been in the bus, not onstage, when the Western Flyer got jacked.

Chester glanced down at the table, saw the woman's fingers lacing his own, felt the nagging heat of her touch. "Darlin' dear," he repeated, snapping to. "As I have told you at least twice now, and which should be obvious to a fan as devoted as you claim to be . . ." He lumbered to his feet as, at long last, the headlights of Geno's Firebird appeared in the lot. "The name is pronounced *Ree-shard*."

She cocked her eye, a dark glance, the rice pudding curdled. "Oh, boo."

"Adieu."

"Boo!"

He tipped his hat and hustled into the night.

Inside the car, Chester collected a pearl-handled Colt .45 from an oilcloth held out to him by Skillet, who kept for himself a .44 Smithy and a buck knife big enough to gore a dray. Geno carried a .38 snub-nose and a length of pipe. You play enough bayou jump joints and oil-coast dives, you habituate your weapons.

Geno, sitting behind the wheel, glanced over his shoulder at Chester who straddled the hump in the backseat. "I'm guessin' there ain't no guesswork to who took the bus."

"No." Chester dropped the magazine on the Colt, checked to be sure it had all seven rounds, plus one in the pipe, slammed it home again, then tucked the pistol under his belt as Geno slipped the Firebird into gear and took off. "I think not."

Skillet, true to his nature, remained quiet. Black as Houston crude and wiry with cavernous eyes, he'd been hit with a fry pan in '77, still had the telltale dent in his skull. Geno, plump as a friar with slicked-back hair, kept up a low, tuneless hum as he drove. He was the band's gadfly mystic, always wandering off on some oddball spirit craze, and he'd recently read somewhere that you ought to chant "Om" to get right with the cosmos. Apparently, though, he'd snagged some cross-signals, for the effort came out sounding like some rural Baptist dirge, hobbling along in waltz time. Chester almost asked for the radio, then reconsidered. Who knew what sort of ass-backward mojo you'd conjure, stopping a man midchant?

They pulled over for food at an all-night canteen on the Port Arthur outskirts: crawfish étouffée, hush puppies, grilled boudin sausage. Using his fingers to scoop the food from its white cardboard carton, Chester dug in, reminding himself that vengeance is but one of many hungers.

"Boudin," he said. "Proof that God loves a Creole man." To himself, he added: *Let's hope some of that love will hold.*

They took Route 73 to catch I-10 near Winnie, figuring the thief was heading west. He'd mentioned home was El Paso, just across the border from Ciudad Juárez, murder capital of the planet.

His name was Emigdio Nava but he went by Feo, the Ugly One. The handle was not ironic. Small and hunched but muscular, arms sleeved with tats, he had a scrapper's eyes, a mulish face, the complexion of a peach pit. He'd approached Chester about two weeks back, at a private party they were playing out on the levee road in East Jefferson Parish. He invited himself back into the greenroom between sets and sat himself down, a cagey introduction, smile like a paper cut. Everybody in the band figured him for a dealer—except for a few old locals too big to unseat, the Mexican gangs ran practically everything dopewise now—but he made no mention of such.

He did, though, have an offer.

"Want you to write me a song," he said, whipping out a roll of bills. He licked his thumb, flicked past five hundreds, tugged them free, and handed them out for Chester to take. "For my girl."

Chester glanced toward Skillet, by far the best judge of character in the band. He'd played up and down the coast for over thirty years, headliners to pickup bands, seen everything twice. It took awhile, but finally Skillet offered a nod.

"Tell me about your girl," Chester said, taking the money.

Her name was Rosa Sánchez but everyone knew her as La Monita, Little Monkey. Again, Chester learned, irony was not at issue. Feo showed him snapshots. She was a tiny woman with unnaturally long arms. Her small round face was feathered with fine black hair. An upturned nose didn't help, though the rest of the package was straight-up fine. And being clever and resourceful, or so Chester surmised from how Feo told it, she turned misfortune to her advantage. A hooker who worked near the ship channel, she gained the upper hand over the more attractive girls by, more or less, outfucking them.

Geno, catching a glance at the picture, muttered, "Ain't we funky."

Chester cut him with a look.

"We got this tradition in Mexico," Feo said, ignoring them both. "Ballads. We call them *corridos*. It's how we sing the praises of the outcasts, the unlucky ones, the tragic ones, but also the bandits, the narcotrafficantes, the pandilleros. Anyone who understands what it means to suffer, but also to fight." The dude had picked up a bit of a Texas accent, and it was weird, hearing the Mexican and the Texican wrestling in his voice. Gave him a case of the mush-mouth.

Skillet watched him like a cat perched beneath the hummingbird feeder.

"You people," Feo continued, "have such a tradition also, no?"

"Called *raconteur*." Chester, too, could be a man of few words. You people, he thought. "When do you need this by?"

Feo rose from his chair, that slashing smile. "How hard can it be?"

Harder than Chester thought, as it turned out, but he'd taken the money and so was stuck. The problem was simple: how to pen something apt that wasn't at the same time offensive. It proved the better of him—he put it off, scratched out a few sorry lines, cast them aside:

Only the homely
And the angels above
Know how to suffer
The pain called love

Mama would shoot me dead onstage, he thought, if I dared sing that out loud. She'd been a torch singer famous up and down the bayou country, Miss Angeline her stage name. She'd died when Chester was seven, the cancer setting a pattern for women he'd lose.

Seeing that Chester was suffering over the lyrics, and sensing in that the chance for some clowning, Geno tried his hand too, singing his version over lunch, a plate of fried chicken and string beans with bacon:

She is my monkey
I'll make her my wife
Gonna be funky
For the rest of my life

Chester glanced up from his own plate, jambalaya with shrimp and andouille. "You looking to get me killed?"

Geno veiled his grin with a shrug. "Not before payday, no."

Two nights later, Feo showed up unannounced at the club they were playing, gripping an Abita beer, working a path through the crowd to the bandstand. He offered no greeting, just gestured once with a cock of his head.

Desperate for an idea—something, anything, quick—and unnerved by the small man's stare, Chester turned to the band and counted off the first thing that popped into his head:

My monkey got a cue-ball head
A good attitude and them long skinny legs

No sooner did the lyrics escape than he felt the sheer disastrous lunacy of what he'd done. And the band hadn't played the tune since forever, execution falling somewhere between rusty and half-ass, a dash of salt in an already screaming wound. The gleam in Feo's eye turned glacial. The bottle of beer dropped slowly from his mouth, and the mouth formed an O, then reverted to slit-mode as he vanished. Chester thought maybe that would be it, a feeble wish, but then he spotted him at the bar between sets, and at the end of the night, like a bad itch, he turned up again, drifting across the parking lot as they loaded up the Flyer.

Approaching Chester, "Got time for a word, cabrón?"

Chester led him off a little from the others, not sure why. "Nice night—no, mon ami?" Cringing. Lame.

"You were supposed to write me a song."

The boys in the band sidled up, watching Chester's back.

Chester worked up a pained look, phony to the bone. "I thought I did."

"That thing you played?"

"It's called 'Who Stole My Monkey?'"

"Bartender tells me it's an old tune, written by some dude named Zachary Richard. Not you. You're Chester."

"He's my uncle," Chester lied.

"Still ain't you."

Chester tried an ingratiating smile. "How's about a few more days?"

"And you insult my girl too?" Feo held Skillet and Geno with his eyes, warning them that he could take all three. "You diss me twice? Know how much money you could make writing me love songs, güey?"

Got a fair idea, Chester thought, just as he knew how many grupero musicians had been murdered the past two years by cats just like this. The situation had snuggled up next to awful, but before he could conjure his next bad idea, the Mexican turned away. Chester saw a whole lot of luck heading off with him.

Over his shoulder, in that inimitable mush-mouth Texican-Mexican, Feo called out, "Fuck all, y'all!"

Inside the car, Geno broke off his solemn humming. "I'm also guessin'," picking up his thread, "that we ain't gonna call the law on this."

"If we were—" Chester began.

"We'd a done it by now."

"Correct."

You don't call the law to help you fetch a stolen bus when there's an ounce of coke on board, not to mention a half-pound of weed, a mayonnaise jar full of Oxycontin, and enough crank to whirl you across Texas a dozen times and back. Small wonder we're broke, Chester thought. They'd stocked up for the road, a lot of away dates on the calendar. Sure, the stash was tucked beneath false panels, nothing in plain view, but all it took was one damn dog.

Getting back to Geno, he said, "Long as you're in the mood for guesswork, riddle me this: think our friend the music lover, before skipping town, scooped up this chimp-faced punch he loves?"

Geno's eyes bulged. "In our bus?"

"He'll ditch it quick, trade down for something more subtle. Or so I figure. Skillet?"

As always, silence. In time, a stubborn nod.

True enough, they found the Flyer with its distinctive black-and-gold design sitting on the edge of the interstate just outside Houston. Maybe he feigned a breakdown, Chester thought, stuck out his thumb, jacked the first car that stopped. Maybe he just pulled over to grab forty winks.

"Ease up behind," he said, drawing the .45 from under his belt. "Let's see what happens."

Geno obliged, lodged the tranny in park. "You honestly think he's up inside of there?"

"That's one of several scenarios I could predict." Chester let out a long slow breath. "What say we not get stupid?"

Chester kept the gun down along his leg—wouldn't do for a state trooper to happen by and spot two armed African American gents with their fat dago sidekick sneaking up on a fancy tour bus in evident distress. They lurked at the ass-end of the Flyer, waiting to see if the old in-line six turned over, a belch of smoke.

Geno glanced at his watch. "Wait too long, we'll be dealing with po-po."

Chester felt the engine panel, noted it was cool to the touch. "I'm aware of this."

"Like, Rangers."

"Indeed."

"Just sayin'."

"Duly noted."

They ventured single file along the bus's passenger side, Skillet in the lead, his crouching duck-walk straight out of some Jim Brown blaxploitation joint. Chester, lightheaded from fear, began imagining as a soundtrack a two-step rendition of the theme from *Shaft*.

Reaching the door, Skillet tried the handle and found it unlocked. He let it swing open easy. A glance toward the driver's seat—empty—then a glance back toward Chester, who nodded. Crouching, pistol drawn, Skillet entered, the others right behind.

The stillness was total, all but for the buzz of flies. No one there, except for the seat at the back, dead center. She wore a black miniskirt with a crimson top bunched in front, no stockings, shoes kicked off. Long skinny arms you couldn't miss.

Geno put words to the general impression. "What happened to her fucking head?"

Chester searched for Lorena while Skillet probed the hidey-holes, unscrewing the panels, bagging the dope he found untouched within. Geno kept an eye out for troopers. Chester could feel his heart in his chest like a fist pounding on a door, sweat boiling off his face, but the accordion was nowhere to be found. Thief wants me to follow, he thought, that or he's got a mind to hock her.

Despite himself, he glanced more than once at the headless corpse, sitting upright at the back, like she was waiting for someone to ask her the obvious question: *Why?* The woman he loved so much, Chester thought, paid five hundred cash for a song, then this. Only way it made sense was if she was just a means to an end. And the end lay somewhere west.

Geno, suddenly ashen, said, "That Mex is tweakin'," then stumbled off the Flyer and vomited in the weeds. Jackknifed, short of breath, he mumbled, "Oh Lord . . ."

A moment later, like a sphinx handing up its riddle, Skillet finally spoke: "'Less you wanna get us all sent up for that girl's murder," he told Chester, "might be time to make a call."

In Houston they phoned the Port Arthur police, reported the

bus stolen, fudged a little about when and where, claimed no
notion of who—they didn't want some cop getting hold of Feo
before they got their chance—then dialed every local pawnshop, even called the Gabbanelli showroom, putting out word
that somebody might be trying to offload Lorena on the sly. If
so, a reward would be offered, no questions asked. But they
got no word the Mexican had tried it yet. Still, the phone lines
would be ringing all the way across the state. If he stopped to
unload the accordion anywhere along his jaunt, they'd hear,
unless Feo sold it to a private party.

"Which," Chester noted despondently as they resumed
the trip west, "I figure he might well do."

"That'd be my plan," Geno acknowledged.

"Just drive," Chester said.

They were screaming past a little town called Johnsue
when the cars showed up, two unmarked sedans, recent model,
U.S. make. The men within remained obscure behind tinted
glass. One car tore ahead, the other locked in behind. A window in the lead car rolled down, an arm emerged, gesturing
them to the berm.

Geno glanced back over his shoulder. "What you want
me to do?"

This business just ain't gonna turn easy, Chester thought.
"What I want and what's wise would seem to be at odds at the
moment." He let out a sigh and pushed the .45 under Skillet's
seat. "Pull on over."

Skillet and Geno tucked their weapons away as well, as
two men emerged from the lead car; the crew behind stayed
put. The visitors wore identical blue sport coats, tan slacks,
but they walked like men who spent little time in an office.
The one who approached the driver's window did so almost
merrily, an air of recreational menace. The other had shoul-

ders that could block a doorway, a bulldog face, that distinctive high-and-tight fade, fresh from the Corps.

The merry one glanced in, studying each man's face, one at a time, settling at last on Chester. "You wanna un-ass that seat, big fella?" He grinned, cracking gum between his molars.

Chester opened the door and bent Skillet forward as he struggled to unfold into the sun, while Mr. Merry Menace leaned on the Firebird's fender, arms crossed. His wraparounds sat crooked on his face.

"Understand you've made some inquiries regarding a certain Emigdio Nava." A whiskey baritone. "Mind telling us what that concerns?"

Us, Chester thought. "He stole an instrument of mine."

The man cocked his head toward his partner, who just continued to glare. Turning back: "Instrument?"

"You knew we've been making inquiries, I'd guess you know about what."

The smile didn't falter. The man repeated: "Instrument?"

All right then, Chester thought. Way it's gonna be. "Accordion. Belonged to my granddad. Serious sentimental value."

A loathsome chuckle. "Sentimental value. Touching."

"Can I see some identification?" Chester said.

The man pushed his wraparounds up his nose. "I don't think so. No."

"You're not the law."

"Better than the law, most occasions."

"Such as this?"

"Oh, this especially."

The sun-baked office bore no name, just another anonymous door in an industrial park ten blocks off the interstate. Four men not much different than the first two emptied from the second car, another two waited inside. They put Chester and Skillet and Geno in separate rooms, each one the same morose beige, folding chairs the only furniture, to which each man got bound with duct tape. A silver Halliburton case rested in the corner of Chester's room, and he doubted an item of luggage had ever terrified him more.

Mr. Merry Menace snapped on a pair of latex gloves. "So you're musical."

"Look," Chester said, his mouth parched, "no need for this, I told you—"

The fist came out of nowhere and landed like a sledge, the latex chafing his face like tire rubber. He heard the hinge crack in his jaw, a phosphorescent whiteness rising within his mind, blotting out the world. When the world came back, it came back screaming—Geno, the next room over.

Chester shouted, "I'm telling them everything!" but all it earned him was a crackback blow, knuckles busting open his cheek.

"You talk to me. Not them."

Chester shook his head, gazing up through a blur. The trickle of blood over his stubble itched. "Why do this?"

"What was it like, finding your bus by the side of the road, Feo's little ape-girl inside?"

Chester shook his head like a wet dog. "You know."

"Oh, I know. Yes."

"He said he loved her."

"Love?" The man's smile froze in place. "She stood up to him, only woman who ever did, so it's said. He put up with it. That's love, I suppose. Up to a point."

"Why—"

"Cut off her head?" A shrug. "Style points."

Chester coughed up something warm, licked the inside of his cheek, tasted blood.

"They hurl severed heads onto disco floors down Mexico way, Chester, just to send a message. It's how vatos blog."

"I don't—"

"I'm gonna make it simple, okay? There are forces at play here. Secrets. Schemes and counterschemes and conspiracies so vast and twisted they make the Kennedy hit look like a Pixar flick." A gloved finger tapped Chester's brow, tiny splash of sweat. "Bottom line, you're dispensable, you and your two wack friends. I'm doing you a favor. Whatever business you have with Señor Nava, it's hereby null, moot, done. Tell me I'm right."

"I don't understand."

An open-hand slap this time, mere punctuation. "He's a poacher. Understand that?"

Chester inhaled, his chest rippling with the effort. "I grew up in Calcasieu Parish. I know what a poacher is."

"Not that kind of poacher. He's Mexican military, Teniente Nava, trains infantry, automatic weapons. When he's not recruiting assassins for the Juárez Cartel."

Chester swallowed what felt like an egg. "That's got nothing to do with me."

"Not now."

"Not never. All I want is Lorena."

The man glanced to his partner, eyebrow cocked. Perplexed. Chester sighed. "My accordion,"

It was like he'd admitted to sex with a fish. "Damn," the man said. He barked out a laugh. "You *are* sentimental."

They were escorted all the way back to the Houston city limits, then the two cars broke away. Message delivered, no further emphasis required. Skillet held a wet bandanna to the gash on the side of his head. He'd about had it with being hit on the skull. Geno, glancing up into his rearview, face swollen and colored like bad fruit, caught Chester's eyes, held the gaze.

"Say the word."

Chester had never killed a man—thought about it, sure, even plotted it out once. Now, though, he felt as close as close got. Feo had to pay. Pay for the theft of Lorena, pay for what Geno and Skillet had just endured, pay for the girl in the back of the Flyer. Feeling within him an invigorating, almost pleasurable hate, he imagined it was what his granddad—tongue unlocked by a jug of corn, Lorena resting in his lap—once described as the sickness at the bottom of the mind. He confessed to killing barehanded, last days of the war, his unit charged with cutting off the German retreat through the Cisa Pass. Low on ammunition, they didn't dare call in air or artillery support, the white officers would too easily call in fire directly atop their position. When the Germans overran their front line it got down to bayonets and bare knuckles, swinging their M1s like clubs. *I choked one man, stabbed two more, beat another unconscious with my helmet, then smothered him with his own coat. Lucky for me they was all starved weak.* The voice of a ghost. But now Chester understood. So be it, he thought. The old man would not just understand, he would insist. I will not betray her. I will find her. I will bring her home.

"You drop me at the airport, then go on back to Port Arthur."

"That won't do." It was Skillet.

Chester shook his head. "I can't let you—"

"Ain't you to let."

"Skillet . . ."

"You catch your plane." The older man's voice was quiet

and cold. "Geno and me, we'll turn on around, head west again. We'll check around San Antonio, see if we can find Lorena. Not, we'll see you in El Paso."

"I can't make it up to you."

"Nobody askin' that."

He slept in the terminal and caught the first flight to El Paso the next morning, touching down noonish, then a cab ride to the rectory of Santa Isabel. The pastor there was Father Declan Foley, but Chester knew him as Jolt. A boxer once, backwater champion before heading off to seminary.

A cluster of schoolgirls sat in the pews as Father Dec led them in confirmation class. Chester caught that haunting scent, beeswax, candle flame, hand-worn wood, a lingering whiff of incense, almost conjuring belief. Or the want of belief.

The priest glanced up as his visitor ambled forward. The girls followed suit, pigtails spinning. I must look a sight, Chester thought, jaw swollen and bruised, a zigzag cut across his dark-stubbled cheek.

"Father," he said, a nod of respect.

The priest told the girls to open their books, review the difference between actual and sanctifying grace, then led Chester back into the sacristy. He eyed his old friend with solemn disappointment.

"You look, as they say, like hell."

Chester tried to gather himself up, quit halfway. "Feel like I been there."

"You've still got time. What's this about?"

Chester laid it all out, something about being inside the church arousing an instinct toward candor, flipping off the switch to that part of his mind inclined toward deceit and other half measures. It was no small part.

Father Declan heard him out. Then: "The man's a killer."

"I'm with you there. I don't want no more trouble, though. Just Lorena."

"I find it hard to believe he cares about an accordion."

Chester laughed through his nose—it hurt. "Maybe he's planning a new career path."

"My point is, from the sound of things, he means to punish you."

"He's succeeded." Chester felt tired to the bone. This, too, he supposed, was the church working on him. "I hope to make that point. If I can find him before he crosses over to Juárez."

"I can ask around."

"I'd be obliged. Old time's sake and all." Chester heard something small in his voice. Begging. "You know the people who know the people and so on."

"Have you bothered praying?"

The question seemed vaguely insulting. Chester tugged at his ear. "Wouldn't say as I have, no."

"Be a good time to start, from all appearances."

"Can't say I feel inclined."

"Try." The priest reached out, his touch surprisingly gentle for such a meaty hand. "Old time's sake and all."

Father Dec gave him an address for a hotel nearby where he could rest while calls were made, then led him out to the front-most pew. Chester knelt. When in Rome, he figured, the deceit sector of his brain flickering back to life.

"By the way," he said, glancing over his shoulder at the schoolgirls, "just to settle my curiosity, what exactly is the difference between actual and sanctifying grace?"

The priest studied him a moment, something in his eye reminding Chester of the brawler he'd known before, glazed with sweat and blood, a smoky light hazing the ring, smell of cigars and sawdust, all those redneck cheers. "You know about all the women being killed across the border, right? Worst of it's right here, just over the line, Ciudad Juárez."

That didn't seem much of an answer. "Dec—"

"Not just women. Kids. Sooner or later, it's always the kids. They're shooting up rehab clinics too, nobody's sure why. Then there's the kidnap racket. Not just mayors and cops and businesspeople, now it's teachers, doctors, migrants, anybody. Know what your life's worth? Whatever your family can cobble together. If that. People have stopped praying to God. Why bother? They've turned to Santa Muerte. Saint Death."

The weariness returned. "Not sure what you're getting at exactly, Dec."

"I'm trying to focus your mind."

Chester had to bite back a laugh. Like having your grand-dad's button box stolen, finding a headless hooker at the back of your bus, and getting punked by somebody's goon squad doesn't focus your mind. "Fair enough."

"Put your problems in perspective."

"All right."

Gradually, the priest's stare weakened. Something like a smile appeared. "Sanctifying grace," he said, "comes through the sacraments. Actual grace is a gift, to help in times of temptation."

He returned to the schoolgirls, who shortly resumed their mumbled recitations, a soft droning echo in the cool church. Chester clasped his hands and bowed his head. He tried. But the churchy nostalgia he'd felt before had a weaker signal now. Nothing much came. No gift in his time of temptation.

Father Dec would phone around, every soup kitchen, every clinic, every police station, the holy hotline, calling all sinners. Someone would remember the monkey-faced street-walker who'd gone off with the Mexican lieutenant known for his deadly sideline. Someone would know where in town the man would sneak back to. He wondered if Father Dec would mention how the woman died, mention who the killer was, playing not on sympathy but revenge. No, Chester thought, that's my realm, and he thought again of his granddad in the spring of '45, last days of the war, knifing a man, strangling another, smothering a third, whatever it took. And why? He pictured her, the bottomless glow of her wood, the warm tangy smell of her leather straps and bellows, the pearly gleam of her buttons. Remembered the moaning cry she made in his loving hands. No other like her in the world, never. If that wasn't love, what was? Worth suffering for, yes, worth dragging all across Italy to bring back home, worth killing for if it came to that. And it had. He suspected, very shortly, it would again.

He glanced up at the plaster Jesus nailed to the crucifix hung above the altar. If you were half of who they claim, he thought, none of this would be needed. Which pretty much concluded all the praying he could manage.

He rose from his knees, let the weariness rearrange itself in his body, then ambled on out, murmuring "Thank you" to his friend as he passed, smiling at the girls who glanced up at him in giggling puzzlement or mousy fear. Orphans, he guessed, remembering what Jolt had said about the killing, knowing there were thousands of kids like this in every border town, their parents out in the desert somewhere, long dead. Some of the girls were lovely, most trended toward plain, a few were decidedly nun material. One among that last group—he couldn't help himself, just the darkening track of his thoughts—reminded him of the Mexican's tramp girl-friend, La Monita.

He was halfway down the block, thinking supper might be in order, when his cell rang. A San Antonio number. He flipped the phone open. "Geno?"

A gunshot barked through the static on the line. A muffled keening sob—a gagged man screaming—then grunts, a gasp, Geno came on the line. "Please, Chester, it's just a box." The voice shaky, faint, a hiss. "Buy yourself a new one. P-p-please?" Chester could hear spittle pop against the mouthpiece. The fact that it was Geno meant Skillet was dead. You don't put the weak one on the line to make a point with the strong one. You kill the strong one so the weak one understands.

He slowly closed the phone.

"I'm sorry," he whispered.

He wandered the street for half an hour, dazed one minute, lit up with fury the next, settling finally into a state of bloodthirsty calm. In a juke joint off East Paisano he scored a pistol from the bartender, a Sig Sauer 9mm, stolen from a cop, the man bragged. In a gun shop nearby he bought two extra magazines and a box of hollow points, loaded the clips right there in the store, hands trembling from adrenaline. Feo's gonna walk the border, he told himself, and the best place to do that is downtown, Stanton Street bridge. That's where I gotta be.

He walked toward the port of entry, found himself a spot to sit, lifting a paper from the litter bin for camouflage, spreading it out in his lap, the gun hidden just beneath. An hour passed, half of another, night fell, the lights came on. He sat still as a bullfrog, watchful, eyeing every walker trudging south into Mexico. And as he did the sense of the thing fell together, like a puzzle assembling itself in midair right before his eyes. If only that helped, he thought.

A little after eight his cell phone rang again. He considered letting it go but then he checked the display, recognized the rectory number.

"Jolt," he said.

Silence. "No one calls me that anymore."

"I just did."

"I want you to come back to the church."

"Not happening."

"What you're thinking of doing is wrong."

"All I want's Lorena. There's others want him dead on principal. That's why he's running."

"He'll be back."

"I suspect that's true."

"Suspect? I know. He's been in touch."

Chester shot up straight. A vein fluttered in his neck. "Feo."

"He wants to work a trade."

"I'm listening."

"No, you don't understand. He can't . . . Not what he's asking. I won't."

"The girl."

Another silence.

"Chester . . ."

"The one I saw in the church today. One who looks just like Rosa Sánchez."

"It's just an accordion, Chester."

The rage blindsided him, a surge in his midriff like coiling fire. "Not to me. Not to my granddad."

"You can't trade a child for a thing."

A *thing*? "Is it still a sin to chew the wafer, Dec? You know, because it really isn't bread anymore. Something's happened."

"Don't talk like a fool."

"Says the man who turns wine into blood."

"Her name is Analinda. The girl, I mean."

Of course, Chester thought, knowing what the priest was up to. Give her a name, she turns precious. She's alive. Like Lorena. "She's his daughter."

"She's *her* daughter."

"Point is, the girl's what he wants, has been all along. Why? I have no clue. Killers are vain, kids are for show. It's an itch, the daddy thing, comes and goes, maybe he felt a sudden need to scratch. The mother gave her away, spare her all that. So he paid me to write her a song, impress her, get her to ease up, forgive him, introduce him to his daughter. Then I went and screwed the pooch on that front, so—"

"He has no right."

"Who are you to say?"

"He'll sell her."

"So offer him a price."

"You said it yourself, he's a killer."

"He's not alone in that. My granddad was a killer. Killed for you. Killed for me."

"Chester . . ."

"God's a killer. Put some heat under that one."

The priest, incredulous: "You want to argue theodicy?"

"Not really." He felt strangely detached all of a sudden, preternaturally so, tracking the walkers bobbing past. It was no longer in his hands. "I'm just passing the time, Jolt."

"I want you to come back to the church."

"And what exactly does that mean—argue the odyssey?"

"Not the odyssey. Theodicy."

"I know," he said. "Just messing with you."

He spotted it then, the hardshell case he knew so well, nicked and battered from the Italian campaign, a long whitish crease like a scar across the felt, left by the bullet from a Mauser 98 at Gallicano. The man carrying it walked hurriedly, face obscured by the hood of his sweatshirt. Chester felt no doubt. He flipped his phone closed, rose to his feet, and let the newspaper flutter down, tucking the pistol beneath his shirt. You've taken what belongs to me, he thought, what belongs to my family, the most precious thing we've ever owned. Two good men are dead because of you, not to mention the woman, the one you crowed over, said you loved. You deserve what's coming. Deserve worse. I'm doing your daughter a favor. I'm bringing Lorena home.

He chose his angle of intercept and started walking, not so fast as to draw attention but quick enough to get there, easing through some of the other walkers. From across the street, a second man appeared. Chester recognized him too, the shoulders, the bulldog face, that distinctive jarhead fade.

Let it happen, he told himself, and it did.

Feo caught sight of the ex-Marine, began to run but the accordion slowed him down. *Drop it*, Chester wanted to shout, but the Mexican wouldn't let go and then the gunman was on him and the pistol was raised and two quick pops, killshots to the skull. Feo crumpled, people scattered. The killer fled.

Blinking, Chester tucked the Sig in his pants, pulled his shirt over, moving the whole time, slow at first, cautious, then a jog, breaking into a run, till he was there at the edge of the pooling blood, the Mexican, the poacher, the Ugly One, lying still, just nerve flutters in the hands, the legs. Strange justice, Chester thought. The sickness at the bottom of the mind.

He pried the case from the dead man's fingers, gripped the handle, and began to run back toward downtown. Something wasn't right. The weight was off-balance, wobbly, wrong. He stopped, knelt, tore at the clasps, lifted the lid. Staring back at him from a bed of sheet music, the eyes shiny like polished bone, was the severed head of Rosa Sánchez.

Some time later—hours? days?—he found himself propped on a cantina barstool, a shot of mezcal in his fist, a dozen empties scattered before him, splashes of overfill dampening the bar's pitted wood, a crowd of nameless men his newfound friends, all of them listening with that singular Mexican lust for heartbreak as he recited the tale of La Monita and Feo, told them of Geno and Skillet, confessed in a whisper his unholy love for Lorena. Time blurred into nothingness, he felt himself blurring as well, just another teardrop in the river of dreams, and he wondered what strange genius had possessed him, guiding him to this place, over the bridge from El Paso to Ciudad Juárez, the murder capital of the planet. Nor would he recall how or when he crossed that other bridge, the one between lonely and alone, but it would carry him farther than the other, days drifting into weeks, weeks dissolving into months then years, more cantinas, more mezcal, till life as he'd known it became a whisper in the back of his mind and the man named Chester Richard drifted away like a tuneless song.

The ghost in the mirror of the bus terminal washroom, rinsing out his armpits, brushing his teeth with a finger, hair wild as an outcrop of desert scrub, sooner or later shambled off to the next string of lights across a doorway, entered and plopped himself down, crooning his garbled tales of love and murder and music, then begging a drink, told to get out by the owner, indulged by the angry man's wife, exiled to a corner with a glass of tejuino—no mezcal for a gorrón—and he'd wait for the musicians to appear, assembling themselves on the tiny bandstand like clowns in a skit, until once, in that endless maze of nights, a boy of ten shouldered on his accordion in the smoky dimness, and the nameless drunk criollo glanced up from his corner to see the seasoned mahogany dark as cane syrup, the pearl inlays, the purple heart accents, the buttons of polished bone, and with the first sigh of the kidskin bellows came that deep unmistakable throbbing tremolo, and he felt his heart crack open like an egg, knowing at last he was free.

SIX DEAD CABBIES

BY TIM TINGLE

Ellington AFB

Fifty years later, the image will not leave me alone. Six cab drivers, their throats sliced from behind, left slumped and twitching in the front seat, while a gaunt man with a bum knee wipes blood from his switchblade to his jeans and walks ten miles to his car, parked in the lot of the Officers' Club at Ellington Air Force Base, southeast of Houston. He limps through the security gate to his waiting car, pulling his jacket collar high and nodding to the guards.

"Another fight with the old lady?" yells a guard.

Just a nod in reply.

"Man, I hope she's worth it. Making you walk at four in the morning."

A shrug. Nothing more. Laughter from the guards.

"Don't ever tell anybody more than absolutely necessary to get what you need." If Denny said it once, he said it a dozen times. "Too many words will cost you."

Too many words. 1966, summer of. I was working as a busboy at Ellington Air Force Base, senior year of high school coming up. I was doing okay, too. After a month I got promoted to Head Salad Maker, an illustrious title worth fifteen more cents an hour, the price of a gallon of regular. But the promotion meant a stylistic change that came as a sweet surprise. I became part of the kitchen crew, who made no pretense at cleanliness and courtesy, like waitresses and busboys had to. Nope, if you felt it coming, no need to stifle, not in the kitchen.

Burns and yelps and cussing out loud, grease-splattered sleeves and aprons and bumping into each other ten times a night, stolen minutes with cigarettes in the cinder-block men's dressing room—nobody would think of wearing real clothes in this kitchen, only the white pants and shirts provided by the management—while jokes and dirt of every sort came flowing from the kitchen and spilling out the back door onto the employee parking lot.

Where Denny waited.

"I'm dating one-uh the waitresses at the Officers' Club." That always got him in the gate. No one even asked who, but he wouldn't have minded telling 'em Sherry if he had to. She was a good-looker all right, a real sexy woman.

Sherry started glancing at the back door usually around one a.m., squinting through the screen for her skinny, limp-legged beau. What she saw in him nobody could guess. He had a scary glint in his eye. We closed at two.

"You gonna stay up past your bedtime again tonight?" came the first round of catcalls from the cooks.

"Not Sherry, Sherry baby," said another. "She always knows when it's bedtime."

Sherry disappeared with entrees for four, through the swinging double doors to the thick maroon carpet and chandeliered dining hall, where astronauts brought their wives and officers sported formal dress attire. Different world. Twenty-piece orchestra playing "Strangers in the Night" and even early Beatles songs . . .

Michelle, ma belle,

These are words that go together well,
My Michelle

. . . sometimes with a crooner, mostly instrumental. Men drank whiskey and women stirred swizzle sticks in fruity drinks or rum and cola, till everyone shed the skin of daytime sufficiently and eased into the star-spangled night. Then lights came up, the show was over, and busboys split tips with the waitresses. Eighty-twenty, advantage waitress. That was the deal.

On nights when Denny waited, Sherry would go fifty-fifty if her busboy did her cleanup work and let her leave early. You'd have to be nuts not to go for a deal like that. Made me want to be a busboy again, all those crisp dollar bills changing hands.

Till one Saturday night, early. Cooks and kitchen help, the night shift, were getting dressed when Sherry walks into the men's room, flips her Camel ashes, and says, "If Denny comes to the back door tonight, tell him I am not going out with him, ever again."

"Why don't you tell him?"

"I did tell him, last night. But he won't give up. He'll be back. Lemme know when he comes, and don't give him the time of day. Just tell him to leave me alone."

"You got it, sis," we all of us agree.

As soon as she was gone, the speculating starts.

"Man, whatever Denny did, he messed up this time."

"Yeah, and she was in LOVE with that skinny fool."

"Not no more."

"Un-uh. Gonna be cold day in hell 'fore she sees him again."

"Maybe some other leg went limp." Hoots and laughter,

especially from the black cooks, and a buskid buddy, Eddie, asked me later, "So did Denny hurt his other knee?"

"Whatever happened, she better off for it. That Chevy he drives 'bout to fall apart."

"You right about that. Giddy-yap, giddy-yap, 409."

"Giddy-yap to the junkyard."

Everybody laughs, and ten minutes later no one gives a second thought to the demise of Denny and Sherry.

Including Denny. He had other plans, though for the next week he appeared, as expected, at the back door of the Officer's Club, his figurative hat in hand. "Would you mind telling Sherry I'm here?"

"She don't want to see you no more," said whichever cook was out back smoking.

"If you'd just let her know, I'll wait here for a while, in case she changes her mind." Denny wasn't so good at kicking the dirt and sighing regretfully, but he did the best he could, and since none of the cooks were so good at detecting guile, everybody seemed to buy the fact that Denny was pining and Sherry was holding her ground.

First indication otherwise came a few days after the breakup, when I snatched a half-full margarita glass from a bus tray and dashed to the men's room. I was just about to push the door open when the screen door banged and I saw Denny standing there. "Have a cigarette, kid," he said, tossing me a pack of Marlboros.

"I don't smoke." I tossed them back.

"Have it your way," he smirked, then flicked his lighter, cupped his hand, and leaned into the flame. "Enjoy your drink." He had to see the panic on my face.

"Look, Denny, don't tell anybody about me drinking, please."

"Kid. Do I look like some kinda snitch? Your secret's safe, no worries."

"Thanks." I stepped in the men's room and downed the drink. On my way out, he was still there.

"How old are you, kid?"

"Fifteen, be sixteen in November."

"Too young for beer."

"Too young to buy it, maybe," I told him.

"But not too young to drink?"

"Nope."

"That's good, kid. 'Cause I'm up for a few beers tonight. Maybe let the other boys know. You spring for the bucks, I spring for the ID."

Simple as that. Saturday was a great night for tips, and Denny found four takers, myself and three busboys—Eddie Serge, Bobby Haney, and Charles Savell. Ready for kicks. We pooled our tips, gave Denny six bucks, and he had a case of Lone Stars iced down in a brand-new cooler by the time we finished our clean-up work.

"New cooler? You buy that?" Charles asked.

"Yeah, kid. I bought it with this," he said, tapping his head with the tip of his longneck. We let it go at that, but an hour later, when we passed a snatch 'n grab, as my old man always called a convenience store, Bobby said, "Denny, man, pull over. I need some smokes."

"Not here," said Denny. "That's where I got the cooler. No reason to risk it."

"Huh?"

"I done told you. I used my head. Paid for the beer like a good little boy, then asked the man where the john was. After I finished, I told him the toilet was overflowing. He ran to check, and I grabbed the cooler from a stack on the sidewalk."

Denny drove another two blocks, to the Gulf Freeway feeder road, and we piled out for cigarettes and chips. Denny grabbed me by the shoulder before I could enter the store.

"Okay. You seem to be the smart one here. So listen up. Never leave the car, unless we staying for a few hours, then you park away from the place. Get it?" I nodded. "If we here for a quick stop, keep the engine running. Better yet, back into the space. If we need to leave in a hurry, no problem, we do it."

He tossed me the keys, and I started the car. Ten minutes later, he dropped a bag of Fritos in my lap and slid in beside me. "Let's go."

"Where?"

"Galveston Island. Beaches are nice and deserted at this hour." Denny popped the cap off another beer.

So we drank and smoked—even though the cigarrettes made me dizzy, I had a few—and prowled up and down Galveston Beach our first night as Denny's hoodlums. Sometime around three o'clock, we snuck up on a car parked on a shadowy stretch of beach. The windows were rolled down and we heard moaning and mumbled words coming from the backseat. I slow-crawled the car as close as we dared, then waited at the wheel with the engine humming while Denny and my buds crept out and surrounded the parkers.

"THIS IS THE POLICE!" they all hollered. Denny shined his flashlight on two college kids from the mainland, scared out of their wits, and I hit the headlights on bright. We all laughed, and Denny tossed an open beer can on the couple while they scrambled to get dressed.

As we pulled away, squealing the tires on the ramp from the beach to the seawall, Bobby said, "Man, I would hate to be those two!"

"Yeah," said Charles. "Gonna be the last time they go parking on the beach."

"Then we did 'em a favor," said Denny. We all turned our eyes to him as he lifted a switchblade from his hip pocket and flipped it open. He held it out the window, twisting the steel in the streetlights and slicing the night air at fifty miles an hour. "They could'a got this." We drove in silence to the base.

Other than that, and letting the air out the tires of a few cars parked on the seawall, the night was uneventful. I remember thinking Denny might have slashed a few.

Nothing much happened at the base on Sundays. The club closed at ten, and even though it was summer and we were high school students, somehow the pattern that Monday begins another hard workweek seemed ingrained from birth. Was certainly true for the grown-ups in our lives. This was blue-collar turf, Pasadena, South Houston, La Porte, Kemah. Less us versus the Russians and more beer versus the Baptists.

The Baptists reigned in Pasadena, keeping the city dry and free of alcohol, but the city limits were well defined in every direction. But just like the television comics said, "Wherever you find four Baptists, you'll always find a fifth," and sure enough, lingering just across the street from the city proper lay a steamy world of cheap fluorescent lights, private clubs and bars, pickup trucks, sleek Chevys and Pontiacs with dark-tinted windshields, and women in tight, tight skirts inside and outside the "beer joints," as my mother and her friends called them in disgust. Even the Klan had an office, KKK Headquarters, on busy College Avenue in Pasadena, frequented by good Baptists and Methodists both, and conveniently located two doors down from the Veterans of Foreign Wars Private Club.

* * *

Denny showed up the next Tuesday, asking again for Sherry, but his pleas were half-hearted. He didn't stay long. Come Friday, he caught me sneaking my nightly drink, this time the remains of an expensive whiskey from Sherry's favorite customer, a major who always had "way too much to drink," according to the club manager. The major had a way about him as smooth as the whiskey he drank. When he got real drunk he'd stroke his wife's wrist with one hand and Sherry's tight butt with the other. Sherry always smiled and put up with it, earning her tip.

But the club manager had another problem. Confronting an officer about his drinking was risky, so he and the waitresses had their ways of keeping order. A favorite ploy was letting him take a sip from the stout drink, then replacing it with a watered-down version while he wasn't looking.

But they couldn't watch the front and back doors at the same time, so if I wasn't choosy and didn't mind somebody else's germs, I could always get my drink, in this case the stout one.

"You on for tonight?" Denny said.

"You bet. I'll tell the guys."

"You do that."

We ponied up the bucks, and Denny stuffed the bills in his pocket and pulled away to blues music blaring from his car radio.

"I hate niggers," Denny called to me out the car window, "but I love their music."

I hated blues, and being a big Boston Celtics fan, I kind of liked Bill Russell and the Jones boys, so I didn't go along with Denny on the racial score either. But questioning Denny's taste in music or anything else, well . . . *I and Velma ain't stupid*, my favorite line from *West Side Story*.

That night we stayed on base. Maybe Denny thought he might've rushed his boys into a little too much mischief, time to back off some. We climbed over the wire fence to the officers' swimming pool, Olympic-sized with black lane strips on the bottom for competitions, and a three-tiered diving board. Even the dressing rooms were plush, with blue carpet and a drink bar.

The doors were locked, but that didn't stop Denny. He jimmied the lock with a screwdriver while we dangled our feet in the deep end. He soon appeared poolside with two fifths, one of rum and one of vodka.

I must've thrown up a dozen times that night, mostly out the window—and I was the designated driver—and capped it off with a nice bubbly mouthful of sour shrimp, which covered my pillow in the morning.

Denny coasted for a few weeks. We drank some beers and flung the empties into the officers' pool. Some evenings, once a week or so, we drove to the moneyed suburbs, and Denny cut his car across yards, destroying manicured flowerbeds and flattening hedges. "Small crimes," he would say, laughing.

As for me and my buds, we were scared at first, real scared, but after a while we knew Denny was above it all. We would never get caught. He wouldn't let us get caught. None of us ever questioned the logic of a forty-five-year-old man running around with teenagers. Bobby, Charles, Eddie, and me, we were *cool* teenagers, cool enough to be Denny's buds, that was our reasoning. One Saturday morning, we drove over to the pawnshop on Red Bluff Boulevard and bought ourselves switchblades, flashy cheap ones with long thin blades. Cheap because we knew we'd get kicked out of school if we got caught carrying 'em.

Summer two-a-days were starting up for the football team.

Me and Bobby and Eddie lived near the high school, and since we had afternoons off, we sometimes hung out around the field watching practice. We had some track stars, state champs in the sprints, and it was cool to see Freddy Randall, a coach's kid and our quarterback, launch a spiral while the jackrabbits outran everybody and grabbed a long one.

Then one day a defensive back, fooled at first, somehow caught up with Jimmy Whitson, one of the sprinters, and swatted a pass away. Nobody said a word, not even the coaches, and for a minute I thought maybe we hadn't seen what we just saw, someone outrun the state quarter-mile champion. That was only the beginning. When the guy took off his helmet and we saw that he was black, we all sucked air.

"Oh shit," said Bobby. No school in Pasadena had ever had a black student, as far as we knew, and certainly no football player.

"Case," a coach hollered, and the newcomer ran to the sideline. He didn't play anymore, not for the rest of practice.

When we climbed into the car to go, Eddie said, "Don't go yet. I want to see what he's driving."

Near the end of August, Denny turned impatient on us, getting jumpy and nervous. Waiting was over. His time had come. After all, we were headed back to school after Labor Day. Next-to-last Friday, Denny was waiting for us at the pool. "Beer's in the car," he said, no-nonsense. "We don't have much time, that's what you boys tell me, so we better get going."

We piled in the car and he laid rubber. In twenty minutes we were on the Gulf Freeway heading north. Two, three beers apiece and we were back in the groove. When we reached the turnoff to Gulfgate, Houston's first shopping mall, Denny turned east and pulled to the shoulder.

"You take the wheel," he told me. "Let's take a drive through the neighborhood."

I turned into a ten-year-old suburb, or what was built to be a suburb but now skirted downtown, and drove slowly down the dark, paved corridors of homes too close together and overhanging Chinese tallow trees.

"Looks like trash pickup is tomorrow," Denny said, noting the cans lining every curb. "Pull over."

He hopped out, grabbing the car keys on the way, and tossed a heavy metal container, brimming with refuse, into the trunk. He flipped me the keys.

"Okay, let's go."

"Where?"

"To the overpass."

I drove the five minutes back to the freeway overpass. Though it was now almost three a.m., a steady flow of traffic sped below us, sixteen-wheelers avoiding city traffic, late-night revelers headed home.

"Stop!"

I crossed the overpass and pulled over.

"What are you doing? I told you to stop."

"I did stop," I said.

"On the overpass. Now back up so we're on the overpass."

A freeway is a freeway, and though this was Interstate 10 and not the heavily trafficked Gulf Freeway, it was still a freeway, and backing up on a freeway is asking to make the morning headlines.

"Do it!"

I did as I was told. I parked near the guardrails.

"Leave it running." Denny moved with speed and purpose, lifting the trash can over the railing and flinging it to the freeway below.

To this day I don't know what mayhem ensued—a metal garbage can crashing thirty feet onto four lanes of vehicles driving anywhere from fifty to ninety miles an hour. When I think of that night I see broken windshields, swerving cars, overturned trucks, and twenty-car pile ups. Or maybe nothing more than a single dead teenager, returning from his date in faraway Conroe.

Or maybe nothing happened.

Bullshit. Plenty happened. We were just getting started. We were Denny's boys and we were on a roll, and with Denny, it was never enough. I have since met many people for whom it was *never enough*, but Denny set the standard.

By now we were too scared to speak, Charles, Eddie, and Bobby and me. Back in the burbs, we passed a block-long, two-story apartment unit. "To the curb," he said.

I eased to a stop opposite the apartments. Denny had spotted an unattached U-Haul trailer parked near the sidewalk between two buildings.

"Come on, boys. Keep it running," he told me.

The last I saw of the U-Haul, Denny and my buds were lifting the tongue of the trailer and dragging it down the sidewalk. A few minutes later the four emerged running from the apartments, scrambling into the car and hollering, everybody hollering, "Get gone! Go! Step on it!"

I gave it the gas. I didn't have to ask what happened. I knew Bobby was good for it. Denny might flip out his blade and stick him in the ribs, but not before Bobby had his say. He didn't even lower his voice, no pretense at cool, he just blurted it out.

"We shoved the trailer in the swimming pool. Man, it was heavy."

He waited for my what's-the-big-deal-with-that look and continued.

"When it hit the bottom, it cracked the foundation of the pool. We in big trouble now." I looked hard at Bobby, but people like that never seem to catch the time-to-shut-up looks. "I guess we're still minors, though, according to the courts."

"Jeez, Bobby," said Charles.

Nothing from Denny. He had us by the cajones and he knew it. But everything in our lives was about to change. The Houston police have a way of making that happen.

I was driving maybe thirty miles an hour, winding through Milby Park, half an hour from the busted swimming pool, when I first saw the red lights flashing. I stopped in the middle of the road. Two patrolmen, hands to their holstered hips, soon flanked the car.

"Get out, everybody. Out now." We crawled out and the officers, billy clubs now drawn, prodded us to "Stand behind the vehicle." By-the-book talk.

"Line up facing the car and put your hands behind your head." We were shaking. The cops had to see that.

One officer told Denny, "Hands behind your back," and handcuffed him. He then snatched Denny's wallet from his back pocket and tossed it at the other cop, who radioed to police headquarters to see if Denny had a record.

During the wait, one officer stood guarding us while the other rummaged through the car. Several minutes passed, and when the cop in the car finished with the glove compartment and started poking around under the seats, Denny leaned to me, unseen by our guard, and whispered, "I have a loaded pistol under the driver's seat. I'm on parole so they'll take me to jail. But this has nothing to do with you. Don't worry."

I clenched my teeth. The cop standing just to the right of

Denny must have heard or seen him whispering to me, about the time the other cop lifted the gun and said, "Look what we got here."

What happened next went by in a blinding flash, too fast for my mind to register. The policeman didn't lift his billy club, gave no warning, he simply swung it in a roundhouse arc and cracked Denny on the back of his head. Before he could hit the ground, the officer in the car took several long strides and planted his black leather shoe in Denny's groin, standing him up just long enough for his knees to wobble and give way, sending Denny in a face-first freefall to the pavement.

Charles made a move to catch him, but the cop gave him a look and brandished the club. The other patted Denny down, searching him where he lay and emptying his pockets. He stood up, tossed the car keys at my feet, and said, "Get the hell outta here. I don't ever want to see you again."

The cops didn't care that the car was Denny's. They had their man.

I remember little else about that night, other than the closing image, a shadowplay of silhouettes from the rear window of the patrol car. One officer drove while the other sat in the backseat with Denny. As the car pulled away, Denny's head lolled easily on his left shoulder, lifting and settling with the rise and fall of the pavement, seemingly napping. Meanwhile, the police officer, like an actor in the wrong play, continued to flail away, pounding Denny's head with the billy club.

Eight days later I started high school, and on the few occasions when I saw my Ellington buddies, we either nodded when it couldn't be avoided or pretended we didn't see each other. We ran in different circles, simple as that. I feel certain they never mentioned Denny to their friends, nor did I to mine. The Ghost of Summer Last.

But still, school had a sour taste that somehow reminded me of Denny. It started off with old gray-haired Mrs. Montgomery, the government teacher, warning us away from downtown Houston late at night, where "only drunks and niggers are welcome." And then a week or so later my biology instructor began improvising during his lecture on the flora and fauna of swamp country—"With all the trouble that Martin Luther King is stirring up, he needs to take a trip to Louisiana. He just might visit a swamp and never find his way out." And remember that young man of African ancestry who wanted to play football? Well, he was removed from the football team after the first week of school, but not before his tires were slashed. Twice. Everyone knew who cut the tires. Eddie Serge. He still had his switchblade. Denny would have been proud. Me and my other buds—we didn't say a word.

I and Velema ain't stupid, and neither were they. Or like Denny used to tell us over and over again: "Too many words will cost you."

So no action was taken. None was necessary. The problem and his family simply moved away.

That was the year they called the "Year of the Cougar" at the University of Houston. The Cougars were ranked number one in the nation after thumping Lew Alcindor's UCLA Bruins at the Astrodome. Too much drinking going on for my family to give a damn, so I kept up with it all by reading the *Houston Chronicle.* But the Cougars never made the front-page headlines.

Denny occupied that spot, though nobody knew his name.

CAB KILLER STRIKES AGAIN!

Six times I read that headline, or one like it. Every article described details of his modus operandi, of the unknown assailant who lured cab drivers to the Officers' Club at Ellington Air Force Base. The cabbies carried the killer to a deserted shore or unoccupied stretch of Gulf Coast prairie, where he slit their throats from behind. Every article concluded with a warning, but no mention of clues or possible suspects. Nobody in the Houston Police Department knew his name. But we knew. Charles and Bobby and Eddie and me, we knew.

In my mind I saw it as clear as if I were watching a movie. Denny giving the cab driver an address, a real address, no room for suspicions. Denny was too smart, had thought it all out, played it in his mind a hundred times before he did it, before he waited till the cab was speeding down a dark stretch of road, plenty to chose from in those days, then sticking the knife in the back of the cabbie's neck.

"Pull over, slow and easy." His voice was steady, his muscles taut, quivering.

When the cab slowed to a halt, Denny grabbed the man by the hair and jerked his head over the seat, and with one deep stroke of his blade, he sliced the man's throat, severing his windpipe. Maybe the first time he cut two, even three times, to make sure the man was dead.

Blood. Oh yeah, lots of blood. Enough to fill a nightmare. Soaking into the seat, and his shirt, not Denny's, no, the cabbie's shirt, drenched in blood, bathed in blood, his hair swimming in blood, his body writhing and twitching and by the time the air emptied from his lungs through the hose of his windpipe, Denny was half a block a way, half a mile down the road, well into the warm night of another universe, one nobody knew, would ever know, but him. Denny.

Like a butcher cutting slabs of meat. No emotion, only the quick, clean cut.

But that's a lie. Of course he felt something. Power, that's what he felt. Power in the blood, that's how we were raised back in those days. And those cops, their blood was begging to flow free.

You hit me, I cut you.

Cabbies, cops, they're all the same in Denny's world, radios and dispatchers, lights on the dashboard, uniforms with emblems, stiff caps, with one major difference. Cabbies had no billy clubs. No billy clubs, no power.

Now I have the power, and blade trumps billy club. Every time. Cuts deeper and its power is everlasting.

Hit me again. You can't. You a dead man.
Six times over, you a dead man.
Lying by the side of the road, you a dead man.
Slumped in the seat of your car, you a dead man.

How do you like your blue-eyed boy now,
Mister Death?

Hit me again. *Slice.*

"What are you doing here?" Sherry asked.

It was the Christmas holidays. Spurred by morbid curiosity, I drove over to Sherry's house in Sunset Valley, five miles south of Gulfgate. *I and Velma ain't stupid.*

Yeah, right.

"What are you doing here?" Sherry stood with her hands

on her hips, and she more hissed than spoke. She looked pretty, angry like she was.

"Charles called me, said he was getting off work at five. He said maybe you'd wanna go have a beer with us."

"Charles knows better than that. Why are you lying to me?"

"Hey," I said, crossing my wrists in front of me, "arrest me, okay? Guilty as charged. Maybe I just came to see a friend from the base."

Sherry said nothing, but something about her tone, her body's tone, the way she stood, the look in her eyes, told me for once in my life to shut up and listen. I lowered my hands.

"Sorry," I whispered.

Sherry nodded her head to the right, so slightly that if her eyes hadn't done the same I'd have missed the gesture. I moved where she instructed, around the corner of the house to a clump of shrubs, hiding us from the street.

"Did you see Denny on your way over, 'cause he's on his way here now. Did he see you?"

"I don't think so. I didn't see him."

"You better hope not. Look, kid, you maybe think you know something, that's why you came here today. To tell somebody what you think you know. He doesn't know it yet, but Denny is gonna fry for what he did. Nothing's gonna change that. He is a sick and vicious man. You listening to me?"

"Yes. I hear you."

"I am trying to keep you from getting hurt. He knows where you go to school. He mentioned a lake near Kemah, a lake so deep they'd never find a body. That's what he told me. As long as Denny is out free, you are not safe, nobody who knows him is. You need to turn around and drive your car back home, enjoy your Christmastime with your folks, then get your butt back to high school and forget you ever knew anything about Ellington Air Force Base."

I did as I was told.

Six years and several fruitless appeals later, Denny had his date with Old Sparky, the electric chair in Huntsville Federal Prison, and Sherry married a chef from the base. And still as I write, encouraged by zealous defenders of the people, the Texas treadmill creeps in its petty pace from day to day, lighting fools the way to dusty death.

Back in Pasadena, my old teachers have long-ago retired or died and the schools are integrated. I don't get home that often anymore. My mother moved to San Antonio and only my sister lives near the coast. She married a former SoHo football player and they moved to Lake Jackson, where he starred for the post office till he retired.

The coastal town of Kemah, a few miles east of Ellington, is once again gutted houses and smelly seaweed, just as it was after Hurricane Carla in 1961. Hurricanes have a way of equalizing things, and in 2008, Ike fulfilled its purpose. I did attend my thirtieth high school reunion, and my fortieth as well. Charles was there, and we had a drink for old times. We didn't speak of Denny. Late that evening, probably around three a.m., I drove by the gate to Ellington, but I didn't linger there. Sometimes it's better just to drive away.

PART II

BACK ROADS TEXAS

Jump in the river, stay drunk all the time . . .
—Henry Thomas

LUCK
BY JAMES CRUMLEY
Crumley, Texas

JASMINE

13th June, Slippery Rock

Little sister,

I fear that I waited too long to respond to your missive of early December. I hoped and prayed that I could find the time to write a short and sweet, perfectly reasonable explanation for the financial morass that seems to be dividing our true and deep sisterly love. (You understand.) So please forgive me if I rattle on in a dozen different directions before I discover the truth dancing in front of me, lost and fluttering like one of those monarch butterflies on his endless migrations.

The folks here in Slippery Rock seem to have recently arrived from some other time zone—the slow drip of molasses time zone, slow hands and deep pockets. But they have other advantages. They have no idea how the marble breaks down. Silver Slip had to twice physically restrain farmers who wanted to wager their bottom land against the illusive numbers. They went home, small slices of skin missing. They refused to believe a dwarf could be so quick. But, Lord, the women are so tight they won't even spit on the ground or step into the honey-bucket flop. You know the kind of women I mean—like Momma—cat glasses, hair so tight in buns that their noses are pointed like the bills of the snapping turtles Daddy brought out of the Black River, hard, stingy eyes over skinny, pale mouths. They probably think a blow job is when you blow smoke in a guy's ear. The things we could teach them, huh? (HA! Remember those two drummers at the Pow Wow Motel in Tucumcari? They should have been diamond miners.) But Jesus, they eat like lost hogs. Mounds of popcorn, miles of cotton candy, and enough Cokes to launch a ship, but they never shit. The whirl-around ride is shot, and this here's a town that keeps little kids on the soft rides, these Slippery Rockers. Shit, the games are down 200 percent. Even the penny pits are losing money to the fucking rug rats. Which is why I've missed the last two payments. I'm sorry. We're living on macaroni and welfare cheese. Maybe we need to put the shows back together. Maybe.

Speaking of rug rats—how's little Harney doing? Same sort of straight dude his dad is? What is he now? Eighteen months? I hear little Pearl looks just like you. I know Harney would love to send you some money, but he's still got those Kentucky peckerwoods on his back. It wasn't Harn's fault that the still caught fire. Hell, he nearly lost two fingers trying to put it out.

Well, baby sis, I gotta run. More soon.

Your loving sister,
Jasmine

GINGER

Flat River, August 31

Toad, it's always a pleasure to get one of your wandering forays into the fucking miasma of your twisted, lying mind. You're as ugly as Momma and twice as crooked. Stop whining and send the fucking money. Now. I've got a new sword swallower that will turn your bad news dwarf into mincemeat pie. And perhaps do a little cosmetic surgery so no one will ever mistake us again. Your excuse was late, mailed to the wrong place on purpose or by accident, no matter. The USPS is a fairly solid bet these days. Of course, there didn't seem to be a check from you for $3,700, and no child support from Harney. Tell him I'll put the sheriff on his ass and this time McAlaster will welcome him home. Or, hell, just forget it. I'll come take the whole works, baby—in fact, forget everything. Like you always do. I didn't fuck any drummers in Tucumcari, dear. I was in the governor's suite with a fist full of cash and a mouth full of the governor's press secretary's cock. So we could get our permits restored, permits you'd lost with a rigged wheel. Then you told Harney it was me. That's why I fucked him the first time. Or was that the first five hundred times? Who can keep it straight, bitch.

Wow. Time for a deep breath, a reassessment, then back to business. But before I forget, Pop didn't leave because Mom wouldn't go down on him. He left because she was boring, mean-spirited, and fairly stupid. And wall-eyed too. Just like you. Yeah, I can hear you sigh. She's in denial again.

Maybe not, sis. Maybe not.

Look at it the real way, sister mine: you seduced him at thirteen for a pair Cherokee platform boots to impress Lauren Poltz. But you got Tommy Poltz in every orifice, didn't you? Then it was off to Spokane to have the baby, then a flappy-ass job in the accounting wagon. While I shoveled Shetland pony shit and battled ankle-biters as they covered me with baby shit, thin puke, and endless screams. I could have gone to college. You couldn't finish grade school.

So when I was sixteen, I seduced the old bastard too, because he was the single most lonely man in the world, and I couldn't stand it. He was a fine man. I don't think he ever gave a shit about fucking you. You were so awful from the day you were born, you *had to be forgiven for everything from the start. Or be throttled in the fucking crib.*

And remember this too: Mom was too fastidious to nurse. She didn't want too-big boobs to get in the way of her tumbles. So we were bottle babies. You were, at least until they discovered you had been stealing mine out of the crib in the dog cart.

You owe me the money. Or you're ruined. That would be fine. On your own, sweetie, you'll be in jail in six months. Where you've always belonged.

Pay or die, sister bitch.

Your sister in chains,
Ginger

HARNEY

I tried to stop it. I really did. I loved those women. Fire and ice, blood and guts, yin and Yankton, South Dakota.

The first time I saw them standing in a wheat stubble field outside Valentine, Nebraska, that long, stroking wind pushing their cheap dresses against their bodies so ripe . . . the sensation was this: lick your finger, then touch their skin, and try to get your finger back; touch them with your hand and pray that they don't explode; hell, sometimes just looking at them made you think the whole fucking world was going to end in a single orgasm. Not with a bang, no, nor a whimper. But one long, glorious groan of infinite pleasure.

Romantic twaddle, I told myself as I bolted the aisle to the wheel. I'd been to several schools: Gunnison High, Colby, Soledad, and ten years drifting and grifting with the carnivals. I've learned some things. If you've never been locked up, you don't know what the world is all about. Never trust anybody working the carnivals. Shit, never trust anybody. And never say *romantic twaddle*.

The first time with Jasmine, I thought I'd broken some ribs. The second time I was sure I'd broken my back. The third time I fainted.

I made a drunken mistake early on, in a citizen's bar outside El Paso. I told the ring-a-ding guy about fainting. Drunk and in love until he said, "Shit, man, when she was a kid she used to jack off the Shetlands to keep them copacetic. Story is, man, she killed three of them one year."

I ran. I came back. A dozen times. Jasmine was worse than Soledad. I knew that if I watched my back and walked their line, I'd get out. Eventually. Jasmine didn't work that way. I stole her money; she had the roustabouts beat me until I cried. Something that never happened inside. I fucked her sister for a long time—great, but not the same—acknowledged our baby girl, and Jasmine laughed at me. She knew the worst.

Except for Ginger, the twin. How could two women be so different—bodies of long, sweeping curves frosted with glowing red-brown skin smoother than polished ivory and steaming with an internal fire—Jasmine seemed to laugh in flames when she came and her breath seemed hot enough to scorch my beard. Ginger was terrific, but ordinary. Jasmine was heaven and hell, cocaine and crank, star light and black hole.

I gave our little girl, Pearl, to a childless family outside Marengo, Iowa, and wished the people all the best luck. They seemed like nice people. If Pearl had been a cat, I would have had her fixed.

Jasmine had to be first, or I could have never finished it. After I cut her throat, I dumped her into a swamp outside Mud Lake, Wisconsin. In that shallow, muddy water, she floated like a queen. All I ever loved. Ginger was easier. She lifted her neck to the blade as if she'd been waiting for years. "Jasmine," she whispered, as if she knew. Ginger's yellow dress, blood like a flood, bobbed in the small Minnesota creek, drifted like a fading light. As always, I'd done what they wanted.

Now it was time for me. The raucous silence of Stillwater prison, the quiet needle smooth in the vein, the end of memories. Peace.

PREACHER'S KID

BY JESSICA POWERS

Andrews

L ooking back on it, with everything that's happened since, Sammy disappearing and all, I'm not sure I did the right thing. I've seen many things in my life, and I've learned to let many things slide, but it's not just me, you see. It's the wife. She cares about these things. So the second time Chief brought Sammy home, drunk as a skunk, saying he'd found him passed out just inside the Andrews County line, I felt I had to speak to the boy.

"You're making your mother look bad to the church ladies," I said, thinking he'd have some compassion for her feelings. They'd always been close. "Those are her friends. They've known you since you were a small boy, a good boy."

He sneered.

There was something in that sneer that made me think twice about what I said next. But I went ahead, glancing at Charlene to see her reaction as I spoke. She was sitting on the couch in her bathrobe, looking as anxious as the bride I married thirty-three years ago.

"Drinking is the devil's business," I told the boy. "Don't bring the devil's business back to this house again."

He looked at me then as if I'd said something curious, and that's when I noticed the color of his eyes in the morning light—amber from one angle, green from the other, same as my own.

Later, I got to thinking. I got to thinking how maybe I should've asked him why. Why he was staying out all night. Why he was drinking. But at the time, I was just so concerned with *what* he was doing, *why* didn't even occur to me. It was only after he disappeared for a while, then came back, then disappeared again for good, that I started thinking about how he'd looked haunted toward the end. Like something—or somebody—was *driving* him to drink.

In my line of business, I've seen worse than a drunk preacher's kid, it's true. Over to Seminole, just thirty-odd miles north, preacher's kid went crazy in the middle of the night, strung up his parents in their bed with purple twine—purple!—and set fire to the bed. In Odessa, just south, preacher's kid made news when they discovered he'd been doing drug deals on church property. The state came in and seized all the church's assets, just like that, an entire church reduced to rubble in a matter of days.

Takes my breath away sometimes, the way evil can sink its teeth in somebody, shake them hard, until it's their own neck broken and bleeding.

That's what worried me about the boy and wherever it is he'd gone to.

It's not easy to drink in Andrews. We're a dry county. To buy any kind of liquor, you have to drive elsewhere. Out toward Odessa, just across the county line, you'll find the first liquor store, just lying in wait. I'm not one to take up causes, but there's something wrong when a town manages to keep itself free of sin yet has to contend with the devil permanently camping out on its perimeters.

For a while after our talk, Sammy didn't drink, or if he did, it was in secret. Then one morning he wasn't in his bed. Charlene wanted to call Chief right away and it's true, I made her wait. I said, "There's no reason to involve the police when, like as not, the boy'll come dragging his sorry self through that door in another hour, barely able to stand on the two legs God gave him."

I saw something in Charlene give then, in the way her eyes became all dark and soft. For a moment, it looked like she was resigned. But how could she be resigned to Sammy's drinking? Or to his disappearing act? She had *something* tucked away in the back of her mind but I couldn't figure it out.

One of us called the church secretary, I don't even remember who, said I'd be in late that day. Then I sat myself down on the living room couch with a cup of coffee, waiting for the boy to show up so I could give him a piece of my mind.

I am not a fire-'n'-brimstone kind of preacher. The good church ladies who make up my congregation say I'm a salt-'n'-pepper kind of preacher instead, mostly pepper. "Too much pepper, Preacher," one of them told me once as she left the church one day, never to return. "Too much pepper."

That day, however, I was in a fire-'n'-brimstone kind of mood and I planned to give it to the boy when he came home.

Only he didn't come. Both of us waited as long as we could. Eventually, Charlene had to get on over to the hospital—we like to joke that her boss isn't as understanding as mine—and by lunchtime, fingernails bitten off to the quick, I decided to get off to the church before I started gnawing on the flesh too. Andrews is a small town and people know where to find me. If the boy turned up in a compromising situation, the church would be the first place they'd call.

But he didn't turn up that day or the next. He didn't show up until Sunday, showed up in the back of the church, right in the middle of my sermon. I was preaching on the loaves and fishes, the miracles our Savior performs, the way He multiplies and provides. It's hard to yell at your boy when he's been gone so long, the only thing you want anymore is to see him walk through the door, and then he shows up right when you're talking about the mercy of God.

So I never gave him a piece of my mind. And now I wish I had, because a few weeks later he disappeared and never came back.

I suppose that at first I thought Chief would take care of it. I suppose that I thought, *It's a small town. Chief will put this case first, he'll realize the importance, he'll put every resource toward finding the boy.*

Until then, I hadn't realized how different police work is from church work. Police work isn't about *saving* anybody. Or, at least, it isn't about saving a teenager who's just gotten a little off track, a little lost, who needs somebody to find him, to help him home.

In fact, the first thing Chief brought up when we went to see him was our recent trouble. "Didn't Sammy disappear for a few days awhile back?" he asked, scratching his stomach, drinking out of a big mug on his desk, and eyeing us over the rim. Chief had an odd tic I'd never noticed before, the eye shuddering in sudden rapid winks and the skin underneath it trembling and heaving. It was distracting.

"You know he did, Chief," I said.

"He's probably run off again. My guess is he'll show up in a few days, just like last time. These things happen." He moved some papers on his desk and looked at Charlene as he spoke. "When he comes back, you should sit down and have a long talk with him."

The wife was so nervous, I was afraid she was going to start chewing her handkerchief. I took it from her gently and put it in my pocket.

"Isn't there anything you can do?" I asked.

"Not much," he said. For the first time, he looked vaguely sympathetic. "He's seventeen. As far as the law in Texas is concerned, he can leave Andrews whenever he wants. We don't do much unless there's some sign of foul play."

"That's that then," I said, and we left the station.

On the way home, Charlene asked me what I wanted to do.

"I guess we wait," I said.

After that day, the wife and I started fighting. We've always been a placid couple, but here was Charlene, snorting like an angry horse, face beet-red, screaming how this and that and the other thing didn't make her happy or satisfied or what have you.

"What do you want me to do?" I asked her once after the screaming was over and she was sitting on the couch across from me, her hands in her lap, open and turned up toward the ceiling.

"It's too late," she said. She was staring at those hands, not me, when she said that.

"Do you want a divorce?" I asked, appalled and, frankly, ashamed. I spend so much of my time counseling couples on how to mend broken marriages and here I was facing it myself, no clue how it all happened. How *did* it happen? What *had* happened?

"That's not what I meant, Charles," she said. "That's not what I meant at all."

She looked up at me then and I realized, all of a sudden,

Why, she and I have the same eyes, the same eyes as the boy. I broke down weeping. All these years, thirty-three years now, I was looking into a mirror when I looked in her eyes, and I'd never realized it before.

"Do you believe in miracles?" she asked.

She'd asked me this question once before, back when she was supplicating the Lord to touch her barren womb and give her a child, just like Hannah in the Old Testament. And when her belly was swollen with the boy and her eyes swollen with joy, I reminded her of her many prayers, and that is when we decided to name him Samuel, which means *God heard*.

"Of course," I said. "Isn't our boy's life a miracle?"

"No, I mean *real* miracles," she said, her voice flat, emotionless. "Do you believe that we could pray and ask God to send our boy back—*my* boy back—and here he'd come, walking through that door, as if he'd never gone anywhere at all?"

I didn't know how to answer her, so I said nothing.

I couldn't get the question Charlene asked out of my head. Many nights, I can't even count how many, I propped myself up on my elbows and stared at her face while she slept. I counted every single wrinkle—forty-two in all, if you included the soft folds of skin on her neck. Sometimes I think we don't pay attention to all the tiny changes, and then one day we wake up and realize we don't recognize the person we married.

I thought about the facts of our life together—how we married when we were so young, too young, I realize now, only eighteen and nineteen years old; how we tried to have a child for so many years before she conceived; the way she always had to work, because my salary as a minister in a small Southern Baptist church could never quite pay the bills; the way she wasn't just a good mother, she was a *great* mother, because she'd wanted a child for so long before Sammy came; how our life had been made up of endless church meetings and hospital rounds. Charlene was a nurse, and we made a good pair, her healing bodies and me healing souls. She'd always worked with babies, newborns, and that'd been hard for her for many years when we were struggling and struggling to get pregnant. But, as she'd always said, sometimes what doesn't kill you makes you strong.

Still, as I thought about all our years together, I realized more than ever how facts about a person can't even come close to explaining them.

Sometimes when I counsel young couples about to get married, I like to tell them that the amazing thing about marriage is the way your spouse remains a mystery, even after decades of living together. After more than three decades, there are moments when I realize I don't really know Charlene. Who she was. Who she is. Who she's going to become.

Night after night, while Charlene slept, I sat in my study and remembered our lives together. The years before the boy were a haze made up only of Charlene's desperate prayers. His birth, seventeen years ago, marked a complete transformation in our lives. It felt like we'd been wandering in the wilderness for years and the Lord had suddenly flung open the door to the Promised Land, the land of milk and honey.

My biggest regret in life is the fact that I was out of town on the day of his birth. We were living in Amarillo at the time and I happened to be attending the annual Southern Baptist Convention on the day he arrived, early but healthy. I rushed home as soon as I could, and when I walked through the door Charlene was nursing him in the big rocking chair we'd bought when she found out she was pregnant.

I went and knelt beside them to kiss and welcome my baby

boy, the one we'd been waiting for—all our lives, it seemed, now that he was here.

Sometimes—and it feels like a sin to say this—the day I was saved by the Lord and the day I knelt by their feet, the first time I saw Sammy, blur together as if they were the same day.

Still, I'll admit I was surprised by the look of him. Charlene and I are both slight, and even as a baby he was big-boned and long, with ears and a nose I didn't recognize. Some men might have wondered but I did not. I knew he was my son. I knew the way I knew Charlene would be my wife the day I met her.

We were never happier than after he'd come into our lives. It had been Charlene's biggest heartache, the wait.

Around that time, there was a need for a pastor here in Andrews. I'd applied before the Convention and when the call came just days after Sammy's birth, she begged me to take it. She wanted to raise Sammy in a small town, with small town values, she said. So we left Amarillo and made ourselves a home here.

Sammy was the darling of the church, a good student, and an excellent football player. I suppose there were girls that liked him, but we never talked about it. I warned him that carnal desires can ruin a man's life and we left it at that.

Andrews had been a good place to raise a son, I thought, though when he started driving to the county line to drink, I was reminded of what the Lord said after He discovered that Cain had murdered his brother Abel, how sin is always crouching at your door, how it desires to have you, but you must learn to master it. No matter where you go, you cannot escape what is lurking in your heart.

A few weeks after the boy disappeared, Charlene stopped

coming to church, not even bothering to explain why. The good church ladies—her friends, my congregation—they all asked after her. I said she wasn't feeling well.

That's when I hired Guy Neely, P.I. Asked him to find the boy, wherever he was, whatever he was doing, it didn't matter.

"Just ask him to please come home," I said. "Tell him his mother's soul hangs in the balance. If he doesn't care about his own soul, maybe he'll care about hers. They were always close."

Neely was a tall man, and his snakeskin cowboy boots only added to his height. He towered over me, the way the boy always had. He was the sort of man who chews gum and tobacco at the same time. While I talked, he was chewing gum so fast I wondered if his jaw would come unhinged.

He spat dark juice into a small cup. "You'll excuse me for being blunt," he said. "But what if your son is dead?"

"Then bring his remains home so his mother can have some peace."

I had high hopes, even if the trail was a few weeks old. I was pretty sure the boy wasn't dead. He was just hiding—from us, from God.

Or maybe he was seeking something he would never find.

Neely came to the house on a Monday.

He looked over the boy's things, what little he'd had: the bookshelves with only one book, a Bible; some T-shirts; a pair of boots. He sat at the foot of Sammy's bed, looking around. Then he hung around in front of the garage, observing the neighborhood where our son had grown up, where we'd spent most of our adult lives, right after Sammy came along. He was chewing tobacco and occasionally spitting on the sidewalk.

I thought about asking him not to spit. But I didn't.

Neely regarded the two of us. "What was the first hint that something might be wrong?" he asked.

I looked at Charlene. She looked at the traces of tobacco juice staining the sidewalk.

"There's always been something wrong," she said, "since the first day I brought him home from the hospital. I always knew he wouldn't stay, he was too perfect, too good, too right for us."

She'd said things like that before during the years Sammy was growing. Charlene had been a fearful mother, possessive in the way she watched over him, as if afraid someone was going to come along and snatch him away. It had sometimes seemed like the fear would devour her.

"And more recently?" Neely asked.

"And more recently . . ." She stopped.

"He started to drink recently," I said, to fill in the blanks. "He'd drive off down toward Odessa, get drunk. Chief brought him home a few times."

"Kids his age will do that," Neely agreed.

"No," I said. "This was different. He was upset about something. Angry." I thought back on the day he'd sneered at me. Come to think of it, the way he'd sneered, it was almost as if he thought it was *funny* that I didn't want him bringing the devil's drink home. Like there was something of Satan already here.

"Any idea what upset him?"

I shook my head. Charlene mumbled something.

"What?" I asked.

"Did you say something?" Neely asked.

"*I* upset him," she said, louder this time.

"Are you a difficult person to get along with?" he asked.

"Not especially," I answered for her. "Charlene has always been a good wife and a good mother. They've always gotten along."

"Then why do you think you upset him?" His tone was gentle.

"He was upset by who I am," she answered.

Neely nodded, like he'd heard all this before. "And who are you, exactly?"

She started to talk then. She had a hunger, she said. She'd had it for years. All her life, maybe, she said. It went deep. It had sharp teeth and bit her insides. Sometimes it felt as though the hunger was consuming her altogether. Sometimes it was all she could do, she said, not to give in to it.

Neely was looking at her from the corner of his eyes, as if he was afraid he would startle her if he looked directly at her. "Is that so?" he said. "And do you? Give in to it?"

"No," she said. She smiled. "Okay," she said. "One time. But only once."

When she said that, I looked away, down the street, to the end of the block, where cement dribbles out until it becomes the flat, dry brown of west Texas, stretching to the place where land meets clear blue sky, as far as the eyes see, just a hazy line on the horizon separating heaven from earth.

The smell of Neely's tobacco soured in my stomach.

I thought of the Beatitudes. *Blessed are those who hunger and thirst after righteousness, for they shall be filled.* That had been the hunger in my life. What was *hers?*

For the first time, doubts about the wife crawled right into my head.

Charlene continued. "Do you know what I'm talking about when I say the word hunger, Mr. Neely? Have you ever felt like you're starving? Have you ever looked in the mirror and all you see is a skeleton—that's all that's left of you, somebody you don't even recognize because you're so very, very hungry?"

"No, ma'am," he said, courteous but firm. "Can't say that I have."

"Well," she said.

We waited for more. But she was done.

My hands were shaking. I'm a preacher, so I know what sin is, the tragedy of it, the way it corrupts a person and turns everything they love to dust. But still I was surprised how calm Neely was. Like he'd seen everything under the sun already.

I paid him for a week in advance, gave him Sammy's Social Security number, and watched as he drove away. I wanted him to find something, and at the same time I was hoping he would not. The wife had scared me.

I went inside, ready to ask Charlene about all that she'd said, but she was hunched up in bed, blankets over her head.

"Charlene?" I said softly.

She didn't respond. So I went away.

Neely returned two days later, with Chief, which surprised me. They came to the church. I saw them from the office window, and went outside to greet them, to invite them inside. Neely cleared his throat. He spit out the remainder of his tobacco juice before entering the building, left the cup outside on the sidewalk. I appreciated that.

"Have you already found him?" I asked as soon as we were inside my office. I had closed the door. Stacey's a good church secretary, but there are things she doesn't need to know.

It was Chief who answered. "We found him all right." He had a stern expression on his face, which seemed to have calmed the winking-blinking facial tic.

"Well, where is he?" I demanded. "How is he? Is he okay? Is he in trouble? Did you bring him back to Andrews?"

"He was in Amarillo," Neely said. "But he's here now."

We were still standing and I made a gesture to open the door. "Take me to him."

"We have a warrant, Preacher," Chief interrupted.

My hand paused on the doorknob. "What has he done?" I asked, so quick, my mind going to a thousand scenarios, knowing how it's possible to get going downhill so fast, you can't stop yourself even when you want to.

"It's not what *he's* done," Neely said.

"Then what? Who? *Me?*"

"Your wife, it's what your wife's done."

"What's *she* done?" My preacher's voice—usually sonorous and controlled—was soaring. "You have a warrant to arrest *Charlene?*"

"No, we have a warrant for your DNA," Chief said.

"What? *Why?*"

"We can do it here," Chief said, "or you can come on down to the station."

"Let me see the warrant." My heart was racing. I scanned the paper quickly, but it didn't tell me anything that they hadn't already said. "What exactly is going on?"

"Do you mind coming down to the station?" Chief asked, only he didn't really ask, it was more like a statement. His mouth was bunched up, the lips pressed firmly together.

Neely's face had never been expressive, but now it was a blank slate.

"Okay," I said.

We stepped outside my office, the two men following me.

"I'm gone for the day," I told Stacey. I could barely think for the questions swirling around like dust devils in my head.

There were four cars in the parking lot—mine, Stacey's, Chief's, and Neely's.

"You'll come with me," Chief said.

"Front or back?" I asked, still wondering how much trouble I was in.

"Your choice," he said.

I sat in front.

As we drove out of the parking lot, tires spinning in the gravel, I looked back at the small redbrick building with its white steeple and the wooden cross hanging over the door frame. Neely's spittoon sat on the sidewalk, right in front of the sanctuary door.

The sky was Texas-style blue, expansive and deep, clouds scudding across its face. Usually, that sky reminds me of the wide, wide mercy of God. Today, it made me feel like anything could happen, anything at all.

As we walked through the station, I caught a glimpse of Charlene sitting in a small room as a police officer went inside. Another officer was sitting across from her, a tape recorder in his hand.

". . . there was the cord wrapped around his neck . . ." I heard her saying.

The door closed and I lost sight of her.

And then there was Sammy, sitting in the hallway, his big frame impossible to ignore. He looked tired and dirty. He hadn't had a haircut or a shave since he'd disappeared, and the beard and scruffy hair made him look like a man and a stranger.

Oh Sammy. My Sammy.

The breath caught in my throat.

"Sammy," I called, my voice high and unnatural and cracking.

He looked up and our eyes met and again I was startled by their amber-green, so like his mother's, so like mine. Samuel. My boy. *The Lord heard.*

Neely pushed gently from behind, and we stumbled into a small room. Chief hustled inside behind us.

"You really did find him," I babbled. "And he looks all right, doesn't he? Isn't he all right?"

"He's fine," Neely said.

"Thank you, Lord," I breathed. "Thank you."

The last thank you was directed at Neely, who nodded in acknowledgment. He seemed like a decent man, even if he wasn't explaining to me what was going on.

After they swabbed my cheek to get their DNA sample, Chief gestured to a chair, and I sat.

"When can I see my boy?" I asked. I felt like a small child, petitioning an arbitrary adult.

"Actually, we have some questions to ask you, if you don't mind," Chief said. The tic was back. It looked like a worm moving beneath the skin.

"Sure," I said, "anything I can do to help. What are you looking for, anyway? Why did you need my DNA sample?"

"We don't think Sammy is yours," Neely said.

I stood then, leapt to my feet. "No," I said. "No, no, no! Sammy is mine, has always been mine."

Had Charlene? *Could* Charlene?

I have a hunger, she'd said. *Sometimes it's all I can do not to give in to it.*

And do you? Give in to it? Neely'd asked.

One time, she'd said. *But only once.*

"Charlene is a good woman," I insisted. "A faithful woman, 100 percent. It's not even possible, what you're saying, that she would've—" I choked on the words.

And then I grew spitfire angry.

"All right," I snapped. "Fine. It happens all the time. Maybe he's my son, maybe he isn't." My face was growing red. "But even if he isn't my son, adultery is a matter for the church, not the police. Sin is the Lord's work." It would have been a comfort to stand behind a pulpit and shout down the voices that whispered evil all around me. But here I was, weak and vulnerable in the face of something I didn't expect. "I don't see how this is any of your business," I said.

I glared at the two silent men standing in front of me.

And suddenly, they both looked uncomfortable.

Neely cleared his throat.

"We don't think he's Charlene's son, either," Chief said.

It felt like a hammer to the spine, to the throat, to the chest, everywhere, my whole body beaten. "*What?*" And my voice didn't sound like my own, it sounded like an old man's.

Neely slapped a newspaper story down on the table in front of me. It was the *Amarillo Globe-News*, dated seventeen years back, July, the week or so after we'd left there to move here.

I scanned it, heart beating beating beating.

DEAD BABY SWAPPED

Parents in a Panic to Find their Missing Newborn
AMARILLO, TX—*Police are investigating a possible kidnapping at Amarillo General Hospital. On June 13, Rachel Smith, 26, gave birth to a healthy baby boy that appeared to have died during the night. In the course of a routine autopsy, hospital officials discovered that the dead baby was not related to Smith. Police are currently searching for both the Smith baby and for the parents of the dead baby.*

I looked at the two men who stood before me. "What are you *saying?*"

"You know what we're saying," Neely replied.

"Sammy is my son," I whispered.

"Correction: Sammy is Rachel Smith's son." Chief smirked. "*Your* son was buried by the city of Amarillo."

My knees buckled and I had to sit.

"You gonna make it?" Neely asked.

"I don't know how to make any sense of this," I said.

"You really didn't know?" he asked.

"Know *what?*"

"Your wife was alone when she went into labor," Neely said, "and the baby was born dead. She went to the hospital where she worked and switched the dead baby with the Smith baby."

There was a picture in my head, a picture of Charlene, alone, holding the dead body of our son close to her chest, weeping and cursing God for taking her miracle away.

"Charlene told you this?" I asked. "She's talking about it?"

"Oh, she's talking," Chief said. He shook his head. "She won't shut up. It seems she started feeling guilty about what she'd done after all these years. Apparently, a few months ago she told your son—excuse me, Rachel Smith's son—the truth."

A bitter laugh escaped my lips. "'What is truth?'" I quoted Pontius Pilate, unsure who I expected to answer that question, the fallen men standing before me or the God I've served all my life. It felt like I'd been robbed of my very life. Something evil had slept right next to me for years, and I'd never known how close it was to me, how I'd loved it, how I'd nurtured it, how I'd been blind to it.

"When we found Sammy, he was in Amarillo looking for his real parents," Neely said.

"We've contacted Amarillo police," said Chief. "They're trying to locate the Smith family. Once they have all the samples, it's just a matter of waiting for the DNA results to confirm what we already suspect."

"How long will that take?" I asked, throat dry.

"It depends on how long the forensics lab is backed up," Chief said. "A few weeks. Possibly a month."

I swallowed. Then I swallowed again. It could take a month to find out if my boy was really my boy? Because suddenly, that was all that mattered to me. Although deep down, I already knew. Maybe I always had.

"Can I bring you some water?" Neely asked.

"Sure." I was parched, thirstier than I'd been all my life. *If anyone is thirsty, let him come to Me and drink.*

Chief opened the door to let Neely through. I looked out at the busy police department. It wasn't a big place, so I could see everything there was to see. Sammy was just outside, leaning his head against the wall, eyes closed, like he was tired beyond belief, a tired that went beyond the body, a tired that bit its sharp teeth into a soul and wouldn't let go. And I wanted so badly to say to him, *Come. Come to Me, all you who are weary and burdened, and I will give you rest.*

But I knew I wouldn't be allowed to speak to him, not yet, maybe not for a long time, maybe not ever. Perhaps he would never want to talk to me, and with a clarity that comes with revelation, I realized I had no right to ask him to.

I had lost my boy.

The door to the interrogation room opened and for just a few seconds, I could see Charlene inside, talking to somebody, a police officer. She was talking to him the way one might talk to a pastor, I saw. She was saying everything, leaving nothing aside, confessing her sin, hoping for forgiveness, for salvation.

But police are not in the salvation business. That would be me, picking up the pieces after the trial. I didn't want to lose her too.

Like Sammy, I closed my eyes and leaned my head back until it touched the wall. Images of the boy and the wife flooded the black space between my eyes and my eyelids. There was Sammy, just a boy, hefty and athletic, running down the sidewalk in front of our home after a football. There was Charlene, standing at the door, calling after him not to go too far, calling after him to come home. There they were, sitting in a church pew while I preached a sermon, Sammy fiddling until Charlene handed him a piece of paper and a crayon, her expression serene as she turned her face back toward mine. I saw her in her nurse's uniform, kissing Sammy goodbye at the door as she headed out to work the night shift at the hospital, headed out to heal the bodies of sick babies and their mothers.

And I could not—*I could not*—believe he was somebody else's boy.

I turned my thoughts toward the flatland surrounding the small town of Andrews, where I'd been a preacher of the Word for the past seventeen years.

I'd always said that land was like God, endless and encompassing everything.

I thought about how a man could just walk out into that land and keep going for miles.

I thought about how a man might never come to the end of it.

SIX-FINGER JACK

BY JOE R. LANSDALE

Gladewater

Jack had six fingers. That's how Big O, the big, fat, white, straw-hatted son of a bitch, was supposed to know he was dead. Maybe by some real weird luck a guy could kill some other black man with six fingers, cut off his hand, and bring it in and claim it belonged to Jack, but not likely. So he put the word out that whoever killed Jack and cut off his paw and brought it back was gonna get $100,000 and a lot of goodwill.

I went out there after Jack just like a lot of other fellas, plus one woman I knew of, Lean Mama Tootin', who was known for shotgun shootin' and ice-pick work.

But the thing I had on them was I was screwing Jack's old lady. Jack didn't know it, of course. Jack was a bad dude, and it wouldn't have been smart to let him know my bucket was in his well. Nope. Wouldn't have been smart for me, or for Jack's old lady. If he'd known that before he had to make a run for it, might have been good to not sleep, 'cause he might show up and be most unpleasant. I can be unpleasant too, but I prefer when I'm on the stalk, not when I'm being stalked. It sets the dynamics all different.

You see, I'm a philosophical kind of guy.

Thing was, though, I'd been laying the pipeline to his lady for about six weeks, because Jack had been on the run ever since he'd tried to muscle in on Big O's whores and take over that business, found out he couldn't. That wasn't enough, he took up with Big O's old lady like it didn't matter none, but it did. Rumor was Big O put the old lady under about three feet of concrete out by his lake-boat stalls, buried her in the hole while she was alive, hands tied behind her back, staring up at that concrete mixer truck dripping out the goo, right on top of her naked self.

Jack hears this little tidbit of information, he quit fooling around and made with the jackrabbit, took off lickety-split, so fast he almost left a vapor trail. It's one thing to fight one man, or two, but to fight a whole organization, not so easy. Especially if that organization belongs to Big O.

Loodie, Jack's personal woman, was a hot flash number who liked to have her ashes hauled, and me, I'm a tall, lean fellow with a good smile and a willing attitude. Loodie was ready to lose Jack because he had a bad temper and a bit of a smell. He was short on baths and long on cologne. Smell-good juice on top of his stinky smell, she said, created a kind of funk that would make a skunk roll over dead and cause a wild hyena to leave the body where it lay.

She, on the other hand, was like sweet, wet sin dipped in coffee and sugar with a dash of cinnamon; God's own mistress with a surly attitude, which goes to show even He likes a little bit of the devil now and then.

She'd been asked about Jack by them who wanted to know. Bad folks with guns, and a need for dough. But she lied, said she didn't know where he was. Everyone believed her because she talked so bad about Jack. Said stuff about his habits, about how he beat her, how bad he was in bed, and how he stunk. It was convincing stuff to everyone.

But me.

I knew that woman was a liar, because I knew her whole

family, and they was the sort, like my daddy used to say, would rather climb a tree and lie than stand on the ground and tell the truth and be given free flowers. Lies flowed through their veins as surely as blood.

She told me about Jack one night while we were in bed, right after we had toted the water to the mountain. We're lying there looking at the ceiling, like there's gonna be manna from heaven, watching the defective light from the church across the way flash in and out and bounce along the wall, and she says in that burnt-toast voice of hers, "You split that money, I'll tell you where he is."

"You wanna split it?"

"Naw, I'm thinkin' maybe you could keep half and I could give the other half to the cat."

"You don't got a cat."

"Well, I got another kind of cat, and that cat is one you like to pet."

"You're right there," I said. "Tellin' me where he is, that's okay, but I still got to do the groundwork. Hasslin' with that dude ain't no easy matter, that's what I'm tryin' to tell you. So, me doin' what I'm gonna have to do, that's gonna be dangerous as trying to play with a daddy lion's balls. So, that makes me worth more than half, and you less than half."

"You're gonna shoot him when he ain't lookin', and you know it."

"I still got to take the chance."

She reached over to the nightstand, nabbed up a pack, shook out a cigarette, lit it with a cheap lighter, took a deep drag, coughed out a puff, said, "Split, or nothin'."

"Hell, honey, you know I'm funnin'," I said. "I'll split it right in half with you."

I was lying through my teeth. She may have figured such,

but she figured with me she at least had a possibility, even if it was as thin as the edge of playing card.

She said, "He's done gone deep into East Texas. He's over in Gladewater. Drove there in his big black Cadillac that he had a chop shop turn blue."

"So he drove over in a blue Caddy, not a black one," I said. "I mean, if it was black, and he had it painted blue, it ain't black no more. It's blue."

"Aren't you one for the details, and at a time like this," she said, and rubbed my leg with her foot. "But technically, baby, you are so correct."

That night Loodie laid me out a map written in pencil on a brown paper sack, made me swear I was gonna split the money with her again. I told her what she wanted to hear. Next morning, I started over to Gladewater.

Jack was actually in a place outside of the town, along the Sabine River, back in the bottom land where the woods was still thick, down a little trail that wound around and around, to a cabin Loodie said was about the size of a postage stamp, provided the stamp had been scissor-trimmed.

I oiled my automatic, put on gloves, went to the store and bought a hatchet, cruised out early, made Gladewater in about an hour and fifteen, glided over the Sabine River bridge. I took a gander at the water, which was dirty brown and up high on account of rain. I had grown up along that river, over near a place called Big Sandy. It was a place of hot sand and tall pines and no opportunity.

It wasn't a world I missed none.

I stopped at a little diner in Gladewater and had me a hamburger. There was a little white girl behind the counter with hair blond as sunlight, and we made some goo-goo eyes at one another. Had I not been on a mission, I might have found out when she got off work, seen if me and her could get a drink and find a motel and try and make the beast with two backs.

Instead, I finished up, got me a tall Styrofoam cup of coffee to go. I drove over to a food store and went in and bought a jar of pickles, a bag of cookies, and a bottle of water. I put the pickles on the floorboard between the backseat and the front; it was a huge jar and it fit snugly. I laid the bag with the cookies and the water on the backseat.

The bottoms weren't far, about twenty minutes, but the roads were kind of tricky, some of them were little more than mud and a suggestion. Others were slick and shiny like snot on a water glass.

I drove carefully and sucked on my coffee. I went down a wide road that became narrow, then took another that wound off into the deeper woods. Drove until I found what I thought was the side road that led to the cabin. It was really a glorified path. Sun-hardened, not very wide, bordered on one side by trees and on the other by marshy land that would suck the shoes off your feet, or bog up a car tire until you had to pull a gun and shoot the engine like a dying horse.

I stopped in the road and held Loodie's hand-drawn map, checked it, looked up. There was a curve went around and between the trees and the marsh. There were tire tracks in it. Pretty fresh. At the bend in the curve was a little wooden bridge with no railings.

So far Loodie's map was on the money.

I finished off my coffee, got out and took a pee behind the car, and watched some big white waterbirds flying over. When I was growing up over in Big Sandy I used to see that kind of thing often, not to mention all manner of wildlife, and for a moment I felt nostalgic. That lasted about as long as it took me to stick my dick back in my pants and zipper up.

I took my hatchet out of the trunk and rested it on the front passenger seat as I got back in the car. I pulled out my automatic and checked it over, popped out the clip and slid it back in. I always liked the sound it made when it snapped into place. I looked at myself in the mirror, like maybe I was going on a date. Thought maybe if things fucked up, it might be the last time I got a good look at myself. I put the car in gear, wheeled around the curve and over the bridge, going at a slow pace, the map on the seat beside me, held in place by the hatchet.

I came to a wide patch, like on the map, and pulled off the road. Someone had dumped their garbage where the spot ended close to the trees. There were broken-up plastic bags spilling cans and paper, and there was an old bald tire leaning against a tree, as if taking a break before rolling on its way.

I got out and walked around the bend, looked down the road. There was a broad pond of water to the left, leaked there by the dirty Sabine. On the right, next to the woods, was a log cabin. Small, but well made and kind of cool looking. Loodie said it was on property Jack's parents had owned. Twenty acres or so. Cabin had a chimney chugging smoke. Out front was a big blue Cadillac Eldorado, the tires and sides splashed with mud. It was parked close to the cabin. I could see through the Cadillac's windows, and they lined up with a window in the cabin. I moved to the side of the road, stepped in behind some trees, and studied the place carefully.

There weren't any wires running to the cabin. There was a kind of lean-to shed off the back. Loodie told me that was where Jack kept the generator that gave the joint electricity. Mostly the cabin was heated by the firewood piled against the

shed, and lots of blankets come late at night. Had a gas stove
with a nice-sized tank. I could just imagine Jack in there with
Loodie, his six fingers on her sweet chocolate skin. It made me
want to kill him all the more, even though I knew Loodie was
the kind of girl made a minx look virginal. You gave your heart
to that woman, she'd eat it.

I went back to the car and got my gun-cleaning goods out of
the glove box, took out the clip, and cleaned my pistol and
reloaded it. It was unnecessary, because the gun was clean as
a model's ass, but I like to be sure.

I patted the hatchet on the seat like it was a dog.

I sat there and waited, thought about what I was gonna do
with $100,000. You planned to kill someone and cut off their
hand, you had to think about stuff like that, and a lot.

Considering on it, I decided I wasn't gonna get foolish and
buy a car. One I had got me around and it looked all right
enough. I wasn't gonna spend it on Loodie or some other split
tail in a big-time way. I was gonna use it carefully. I might get
some new clothes and put some money down on a place instead of renting. Fact was, I might move to Houston.

If I lived close to the bone and picked up the odd bounty
job now and again, just stuff I wanted to do, like bits that
didn't involve me having to deal with some goon big enough
to pull off one of my legs and beat me with it, I could live safer,
and better. Could have some stretches where I didn't have
to do a damn thing but take it easy, all on account of that
$100,000 nest egg.

Course, Jack wasn't gonna bend over and grease up for
me. He wasn't like that. He could be a problem.

I got a paperback out of the glove box and read for a while.
I couldn't get my mind to stick to it. The sky turned gray. My

light was going. I put the paperback in the glove box with the gun-cleaning kit. It started to rain. I watched it splat on the windshield. Thunder knocked at the sky. Lightning licked a crooked path against the clouds and passed away.

I thought about all manner of different ways of pulling this off, and finally came up with something, decided it was good enough, because all I needed was a little edge.

The rain was hard and wild. It made me think Jack wasn't gonna be coming outside. I felt safe enough for the moment. I tilted the seat back and lay there with the gun in my hand, my arm folded across my chest, and dozed for a while with the rain pounding the roof.

It was fresh night when I awoke. I waited about an hour, picked up the hatchet, and got out of the car. It was still raining, and the rain was cold. I pulled my coat tight around me, stuck the hatchet through my belt, and went to the back of the car and unlocked the trunk. I got the jack handle out of there, stuck it in my belt opposite the hatchet, started walking around the curve.

The cabin had a faint light shining through the window, that in turn shone through the lined-up windows of the car. As I walked, I saw a shape, like a huge bullet with arms, move in front of the glass. That size made me lose a step briefly, but I gathered up my courage, kept going.

When I got to the back of the cabin, I carefully climbed on the pile of firewood, made my way to the top of the lean-to. It sloped down off the main roof of the cabin, so it didn't take too much work to get up there, except that the hatchet and tire iron gave me a bit of trouble in my belt, and my gloves made my grip a little slippery.

On top of the cabin, I didn't stand up and walk, but instead carefully made my way on hands and knees toward the front of the place.

When I got there, I peered over the edge. The cabin door was about three feet below me. I moved over so I was overlooking the Cadillac. A knock on the door wouldn't bring Jack out. Even he was too smart for that, but that Cadillac, he loved it. I pulled out the tire iron, nestled down on the roof, peeking over the edge, cocked my arm back, and threw the iron at the windshield. It made a hell of a crash, cracking the glass so that it looked like a spiderweb, setting off the car alarm.

I pulled my gun and waited. I heard the cabin door open, heard the thumping of Jack's big feet. He came around there mad as a hornet. He was wearing a white shirt with the sleeves rolled up. He hadn't had time to notice the cold. But the best thing was, it didn't look like he had a gun on him.

I aimed and shot him. I think I hit him somewhere on top of the shoulder, I wasn't sure. But I hit him. He did a kind of bend at the knees, twisted his body, then snapped back into shape and looked up.

"You," he said.

I shot him again, and it had about the same impact. Jack was on the hood of his car, then its roof, and then he jumped. That big bastard could jump, could probably dunk a basketball and grab the rim. He hit with both hands on the edge of the roof, started pulling himself up. I was up now, and I stuck the gun in his face and pulled the trigger.

And let me tell you how the gas went out of me. I had cleaned that gun and cleaned that gun, and now . . . it jammed. First time ever. But it was the time that mattered.

Jack lifted himself onto the roof, and then he was on me, snatching the gun away and flinging it into the dark. I couldn't believe it. What the hell was he made of? Even in the wet night, I could see that much of his white shirt had turned dark with blood.

We circled each other for a moment. I tried to decide what to do next, and then he was on me. I remembered the hatchet, but it was too late. We were going back off the roof and onto the lean-to, rolling down. We hit the stacked firewood and it went in all directions and we splattered to the ground.

I lost my breath. Jack kept his. He grabbed me by my coat collar and lifted me and flung me against the side of the lean-to. I hit on my back and came down on my butt.

Jack grabbed up a piece of firewood. It looked to me like that piece of wood had a lot of heft. He came at me. I made myself stand; I pulled the hatchet free. As he came and struck down with the wood, I sidestepped and swung.

The sound the hatchet made as it caught the top of his head was a little like what you might expect if a strong man took hold of a piece of thick cardboard and ripped it.

I hit him so hard his knees bent and hot blood jumped out of his head and hit my face. The hatchet came loose of my hands, stayed in his skull. His knees straightened. I thought: *What is this motherfucker, Rasputin?*

He grabbed me and started to lift me again. His mouth was partially open and his teeth looked like machinery cogs. The rain was washing the blood on his head down his face in murky rivers. He stunk like roadkill.

And then his expression changed. It seemed as if he had only just realized he had a hatchet in his head. He let go, turned, started walking off, taking hold of the hatchet with both hands, trying to pull it loose. I picked up a piece of firewood and followed after him. I hit him in the back of the head as hard as I could. It was like hitting an elephant in the ass with a twig. He turned and looked at me. The expression on his face was so strange, I almost felt sorry for him.

He went down on one knee, and I hauled back and hit him with the firewood, landing on top of the hatchet. He vibrated, and his neck twisted to one side, and then his head snapped back in line.

He said, "Gonna need some new pigs," and then fell out.

Pigs?

He was laying face forward with the stock of the hatchet holding his head slightly off the ground. I dropped the firewood and rolled him over on his back, which took about as much work as trying to roll his Cadillac. I pulled the hatchet out of his head. I had to put my foot on his neck to do it.

I picked up the firewood I had dropped, placed it on the ground beside him, and stretched his arm out until I had the hand with the six fingers positioned across it. I got down on my knees and lifted the hatchet, hit as hard as I could. It took me three whacks, but I cut the hand loose.

I put the bloody hand in my coat pocket and dug through his pants for his car keys, didn't come across them. I went inside the cabin and found them on the table. I drove the Cadillac to the back where Jack lay, pulled him into the backseat, almost having a hernia in the process. I put the hatchet in there with him.

I drove the El Dorado over close to the pond and rolled all the windows down and put it in neutral. I got out of the car, went to the back of it, and started shoving. My feet slipped in the mud, but I finally gained traction. The car went forward and slipped into the water, but the back end of it hung on the bank.

Damn.

I pushed and I pushed, and finally I got it moving, and the

car went in, and with the windows down, it sunk pretty fast.

I went back to the cabin and looked around. I found some candles, turned off the light, then switched off the generator. I went back inside and lit three of the big fat candles and stuck them in drinking glasses and watched them burn for a moment. I went over to the stove and turned on the gas, letting it run a few seconds while I looked around the cabin. Nothing there I needed.

I left, closed the door behind me. When the gas filled the room enough, those candles would set the air on fire. The whole place would blow. I don't know exactly why I did it, except maybe I just didn't like Jack. Didn't like that he had a Cadillac and a cabin and some land, and for a while there, he had Loodie. Because of all that, I had done all I could to him. I even had his six-fingered hand in my pocket.

By the time I got back to the car, I was feeling weak. Jack had worked me over pretty good, and now that the adrenaline was starting to ease out of me, I was feeling it. I took off my jacket and opened the jar of pickles in the floorboard, pulled out a few of them, and threw them away. I ate one, and drank from my bottle of water and had some cookies.

I took Jack's hand and put it in the big pickle jar. I sat in the front seat, and was overcome with nausea. I didn't know if it was the pickle or what I had done, or both. I opened the car door and threw up. I felt cold and damp from the rain, so I started the car and turned on the heater. Then I cranked back my seat and closed my eyes. I had to rest before I left, had to. All of me seemed to be running out through the soles of my feet.

I slept until the cabin blew. The sound of the gas generator and stove going up with a one-two boom snapped me awake.

* * *

I got out of the car and walked around the curve. The cabin was nothing more than a square, dark shape inside an envelope of flames. The fire wavered up high and grew narrow at the top like a cone. It crackled like someone wadding up cellophane.

I doubted, out here, that anyone heard the explosion, and no one could see the flames. Wet as it was, I figured the fire wouldn't go any farther than the cabin. By morning, even with the rain still coming down, that place would be smoked down to the mineral rights.

I drove out of there, and pretty soon the heater was too hot and I turned it off. It was as if my body went up in flames, like the cabin. I rolled down the window and let in some cool air. I felt strange; not good, not bad. I had bounty hunted for years, and I'd done a bit of head whopping before, but this was my first murder.

I had really hated Jack and I'd hardly known him.

It was the woman that made me hate him. The woman I was gonna cheat out'of some money. But $100,000 is a whole lot of money, honey.

When I got home, the automatic garage opener lifted the door, and I wheeled in and closed the place up. I went inside and took off my clothes and showered carefully and looked in the mirror. There was a mountainous welt on my head. I got some ice and put it in sock and pressed it to my head while I sat on the toilet lid and thought about things. If any thoughts actually came to me, I don't remember them well.

I dressed, bunched up my murder clothes, and put them in a black plastic garbage bag.

In the garage, I removed the pickle jar and cleaned the car. I opened the jar and stared at the hand. It looked like a black crab in there amongst the pickles. I studied it for a long time, until it started to look like $100,000.

I couldn't wait until morning, and after a while, I drove toward Big O's place. Now, you would think a man with the money he's got would live in a mansion, but he didn't. He lived in three double-wide mobile homes lined together with screened-in porches. I had been inside once, when I'd done Big O a very small favor, though never since. But one of those homes was nothing but one big space, no rooms, and it was Big O's lounge. He hung in there with some ladies and body-guards. He had two main guys. Be Bop Lewis, a skinny white guy who always acted as if someone was sneaking up on him, and a black guy named Lou Boo (keep in mind, I didn't name them) who thought he was way cool and smooth as velvet.

The rain had followed me from the bottomland, on into Tyler, to the outskirts, and on the far side. It was way early morning, and I figured on waking Big O up and dragging his ass out of bed and showing him them six fingers and getting me $100,000, a pat on the head, and hell, he might ask Be Bop to give me a hand job on account of I had done so well.

More I thought about it, more I thought he might not be as happy to see me as I thought. A man like Big O liked his sleep, so I pulled into a motel not too far from his place, the big jar of pickles and one black six-fingered hand beside my bed, the automatic under my pillow.

I dreamed Jack was driving the Cadillac out of that pond. I saw the lights first and then the car. Jack was steering with his nub laid against the wheel, and his face behind the glass was a black mass without eyes or smile or features of any kind.

It was a bad dream and it woke me up. I washed my face, went back to bed, slept this time until late morning. I got up and put back on my same clothes, loaded up my pickle jar, and left out of there. I thought about the axe in Jack's head, his severed hand floating in the pickle jar, and regret moved through me like shit through a goose and was gone.

I drove out to Big O's place.

By the time I arrived at the property, which was surrounded by a barbed-wire fence, and had driven over a cattle guard, I could see there were men in a white pickup coming my way. Two in the front and three in the bed in the back, and they had some heavy-duty fire power. Parked behind them, up by the double-wides, were the cement trucks and dump trucks and backhoes and graders that were part of the business Big O claimed to operate. Construction. But his real business was a bit of this, and a little of that, construction being not much more than the surface paint.

I stopped and rolled down my window and waited. Outside, the rain had burned off and it was an unseasonably hot day, sticky as honey on the fingers.

When they drove up beside my window, the three guys in the bed pointed their weapons at me. The driver was none other than one of the two men I recognized from before. Be Bop. His skin was so pale and thin, I could almost see the skull beneath it.

"Well, now," he said. "I know you."

I agreed he did. I smiled like me and him was best friends. I said, "I got some good news for Big O about Six-Finger Jack."

"Six-Finger Jack, huh," Be Bop said. "Get out of the car."

I got out. Be Bop got out and frisked me. I had nothing sharp or anything full of bullets. He asked if there was anything in the car. I told him no. He had one of the men in the back of the pickup search it anyway. The man came back, said, "Ain't got no gun, just a big jar of pickles."

"Pickles," Be Bop said. "You a man loves pickles?"

"Not exactly," I said.

"Follow us on up," Be Bop said.

We drove up to the trio of double-wides. There had been some work done since I was last here, and there was a frame of boards laid out for a foundation, and over to the side there was a big hole that looked as if it was gonna be a swimming pool.

I got out of the car and leaned on it and looked things over. Be Bop and his men got out of the truck. Be Bop came over.

"He buildin' a house on that foundation?" I asked.

"Naw, he's gonna put an extension on one of the trailers. I think he's gonna put in a poolroom and maybe some gamin' stuff. Swimmin' pool over there. Come on."

I got my jar of pickles out of the backseat, and Be Bop said, "Now wait a minute. Your pickles got to go with you?"

I sat the jar down and screwed off the lid and stepped back. Be Bop looked inside. When he lifted his head, he said, "Well, now."

Next thing I know I'm in the big trailer, the one that's got nothing but the couch, some chairs, and stands for drinks, a TV set about the size of a downtown theater. It's on, and there's sports going. I glance at it and see it's an old basketball game that was played a year back, but they're watching it, Big O and a few of his boys, including Lou Boo, the black guy I've seen before. This time, there aren't any women there.

Be Bop came inside with me, but the rest of the pickup posse didn't. They were still protecting the perimeter. It seemed silly, but truth was, there was lots of people wanted to kill Big O.

No one said a thing to me for a full five minutes. They were waiting for a big score in the game, something they had seen before. When the shot came they all cheered. I thought only Big O sounded sincere.

I didn't look at the game. I couldn't take my eyes off Big O. He wasn't wearing his cowboy hat. His head only had a few hairs left on it, like worms working their way over the face of the moon. His skin was white and lumpy like cold oatmeal. He was wearing a brown pair of stretch overalls. When the fat moved, the material moved with him, which was a good idea, 'cause it looked as if Big O had packed on about a hundred extra pounds since I saw him last.

He was sitting in a motorized scooter, had his tree-trunk legs stretched out in front of him on a leg lift. His stomach flowed up and fell forward and over his sides, like 400 pounds of bagged mercury. I could hear him wheezing across the room. His right foot was missing. There was a nub there, and his stretch pants had been sewn up at the end. On the stand, near his right elbow, was a tall bottle of malt liquor and a greasy box of fried chicken.

His men sat on the couch to his left. The couch was un-usually long, and there were six men on it, like pigeons in a row. They all had guns in shoulder holsters. The scene made Big O look like a whale on vacation with a harem of male sucker fish to attend him.

Big O spoke to me, and his voice sounded small coming from that big body. "Been a long time since I seen you last."

I nodded.

"I had a foot then."

I nodded again.

"The diabetes. Had to cut it off. Dr. Jacobs says I need more exercise, but, hey, glandular problems, so what you gonna do?

Packs the weight on. But still, I got to go there ever' Thursday mornin'. Next time, he might tell me the other foot's gotta go. But you know, that's not so bad. This chair, it can really get you around. Motorized, you know."

Be Bop, who was still by me, said, "He's got somethin' for you, Big O."

"Chucky," Big O said, "cut off the game."

Chucky was one of the men on the couch, a white guy. He got up and found a remote control and cut off the game. He took it with him back to the couch, sat down.

"Come on up," Big O said.

I carried my jar of pickles up there, got a whiff of him that made my memory of Jack's stink seem mild. Big O smelled like dried urine, sweat, and death. I had to fight my gag reflex.

I sat the jar down and twisted off the lid and reached inside the blood-stained pickle juice and brought out Jack's dripping hand. Big O said, "Give me that."

I gave it to him. He turned it around and around in front of him. Pickle juice dripped off of the hand and into his lap. He started to laugh. His fat vibrated, and then he coughed. "That there is somethin'."

He held the hand up above his head. Well, he lifted it to about shoulder height. Probably the most he had moved in a while. He said, "Boys, do you see this? Do you see the humanity in this?"

I thought: *Humanity?*

"This hand tried to take my money and stuck its finger up my old lady's ass . . . Maybe all six. Look at it now."

His boys all laughed. It was like the best goddamn joke ever told, way they yucked it up.

"Well, now," Big O said, "that motherfucker won't be

touchin' nothin', won't be handlin' nobody's money, not even his own, and we got this dude to thank."

Way Big O looked at me then made me a little choked up. I thought there might even be a tear in his eye. "Oh," he said, "I loved that woman. God, I did. But I had to cut her loose. She hadn't fucked around, me and her might have gotten married, and all this," he waved Jack's hand around, "would have been hers to share. But no. She couldn't keep her pants on. It's a sad situation. And though I can't bring her back, this here hand, it gives me some kind of happiness. I want you to know that."

"I'm glad I could have been of assistance," I said.

"That's good. That's good. Put this back in the pickle jar, will you?"

I took the hand and dropped it in the jar.

Big O looked at me, and I looked at him. After a long moment, he said, "Well, thanks."

I said, "You're welcome."

We kept looking at one another. I cleared my throat. Big O shifted a little in his chair. Not much, but a little.

"Seems to me," I said, "there was a bounty on Jack. Some money."

"Oh," Big O said. "That's right, there was."

"He was quite a problem."

"Was he now . . . Yeah, well, I can see the knot on your head. You ought to buy that thing its own cap. Somethin' nice."

Everyone on the couch laughed. I laughed too. I said, "Yeah, it's big. And if I had some money, like say, $100,000, I'd maybe put out ten or twenty for a nice designer cap."

I was smiling, waiting for my laugh, but nothing came. I glaced at Be Bop. He was looking off like maybe he heard his mother calling somewhere in the distance.

Big O said, "Now that Jack's dead, I got to tell you, I've sort of lost the fever."

"Lost the fever?" I said.

"He was alive, I was all worked up. Now that he's dead, I got to consider, is he really worth $100,000?"

"Wait a minute, that was the deal. That's the deal you spread all over."

"I've heard those rumors," Big O said.

"Rumors?"

"Oh, you can't believe everything you hear. You just can't."

I stood there stunned.

Big O said, "But I want you to know, I'm grateful. You want a Coke, a beer before you go?"

"No. I want the goddamn money you promised."

That had come out of my mouth like vomit. It surprised even me.

Everyone in the room was silent.

Big O breathed heavy, said, "Here's the deal, friend. You take your jar of pickles, and Jack's six fingers, and you carry them away. 'Cause if you don't, if you want to keep askin' me for money I don't want to pay, your head is gonna be in that jar, but not before I have it shoved up your ass. You savvy?'

It took me a moment, but I said, "Yeah. I savvy."

Lying in bed with Loodie, not being able to do the deed, I said, "I'm gonna get that fat son of a bitch. He promised me money. I fought Jack with a piece of firewood and a hatchet. I fell off a roof. I slept in my car in the cold. I was nearly killed."

"That sucks," Loodie said.

"Sucks? You got snookered too. You was gonna get fifty thousand, now you're gonna get dick."

"Actually, tonight I'm not even gettin' that."

"Sorry, baby. I'm just so mad . . . Ever' Thursday mornin', Big O, he goes to an appointment at Dr. Jacobs'. I can get him there."

"He has his men, you know."

"Yeah. But when he goes in the office, maybe he don't. And maybe I check it out this Thursday, find out when he goes in, and next Thursday I maybe go inside and wait on him."

"How would you do that?"

"I'm thinkin' on it, baby."

"I don't think it's such a good idea."

"You lost fifty grand, and so did I, so blowin' a hole in his head is as close as we'll get to satisfaction."

So Thursday morning I'm going in the garage, to go and check things out, and when I get in the car, before I can open up the garage and back out, a head raises up in the backseat, and a gun barrel, like a wet kiss, pushes against the side of my neck.

I can see him in the mirror. It's Lou Boo. He says: "You got to go where I tell you, else I shoot a hole in you."

I said, "Loodie."

"Yeah, she come to us right away."

"Come on, man. I was just mad. I wasn't gonna do nothin'."

"So here it is Thursday mornin', and now you're tellin' me you wasn't goin' nowhere."

"I was gonna go out and get some breakfast. Really."

"Don't believe you."

"Shit," I said.

"Yeah, shit," Lou Boo said.

"How'd you get in here without me knowin'?"

"I'm like a fuckin' ninja . . . And the door slides up, you pull it from the bottom."

"Really?"

"Yeah, really."

"Come on, Lou Boo, give a brother a break. You know how it is."

Lou Boo laughed a little. "Ah, man. Don't play the brother card. I'm what you might call one of them social progressives. I don't see color, even if it's the same as mine. Let's go, my man."

It was high morning and cool when we arrived. I drove my car right up to where the pool was dug out, way Lou Boo told me. There was a cement-mixer truck parked nearby for the pool. We stopped, and Lou Boo told me to leave it in neutral. I did. I got out and walked with him to where Big O was sitting in his motorized scooter with Loodie on his lap. His boys were all around him.

Be Bop pointed his finger at me and dropped his thumb. "My man," he said.

When I was standing in front of Big O, he said, "Now, I want you to understand, you wouldn't be here had you not decided to kill me. I can't have that, now can I?"

I didn't say anything.

I looked at Loodie, she shrugged.

"I figured you owed me money," I said.

"Yeah," Big O said. "I know. You see, Loodie, she comes and tells me she's gonna make a deal with you to kill Jack and make you think you made a deal with her. That way, the deal I made was with her, not you. You followin' me on this, swivel dick? Then, you come up with this idea to kill me at the doctor's office. Loodie, she came right to me."

"So," I said, "you're gettin' Loodie out of the deal, and she's gettin' a hundred thousand."

"That sounds about right, yeah," Big O said.

I thought about that. Her straddling that fat bastard on his scooter. I shook my head, glared at her, said, "Damn, girl."

She didn't look right at me.

Big O said, "Loodie, you go on in the house there and amuse yourself. Get a beer or somethin'. Watch a little TV. Do your nails. Whatever." Loodie started walking toward the trailers. When she was inside, Big O said, "Hell, boy. I know how she is, and I know what she is. It's gonna be white gravy on sweet chocolate bread for me. And when I get tired of it, she gonna find a hole out here next to you. I got me all kind of room here. I ain't usin' the lake-boat stalls no more. That's risky. Here is good. Though I'm gonna have to dig another spot for a pool, but that's how it is. Ain't no big thing, really."

"She used me," I said. "She's the one led me to this."

"No doubt, boy. But you got to understand. She come to me and made the deal before you did anything. I got to honor that."

"I could just go on," I said. "I could forget all about it. I was just mad. I wouldn't never bother you. Hell, I can move. I can go out of state."

"I know that," he said. "But I got this rule, and it's simple. You threaten to kill me, I got to have you taken care of. Ain't that my rule, boys?"

There was a lot of agreement.

Lou Boo was last. He said, "Yep, that's the way you do it, boss."

Big O said, "Lou Boo, put him in the car, will you?"

Lou Boo put the gun to back of my head, said, "Get on your knees."

"Fuck you," I answered, but he hit me hard behind the head. Next thing I know I'm on my knees, and he's got my hands behind my back and has fastened a plastic tie over my wrists.

"Get in the car," Lou Boo said.

I fought him all the way, but Be Bop came out and kicked me in the nuts a couple of times, hard enough I threw up, and then they dragged me to the car and shoved me inside behind the wheel and rolled down the windows and closed the door.

Then they went behind the car and pushed. The car wobbled, then fell, straight down, hit so hard the air bag blew out and knocked the shit out of me. I couldn't move with it the way it was, my hands bound behind my back, the car on its nose, its back wheels against the side of the hole. It looked like I was trying to drive to hell. I was stunned and bleeding. The bag had knocked a tooth out. I heard the sound of a motor above me, a little motor. The scooter.

I could hear Big O up there. "If you hear me, want you to know I'm having one of the boys bring the cement truck around. We're gonna fill this hole with cement, and put, I don't know, a tennis court or somethin' on top of it. But the thing I want you to know is this is what happens when someone fucks with Big O."

"You stink," I said. "And you're fat. And you're ugly."

He couldn't hear me. I was mostly talking into the air bag.

I heard the scooter go away, followed by the sound of a truck and a beeping as it backed up. Next I heard the churning of the cement in the big mixer that was on the back of it. Then the cement slid down and pounded on the roof and started to slide over the windshield. I closed my eyes and held my breath, and then I felt the cold, wet cement touch my elbow as it came through the open window. I thought about some way out, but there was nothing there, and I knew that within moments there wouldn't be anything left for me to think about at all.

DUCKWEED

BY GEORGE WIER

Littlefield

Carlos McDaniel was skimming duckweed when the two men came and shot him full of holes.

It was at his ex-wife's uncle's place, fifteen miles south and east of College Station, Texas, and it had a summer cabin on it, complete with air-conditioning and an ancient refrigerator always stocked with Cokes, cheap beer, and sandwich materials. The cabin stood ten feet from the edge of the one-acre lake.

The lake was little more than an overgrown duck pond, but it was all the water anyone could need on a hot summer day when the only breeze came from the flapping wings of wild waterfowl and even the water moccasins lay listless on the floating platform, unmindful of interlopers. It was a hidden spot, well away from competing salesmen and customers who gravitated to the two extremes: bored-stiff disinterest or unrealistic expectation. Carlos got more of those two kinds than any other as a real estate salesman. And when they got to be a little too much for a bright-eyed young man with all of life ahead of him and a ticket for this Saturday's Lotto Texas in his pocket, he would climb in his '77 Datsun short-bed pickup and head for the country and the cool, spring-fed waters of Hidden Lake. And his share of the beer.

When blacktop gave way to caliche gravel and a long-following geyser trail of fine, reddish dust spreading out like a comet's tail, only then could he breathe deeply and begin to take in life again.

Hidden Lake, as his ex's family called it, lay at the tail end of everything. The last county road doubled back on itself toward the north and west at the turnout of the lane to his ex's family property. The property was the last customer on the water and electric line, and it was five hundred yards from the Navasota River, which defines the county's easternmost border.

The family—the few that were left of them—hardly ever came out, and almost never in the middle of the week. Carlos would have some alone time. Some time to look at nature and think and let things settle out. Skimming the duckweed was a damned dirty job, and damned if he didn't love doing it.

This day he hadn't bothered locking the gate to the property behind him, as he more often than not did. Possibly things would have turned out differently if he had, but then again, who could know? There are no could-have-beens, should-have-beens, or would-have-beens to life, other than what we consider in the universe-wide space behind our eyes. There is only the moment right here and now.

Carlos looked up from the task at hand when he had the feeling he was being watched.

He had managed to get the floating landscape timbers in a fairly straight line and was just skirting the edge of the floating platform, whereon lay three large and completely still cotton-mouth moccasins, when he felt it. There was movement there under the shade trees some thirty feet away. The sun was hot and bright overhead and he squinted.

"Hello," he called out.

They weren't family—or rather ex-family. He'd never seen the two men before in his life.

They were dressed as if they had just come from a high-end real estate closing. His first errant thought was that they were potential clients who had gone to a lot of trouble to find him.

In a way, he was right.

The water came up to Carlos's chest. It was a good thing they had waited until he was nearly done before happening along. Ten minutes before and they would have come upon him slogging through the muck on the opposite shore with his bare ass dripping mud and water.

"Hello," one of the two men said, and waved. The man smiled.

Carlos almost waved back, but he was mindful of the snakes, just three feet away. Snakes couldn't hear worth a damn, but they could sense movement, and cottonmouths are known for their aggressiveness.

"Give me a minute, will you? Go on in the house. There's beer and Cokes in there. Also, I'm not exactly dressed for visitors at the moment."

Carlos had a towel in his pickup, and he was thinking about how he'd look trying to move across the yard to get to it before the two glanced back out the front window. Chances were they'd get an eyeful no matter what he did. But that was all right. They were guys, after all. And something else was beginning to take hold inside of him. A far-off song, like a radio picking up a skip on a clear night: the opening chords of the world's oldest song—opportunity. Anyone coming this far to see him must want something awfully bad.

And he was right about that as well.

The two men went inside without further word.

Carlos pulled the leading timber up into the mud of the bank and made a break for the truck. The towel was there behind the seat where he'd left it, but it wasn't a beach towel. He kept it there for those moments when the old Datsun itself had had enough and decided it was time to overheat. You had to have a thick, dry towel to remove a hot radiator cap, and the towel—complete with the three Powerpuff Girls: Blossom, Bubbles, and Buttercup (the only thing he'd truly walked away with to call his own from his former marriage)—wrapped around him just enough for him to make a small knot. Even that, in the final analysis, would do him little good.

The towel would have to do.

Carlos stepped up to the front porch and slid the glass doorway back on its tracks. The track needed a good cleaning out and a bit of graphite to smooth the slide of the door, but like all things, there was never enough time.

The air inside was cool. Not cold, but just enough to make him shiver. He was still wet and water trickled down his legs. There were tiny green specks of duckweed all over him. He usually went from the lake right into the shower because if he dried off with the duckweed still on him it tended to stick like glue.

The two men came in from the kitchen. Each had a Coke in hand. One of the men was smiling, the other looked at him with dead-fish eyes.

Carlos shivered again.

"How can I help you fellas?" he asked. It came out sounding uncertain, and he knew it.

"Just a little information," the smiling fellow said. His big teeth were as false as the rest of him, Carlos suddenly knew. That song—that radio-skip melody—was no closer now than the background hum leftover from the Big Bang.

"You guys cops?" Carlos asked.

The dead-fish-eyed fellow laughed. It was the funniest thing he'd ever heard.

For Carlos the temperature in the room plummeted.

"No," Smiley said, cutting his own light chuckle off short. "Not cops. Businessmen, Mr. McDaniel. Just like yourself. You had a client. A lady."

"I've got a lot of lady clients. And you said 'had.' I don't keep track of my old clients very well. Which is maybe why I'm not pulling down a hundred Gs a year."

"We understand, Mr. McDaniel. We really do. This lady you'd not easily forget."

"Who is she?"

"Your first name is Carlos, right?" Smiley asked. "But your last name is McDaniel. You got some greaser blood in you?"

"I don't think I like you," Carlos said.

"You don't have to," Smiley said. "Who's the bean eater? With a last name like McDaniel, it'd have to be your mother, right?"

He felt it then, strong. The floodgates of adrenaline opening somewhere in his body. It was going to be either fight or run. Running, at the moment, looked best. Two on one with him naked in his ex's uncle's cabin, a mile to the nearest neighbor? Not good odds.

But Carlos fought the urge to run. Who can truly tell the future?

"I'll tell you what you want to know," he said. "Then you can leave."

"Smart fellow, right, Sammy?"

"Yeah," Sammy said. He was the broad-shouldered, dead-eyed one. Or perhaps his eyes were more reptilian than merely dead. "Fart smellow," Sammy said and laughed again. Carlos's instant assessment of him was bleak at best. He was all gristle and fat with little brain. If Sammy ever graduated high school, Carlos was willing to bet he'd been in his mid-twenties at the time.

"Okay, kid," Smiley said. "Her name is Linda Sneed. That's two *e*'s. Remember her?"

"The penthouse deal. Haven't talked with her in six months. Lost my ass on the deal too. What do you want to know?"

"See, Sammy? I told you today something was gonna break." His eyes never wavered, but the tone of his voice dropped a whole scale. "Where is Ms. Sneed, pepper-belly?"

Carlos considered. The moment had arrived. The moment he'd known was coming the instant he'd seen Sammy's dead-fish eyes.

Sammy's hand went into his suit jacket, and what came out was exactly what Carlos McDaniel knew was going to come. It was a gun. A black 9mm.

"Tell him," Sammy said.

Carlos's control of his bladder slipped for just an instant. He knew without looking there would be a small spreading stain on the front of the towel. It felt like hot lava in the chilly room.

"She's . . . gone. Long gone. I'm not lying. I tried to reach her. Everybody did."

"Yeah?" Smiley said. "Who's everybody?"

"Me. My broker. The title company. The lawyers. Last I heard she was somewhere in West Texas."

"Yeah? That's a pretty big area. You mind narrowing it down for me a bit?"

"Littletown. No. Littlefield. That's northwest of Lubbock."

"Thank you, Mr. McDaniel," Smiley said. He turned toward Sammy and nodded.

Carlos stood frozen.

Sammy shot him three times: once in the leg—he had been aiming for Carlos's groin and missed by half an inch—once in the stomach, and once in the chest.

The two men left him for dead.

Carlos McDaniel didn't hear the sliding door close behind the two men. He was concentrating on the ocean of pain that had suddenly invaded his life. He hurt. The pain was deep—a fundamental thing that could not be ignored—and blackness was coming. He was already graying out.

His hand moved, touched the widening pool of blood soaking into the old carpet beside him. He brought it to his stomach and traced five letters.

He pulled his finger away and looked at it. There was a tiny speck of green in all the red.

Duckweed, he thought, because for some reason he couldn't speak, and then the blackness rolled over him and carried him away.

Carlos McDaniel was either a fortunate or unfortunate man, depending upon one's point of view.

He was unfortunate to be in the path of the two-man tornado which was composed of a couple of Brooklyn hoodlums named Sammy "The Gootch" Rosario and Victor Cicchese.

Carlos was fortunate in that he initially survived the tornado. The three muffled reports were heard by a man named Charles Lyman, who was walking the power-line cut on the north side of the property that had the idyllic little lake and the cabin. It was the last property on the line, and when he was done he was supposed to turn around and head back. But there was a little glade near the end of the line where it was his custom to stop and have a smoke before returning. Lyman was grinding the spent cigarette butt into the earth near all the others that he'd smoked at the spot over the last twelve years when he heard the reports. He was two hundred yards away and instantly knew what the sounds were.

A person can hear all kinds of things when walking through the east and central Texas woods. A gun going off is not uncommon. It was, however, an uncommonly hot day and the only game in season at the moment was the kind of game that was always in season: rabbits, squirrels, raccoons, and other varmints that weren't worth shooting in 105-degree weather. Moreover, these shots had come from indoors. A gun being fired indoors has a peculiar and particular sound to it. Most of the noise rattles around inside, crossing and recrossing itself, and consequently has a distinctive muffled, and yet hollow, rattle quality to it.

Charles Lyman ducked through the brush and a barbed-wire fence and was behind the cabin within a minute after the last shot was fired. A pair of ducks had taken to the air and were beating their wings hell for leather to the south, just disappearing over the line of trees past the lake.

Glancing out from around the rear corner of the house, well hidden by brush, he saw two men walking back down the lane toward the main gate and the road beyond. They wore business suits.

It was hot, powerfully so, but the blood in Charles Lyman's veins felt as though it had been transfused with ice.

He stepped around the side of the house with the lake, away from the two departing men, stepped up onto the porch from the side, peered through the window, and saw a man who was busy dying.

It took thirty minutes for the ambulance to arrive from town. During that time he had resuscitated the dying young man three times.

The EMTs, when they did show up, would have bet

against Carlos McDaniel. The odds were too long and the kid had lost an ungodly amount of blood. They went to work in earnest. They were both veterans who had seen their measure of curtain calls.

There was severe internal bleeding, the kid's pulse was thready, and according to the grisly-looking gas company fellow who had called them, he'd been repeatedly pulled back from the grave.

The representative from the Brazos County Sheriff's Department arrived as the kid's gurney was being loaded into the ambulance.

The deputy didn't have time to say "howdy." He walked up as the kid was trundled past, took a snapshot picture of him with his eyes, fished a pocket notebook out, and wrote one word on it: *Linda.* It must have been a hell of an effort making those letters in his own blood on his stomach, he thought.

"Don't wash that name off his stomach, fellas," he said. "Take a picture of it. Especially if he . . . doesn't make it. Where you fellas takin' 'im?"

"To meet the life-flight chopper."

"Oh. Where's he going to from there?"

"God only knows. Excuse us, officer." The younger of the two paramedics hopped down from the truck and closed the door behind him. "Gotta go," he said.

"See ya," the deputy said.

Charles Lyman was sitting on the porch of the cabin looking out onto the still duck pond. There was a half-ring of floating landscaping timbers out there tied end-to-end. One end of the daisy chain was anchored to the opposite shoreline and the closest end was lodged in the mud on the nearby bank.

"That's what he was doing," Lyman said.

The deputy wheeled around.

"What?"

Lyman pointed.

The deputy glanced away, quickly, and then back to the man sitting there. It was difficult to look away from him. He was a craggy-looking fellow, mid-fifties, with sparse, rust-colored hair and large freckles all over him. He wore a dark blue jumpsuit with some kind of logo embroidered on the chest. But none of these things were as notable as the amount of drying blood covering the man. His hands were two dark red gloves. His arms, chest, and face were spattered with it. And he just sat there, looking toward the lake.

"He was skimming the lake when they came along," the blood-covered man said. "He was in his birthday suit and was still wet. He had duckweed all over him."

"You're the fella that saved his life. Lyman, right?"

"Not if he don't make it, I ain't. Yeah, I'm Lyman."

"Okay," the deputy said. "My name's Ralph Bigham. We need to talk."

Charles Lyman looked at the deputy, then back toward the lake. "Have a seat," he said.

Carlos McDaniel gave up the ghost three days later. When he went, his hand was gripped by that of his new best friend, the craggy-faced angel who was there whenever his eyes opened, swimming into focus when consciousness slowly yet inexorably returned.

"Who's Linda?" the angel asked him.

Carlos blinked, smiled, and uttered the name in a whisper: "Linda Sneed."

Two weeks later, when he got the word that the case had been closed on the shooting, Charles Lyman left his job with Cen-

tral Texas Gas. At ten minutes till five, he stuck his head in
the air-conditioned substation office in the little town of Kur-
ten, Texas, and told the foreman he wasn't coming back. The
foreman—a forgettable fellow named Seth Sweet—shrugged
at the closed door, lit another cigarette, and turned back to
his weekly report.

"Politics, that's why," Ralph Bigham told him.

"Politics?"

"Yeah. It doesn't look good to have open files, so it's easier
to close them."

"I'll be damned," Charles Lyman said.

"Tell me about the two men again," Ralph Bigham said
before the other fellow could start losing his temper.

"One was big," Lyman replied. "He looked like a big scoop
of muscle and a dollop of fat poured into a suit, but he walked
sort of like a penguin. The other guy was shorter and slim.
Their backs were to me."

"What do you think all of this is about?"

"I don't know," he said. "But I found something you missed."
Charles dropped the leather binder on the cafe tabletop.

Carlos McDaniel's Day-Timer business calendar contained
the details of his appointments for the six months leading up
to the shooting. Bigham leafed through it. There were upcom-
ing real estate showings, open houses, closings, and appointments scattered throughout. There was nothing for the weeks
previous to the shooting that seemed to amount to anything,
but then, leafing his way back, he saw one entry all by itself:
L.S. Littlefield.

"Who's L.S. Littlefield?" Bigham asked.

"L.S. is probably Linda Sneed. At least I hope it is. Now,
the name Littlefield is about as Austin as you can get. There's

a Littlefield Building here, the Littlefield home, the Littlefield statue. You name it, and there's a Littlefield 'it.'"

"That name is familiar to me somehow," Bigham said. "But I'm not an Austonian."

"Austinite," Charles corrected.

They were in a little Mexican restaurant on College Avenue near downtown Bryan, Texas. A waitress came by and cleared away their plates and left a ticket. Lyman fished out a twenty and dropped it on the table.

"Thanks," Deputy Bigham said.

"Sure. The guy everything is named after is George W. Littlefield. He was a Civil War hero and land baron. He owned the Yellowhouse Ranch up in the Panhandle. I think it was land trimmed off of the original XIT Ranch, which was how the state funded the construction of the new capitol building after the old one burned. I think that was back around the 1880s, 1890s. Littlefield was almost single-handedly responsible for the establishment of UT Austin."

"Seems to me like there might be a town with that name as well," Bigham said.

"You're right. Why didn't I think of that before? It's up northwest of Lubbock, not far from the New Mexico state line."

Bigham nodded and kept rifling through the pages of the Day-Timer, while Charles Lyman, who actually liked the deputy, found himself wanting to slam it on his fingers.

"You know," Bigham began, "the name Linda Sneed keeps sticking in my craw. Seems to me there was some news item in the local paper some months back. If it's the same person then I think she's some kind of fugitive from justice. Something about some real estate dealings."

"Wanted, huh?" Charles said.

"I think so. I've never been much of a newspaper reader, myself, but all you have to do is glance in the direction of the damned things and the stuff jumps out at you."

"That's for sure. I'm stuck on that name myself. Not sure why."

"Okay," Ralph said. "So what are you going to do now?"

"I'm leaving town," Lyman said.

"I thought you might." Ralph Bigham reached beside him, pulled up a leather case, and slid it across the table to Charles Lyman.

"What's this?"

"Something you might need."

Lyman tugged the zipper on the side of the case and saw a round metal cylinder. It was the barrel of a .357 Smith & Wesson magnum.

"I can't accept this," he said.

"Why not?"

"I can't hold a gun in my hands."

"Not a religious thing, is it?" Deputy Bigham asked.

"Also, I can't vote."

"You're a felon."

"Yeah. I was a kid, and it was a long, long time ago. I'm only lucky we live in an age where they don't brand your forehead or otherwise mark you."

"What did you do?" Bigham asked.

"I killed a man," Charles Lyman said.

The next question was there between them, an invisible yet wholly tangible thing, and Ralph Bigham found himself asking it.

"Who did you kill, Chuck?"

Lucid, teal-blue eyes looked up at Ralph Bigham, measuring, weighing.

"My brother," Lyman said.

A deep silence settled in around them. It was one of those moments where each was expecting the other to say or ask something first. Bigham waited long enough to be sure that Lyman wasn't going to give him his life story.

When Lyman didn't, Bigham pushed the leather pouch directly in front of him and said, "Keep it anyway. Something tells me you're going to need it."

Farmhouses, windmills, grain silos miles away, vaguely reminiscent of old, well-crafted dime-store miniatures of such, slowly dwindled in the distance as he passed. The Caprock is a true plain. He felt its solidity, its permanence, as he drove into town in his ancient battered Ford F-150 pickup.

Charles Lyman whistled.

He passed a population sign: 6,032.

Somebody likes it here, he thought.

A wind was up and dust was blowing from the west. It was fine dust, and it was coming in through the air-conditioning vent enough to make his nose itch.

It wasn't difficult finding downtown Littlefield. Phelps Avenue is an undivided street, with bluish-green metal seats covered by 1950s-style awnings near each intersection. Half of the businesses were closed, permanently, and there were no more than a few dozen cars along the four-block stretch leading from the train tracks to the courthouse.

"I'd say this town has seen better days," he said to himself. "Reminds me of *The Last Picture Show*."

Two blocks from the courthouse—which was not on a town square like most of the rest of Texas' small burghs—he found a Mexican restaurant. A red neon sign in the front window declared it to be open.

Inside there was red carpet in need of a good cleaning and a pleasant smell wafting from the kitchen.

There was a hand-lettered sign on one wall that declared: *Absolutely NO Table Moving.*

The waitress was a pudgy young lady of perhaps nineteen. She wore a burgundy apron and a beatific smile. She had dimples in her cheeks and her name tag read *Cassandra.*

"Hungry?" she asked.

"You said it," Charles replied. "Coffee first, though. Then bring me whatever you think I'd like to eat."

She glanced down at his ring finger quickly, saw that it was bare, then looked back up to his eyes. He winked at her, and she smiled, turned, and darted off.

He was nearly done with breakfast and thinking about Carlos McDaniel when they came in the restaurant door. A smile flashed at him, all false teeth and malice. Lyman smiled back.

The two men were the Undertaker and Lardman, Lyman's new pet names for them in the two seconds that it took him to fully assess them. They were wearing the same clothing he'd last seen them in as they walked away from the cabin, three hundred miles to the south and what seemed a lifetime ago.

And again, Charles Lyman's blood froze in his veins.

He waited until they took a seat before he fished out his wallet and dropped a hundred-dollar bill on the table. He'd liked the waitress, and he was already sorry for the trouble he was about to cause her if things didn't go well. Then he reached down into his right boot and brought out the magnum. He stood, forgetting to put his truck keys in his pocket, turned, and walked to the table where they were sitting, the pistol with his finger lightly on the trigger behind him.

"Hi," he said. "My name is Charles Lyman." He stood there and looked down at the two killers.

The men looked up at him quizzically.

He swung the gun around and pointed it between the two. Their eyes riveted to it. The two men tensed, as if to spring.

"Not a good idea," Lyman said. "Let's make an agreement. You two guys be nice and we'll take us a little ride and have us a little talk. That sound all right with you?"

"Talk? What about?" the Undertaker asked.

"About Carlos McDaniel. And Linda Sneed."

When he got outside he realized his predicament.

There were two of them, and he had to cover them both. Also, he couldn't find his truck keys.

He turned back toward the diner for just an instant, but in that short space he noted the face between the still window curtains. It was Cassandra, the waitress.

The face vanished, as if it had never been there.

He made Lardman drive their black Crown Victoria while the Undertaker rode shotgun and he covered the two of them from the backseat.

The late-model Crown Vic wended its way through town and out into the countryside where the sun beat down relentlessly on the stubby cotton and the tall corn.

"You guys are pretty quiet," Lyman said. "Remember our agreement."

"We ain't got nothing to say," the Undetaker replied.

"See?" Lyman said. "We're having a conversation already. Tell me where she is."

Lardman and the Undertaker exchanged glances, and suddenly Lyman knew what was coming.

Lardman made an abrupt turn down a dirt road, then began accelerating.

So much for agreements, Lyman thought.

The Undertaker moved, quick and catlike. His hand went inside his jacket.

Charles Lyman fired the Smith & Wesson point-blank into the back of the driver's seat. Lardman jerked the wheel to the right as he crumpled over it. His foot came off the gas and the car slewed toward the ditch.

Lyman reached forward as the Undertaker came up with a gun, took it from him, grabbed the back of his suit collar, and shoved forward with everything he had.

The Undertaker's face got very personal with the windshield.

The car came to a stop in the sand at the side of the road and fetched up against a culvert, hard. The Undertaker flopped back in his seat, out cold.

"Should have buckled up," Lyman told him. "It's the law."

He dropped the snub-nosed .38 he'd taken from the Undertaker onto the floorboard and kicked it under the seat in front of him.

Lardman was slumped over the steering wheel. He had a hole in his back. Probably the bullet had gone through the seat of the Crown Vic, through his back an inch to the right of his spine, and most likely was lodged in his right lung. His days of eating linguini were over.

Lyman got out, opened the driver's door, fished out Lardman's wallet, and found a driver's license. The license was out of state. *Samuel Rosario.* No middle name. Some address in Brooklyn, New York. There was nothing else. He replaced the wallet, went through the man's pockets, and came up with a pack of Pall Mall cigarettes, a gold lighter, and a wad of cash about the size of a small horse apple.

"I'm giving this to Carlos's family," Lyman told him.

He went back around to the passenger side and checked the glove box. Nothing.

He went through the Undertaker's pockets and found an ancient calfskin wallet and with it a name: *Victor Cicchese.*

Victor sported a nose that grew in size and kept emitting a stream of blood and mucus as Lyman continued the search through his pockets.

"One pocket comb. Check," Lyman intoned. "One prophylactic, unused. Check. One tin of Altoids. Check. Aha," he said. "What have we here? One slightly tarnished photograph of a little cutie-pie."

The photo was a black-and-white studio shot of a platinum-blond young lady of that indeterminate age somewhere between seventeen and twenty-five.

He flipped it over.

Blue ink told the tale: *Linda, sophomore year, NYU.*

In the inside pocket of the Undertaker's jacket he found a magnetic key card with a bright Motel 6 logo emblazoned across it.

At that moment, Mr. Victor Cicchese let out a low moan.

"Doesn't feel so good, does it?" Lyman said.

Victor's head lolled to one side. His eyelids fluttered for a moment and then slowly opened.

"Hello," Lyman said.

"Uh . . . what?"

Lyman punched him, hard. His eyes closed.

"Sometimes I just can't help myself," Lyman said.

A truck was coming, trailing dust.

"Ah, hell," Lyman said.

The truck slowed. It was his own pickup, and as it drew

closer, he recognized the face behind the wheel. It was Cassandra from the restaurant.

Cassandra got out, raced over to Lyman, and threw her arms around his neck. She kissed him on the cheek. It took not a little effort to get her to stop.

"I thought you'd be dead," she said.

Lyman chuckled, holding her in the air. After a moment he had to set her back down.

Charles Lyman's first thought was to turn the Undertaker into a hood ornament and strap him across the front of his truck like a trussed deer, but then he reminded himself that he wasn't looking for more attention than he could handle at the moment.

Cassandra found a spool of twine in his truck, which he used to bind up their captive and ensconce him in the bed of his pickup truck. He took a moment to get the Crown Victoria off the road and into the corn.

He walked back to the road.

"Darlin'," he said, "where's the Motel 6?"

Cassandra directed him to the motel.

"Be right back," she said, and climbed out. "I know the girl who works the counter here. This won't take a minute."

True to her word, she was back beside him in the pickup in seconds.

"Around in back and down on the end, number 167," Cassandra said.

"What'd you tell her?"

"I told her that we were borrowing our friend's room. I told her I got lucky and found a man."

Charles laughed. "I wouldn't want to make a liar out of you," he said.

* * *

The door had a *Do Not Disturb* sign hanging from the handle.

They found Linda Sneed inside, barely alive. Charles had to fish out a pair of bolt cutters from his pickup in order to get the handcuffs off of her while Cassandra held water to her swollen lips. She was dehydrated, had fouled the bed linens underneath her, and was talking out of her head.

The ambulance arrived fifteen minutes after she regained full consciousness. Ten minutes after that, the sheriff came knocking.

"What was it all about?" Ralph Bigham asked him.

"It was about money and revenge. She knew her life wasn't worth anything if she told them where it was stashed. So she rode it out."

"What money?"

"Lardman's," Lyman said.

"Who?"

"His name was Sammy Rosario. I call him Lardman because I like that name better. Linda met him at a bar in the Bronx. He bragged about being a hit man who had just made a big score and was going to retire. She took him to bed, robbed him blind, and cut out."

"How much?" Bigham asked.

"Quarter-million. That is, if she's telling the truth."

"What about the other guy?"

"The Undertaker? His name was Victor Cicchese. Lardman's cousin."

"Okay. What about McDaniel? Why'd they kill him?"

Lyman released a long, slow breath. The answer came to him, and as he said it, he knew he was right.

"Because. Some guys are lucky. Some ain't. They make their own luck, good or bad. Carlos put himself in the path of the tornado. In that respect, he was a lot like my brother."

"I don't understand," Bigham said, knowing it was the only way to finally pull it out of the craggy-faced, teal-eyed man in front of him. But Lyman shifted the subject from himself, from his own past, and back to McDaniel.

"McDaniel screwed up pretty bad. Linda Sneed was his client, and he broke a rule. He took her to bed. Word got back to Lardman somehow, where she was, what she was doing, who she was screwing, and they came looking for her. But they found him first."

The silence grew around them. The restaurant had grown still.

"I'll go ahead and tell you," Lyman said. "Because you want to know, and it's secrets that always get us. My brother made his own bad luck. I caught him in bed with my girl. We were going to be married, you know."

A moment passed. Then another.

"I killed him with my own bare hands. It was rage, Ralph. Consuming rage."

"When was that?" Bigham asked.

"Twenty years ago. My parole expired last month. I'm a free man now. I can go where I want, do what I want."

"Yeah?"

"But we're never free, I think. That is, until we somehow make it right."

Ralph Bigham looked down at the table, weighed his own words before speaking. "I hope," he said. "I hope you've made it right again, Chuck."

Lyman smiled. "Me too," he said. "Oh. I almost forgot." He reached into the large paper bag beside him, pulled out the leather gun case, and pushed it across the table. "I gave it a thorough cleaning."

"Thanks," Ralph said.

A horn blared.

Lyman turned toward the restaurant window and waved.

Cassandra waved back.

"Impatient, isn't she?" Bigham said, and then laughed.

"Yeah. Women. I gotta go," Lyman said. "My girl's waiting, and I think she's waited long enough."

CHERRY COKE

BY MILTON T. BURTON

Tyler

S am MacCord was at the poker game at Matty's Truck
Stop in Kilgore, Texas, the night Cherry Coke got his
nickname. Cherry claimed it was his first time playing
poker. When he said that, one of the players laughed and re-
marked that he'd come to the right place to bust his cherry.
With a last name like Coke, the handle was a natural, and
it stuck with him from then on. It was also easy for the players who'd been there to remember Cherry because he walked
away from the table the big winner. And that just doesn't happen the first time around. At least not in the kind of games
Sam MacCord played in. So everybody assumed Cherry was
an experienced gambler who ran out a strong line of con about
not ever having played before. But after an incident that happened at a game down in Lufkin one cold, rainy night about a
year later, Sam wasn't so sure about that.

Cherry was a slim guy of medium height who appeared to
be about forty. He had a face-shaped face that fronted for a
head-shaped head and a pair of unassuming eyes whose color
hovered somewhere between pale gray and hazel, depending
on the lighting. His neatly combed hair was dark brown with
a little gray at the temples, and he usually wore dark pants,
white dress shirts, and a sand-colored tweed sport coat. Nothing about him stood out. In fact the opposite was true. If you'd
asked Sam to describe Cherry and then given him a minute to

think before answering, he would have said there was something blurry about the man, something vague and indefinite that made it hard to remember what he looked like even while you were staring directly at his face.

According to Cherry, he'd gotten into poker almost by accident. His car was a coal-black Mercury Marquis he'd bought from a dealership in Henderson. Cherry was an amiable sort who paid the sticker price on the car without quibbling, and the dealer, who was himself a gregarious individual, took an instant liking to him. While the dealer's secretary was finishing the paperwork, the conversation drifted around to poker. Cherry mentioned that he'd recently acquired an interest in the game and would like to give it a try sometime. Right then the dealer invited him to sit in at Matty's that coming weekend in Kilgore. This, Cherry claimed, had been his start.

During the year we knew him, he played mostly in East Texas. Though Sam now lived in Dallas, he was from East Texas and gravitated back homeward whenever he got a yen for the cards, even though the really lucrative action was to be found in the western part of the state. "A man can hide better where there's lots of trees," he always said with a friendly smile when anybody asked why he'd never tried the big games out around Lubbock and Odessa. The truth was that as far as poker went, Sam was nothing more than a recreational gambler, even though he sometimes won or lost several thousand dollars at a sitting. Back in his younger days he'd been a hijacker whose name was linked in the papers with a collection of Southern criminals who journalists tagged with the lurid name *Dixie Mafia*. He'd also been the main suspect in a couple of contract killings, but that was back then. Now things were a lot different. That was because one fine fall afternoon a decade earlier, a light of sorts had gone off inside

Sam's head, and he'd suddenly realized that he was the only one of his associates who'd never been to prison. Not one to travel too far on luck, he pulled up on the heavy stuff. Then, after getting the go-ahead from the right people a few weeks later, he opened what eventually became a very successful sports book. And Sam really liked Cherry Coke, which was why he was supremely irked the night Jackie Fats Reed pulled out the .357 snub-nose and stuck it in Cherry's face during that Lufkin game.

Jack J. Reed, who was still called "Jackie Fats" years after his health had forced him to slim down from 300 pounds to his current 180, was a surly whiner who'd never been known to lose a hand with any degree of grace. Indeed, he was only allowed to play because he lost consistently, and because he was a hoodlum and a known killer who could not be safely ex-cluded from the table. Jackie Fats was not a happy man. The cardiac he'd suffered in his late thirties and the subsequent triple bypass had forced him to get his life and his diet un-der control, but they'd left him very disagreeable because he missed lolling indolently around and scarfing up gargantuan quantities of whatever caught his fancy—things he certainly couldn't do anymore unless he wanted an early checkout date. He also wanted to win at poker, which he almost never did. Consequently, everybody had mixed feelings whenever Jackie Fats showed up at one of the games. Regulars were happy to see such a steady loser bring his bulging bankroll to the table, but his propensity for violence also set everybody on edge.

Cherry and Sam became casual friends, and often after a game broke up they went out for breakfast, where Cherry always requested double and sometimes even triple orders of sausage. From time to time they'd meet at some club to hoist a few, though both were light drinkers. Cherry's real name was Richard, and once Sam got to know him well enough to mount a personal question, he asked if there was any chance he was related to Richard Coke, Texas' beloved Restorationist governor who ran all the carpetbaggers out of the state at the end of Reconstruction.

Cherry shook his head and said, "No honchos in my family, Sam. My dad was just a dirt farmer."

"Where, if you don't mind me asking?"

"A little ways outside Athens."

At the time, Sam naturally assumed he meant Athens, Texas, a small agricultural town about seventy miles southeast of Dallas. Then, a week later at a game in Longview, somebody said something about Socrates. That was when Cherry, who rarely volunteered anything, smiled and said, "He was queer as a three-dollar bill, you know."

"Who?" one of the other players asked.

"Socrates."

"Some people claim that," said Tom Wilkins, who was a fine player besides being a history teacher at the junior college in nearby Tyler. "But I don't think anybody really knows for sure."

"Oh, I know for sure," Cherry said.

"How so?"

"Because the old rascal made a pass at me the first time my dad took me into town. I was about fifteen at the time, and he was famous. Everybody knew who he was."

For a few moments there was a befuddled silence at the table. Then one of the players, a boisterous older fellow from Nacogdoches who was reputed to be rich as Midas himself, laughed and slapped Cherry on the back and said, "This boy comes on so sweet and innocent that if a man didn't watch himself he'd wind up believing everything he says."

They all had a good laugh and Cherry gave them a bland

smile and the game resumed. But that business about Athens and Socrates came back to haunt Sam after Cherry had his little dust-up with Jackie Fats in Lufkin.

Cherry gambled around East Texas for a year or so. After that first night, he rarely took home the big money, but he won steadily if undramatically, and he always left with enough to live well for a couple of weeks. Which was highly unusual. *Everybody* goes all the way down to broke sometimes. It's just in the nature of a gambler to do so. But not Cherry. He didn't cheat either. Too many of the people he played with were far too savvy not to have eventually spotted something if he had. In fact, he seemed to win more consistently when he hadn't even touched the cards than he did when he was dealer.

Spooky.

Now, as a general rule, it's not considered polite to ask personal questions across the poker table. But it happens, especially when a group of guys have played together here and there over several months and feel like they have gotten to know one another. After all, even seasoned gamblers are human, and we humans are a snoopy lot whose curiosity sometimes gets the better of us. Finally, one night when a cattleman named Bob Robbins got to bitching about the sorrows of the beef market, a couple of other businessmen at the table chimed in with their grievances about the general economic condition of the country. Then somebody broke the ice and asked Cherry what he did for a living. Cherry ran out a song-and-dance about how he'd sold advertising novelties "up until a couple of weeks ago," and then went on to say he was out of work and looking for a job. Nobody believed a word of it, of course. But the message was clear, and it was the only thing Sam MacCord ever knew for certain about Cherry Coke: the man might have started late in life and learned fast, but he was a professional gambler.

The Lufkin game that finally ended Cherry's run in East Texas took place every weekend in the back room of a very successful used car dealership owned by a guy named Eddie Ray Atwell Junior. Eddie Ray Senior had been one of Sam's Dixie Mafia cohorts. Almost forty years earlier, when Eddie Junior was just a little tyke, somebody had let the hammer down on the old man in a motel out in San Gabriel, a sin-filled little West Texas city that sprawled on both sides of the aptly named Rio Diablo—the Devil's River. Nobody ever had a clue as to who was behind that dastardly deed, or why they were behind it, not even Sam, who knew as much about the Southern criminal underworld as anybody. Not that it really mattered. In the final years that Senior graced this world with his presence, he'd come to be known as Eddie the Rat, a man willing to screw his own partners anytime the opportunity presented itself. So his passing was mourned by few, and probably not even by his wife, a smart, tough woman who had been the brains behind the car lot in the first place, and who kept the business going while her husband was off running up and down the roads in a fancy Lincoln convertible, cranked to the gills on speed and trying to get something going in the Mexican heroin trade, an endeavor for which he was uniquely unsuited. She never remarried. Instead, she devoted her energies to teaching her kid the ins and outs of the used car trade. Eddie Junior was a fast learner who wound up even more successful than his mother. He also loved poker, and a lot of money passed across his table every weekend.

It was a Friday night in late fall. The area had been plagued with storms and tornado warnings all week. Thunder could still be heard rumbling in the distance, but by dark the rain had slacked off to a steady drizzle. The weather forecasts called for more bad weather in the next few days, and the temperature was expected to drop below freezing before dawn.

The cards were cold that night too. The game was no-limit Texas Hold'em, but nobody could seem to get any traction, not even Cherry. Then, a little before the witching hour, one of those freak hands came along, and two kings and an ace flopped. Jackie Fats bet $200 and Cherry raised him $500. Jackie smiled—which was a rare thing for the cranky bastard—and called even. Cherry smiled right back at him. This sudden heat caused everybody else to fold, and the next card was the king of spades. After that, Cherry knew the die was cast, even though the rest of us didn't find out until a couple of minutes later. Fats bet $1,000 and Cherry raised him another $1,000. The last card was the seven of clubs, which neither helped nor hurt either of them. Jackie Fats smiled again, and with all the confidence in the world, he laid down twenty brand-new hundred-dollar bills. Cherry didn't even hesitate. He called and raised $2,500, which only left him a couple of hundred on the table. For all practical purposes he was all in, a move that should have made Jackie Fats study the situation over for at least a few seconds. But Jackie was a natural bully, one who was always eager to stomp down on somebody, and he fell all over himself pushing the call into the pot. Eddie Junior, who was dealing that hand, said, "Showtime, boys."

Jackie Fats had made the last call, which meant it was Cherry's obligation to show his cards first. But Jackie was hungry for blood. His eyes were bright and gleeful, and his face was positively vulpine as he reached down with his short, once-plump fingers and flipped over his hole cards to reveal an ace and a king, which gave him an A-A-K-K-K full house. "Can you beat that?"

Cherry didn't even bother to answer. He just casually

turned over his cards to reveal the other two aces for an A-A-A-K-K full. As I said, it was a freak hand.

Jackie Fats gaped at the cards for the longest time, his face getting gradually redder and redder. A drop of spittle dripped off his lower lip and hung by a thread as it made its slow way down to the table. Then he bellowed like a wounded bull and lunged to his feet. That's when the revolver appeared in his hand. Which surprised no one. It was considered the worst of manners to come armed to another man's place, but etiquette had never been Jackie's strong suit.

"Get up," he said, waving the gun wildly under Cherry's nose. "I've never killed anybody who wasn't on his feet."

Cherry was unperturbed. "I don't think so."

"I said, get up!"

"No. I'm comfortable where I'm at."

Jackie Fats licked his lips. He'd never had a man refuse one of his "requests" when he was pointing a .357 at his head. It was a new experience for him. Combined with Cherry's utter calm, it rattled him. "I want to know how," he said.

"How what?"

"How you always win."

"He don't," Bob Robbins said.

"Shut up, Bob," Fats said without much rancor. "I've paid the price here tonight and I want an answer."

Ever the gentleman, Sam had left his piece in the car, but now he regretted it. He was beginning to realize just how long he'd been deeply annoyed with Jackie Fats and just how much he wanted an excuse to smoke the man. Still, he said as diplomatically as he could, "Let it pass, Jackie. It's not worth gunplay."

"I'll be the one to decide that," Jackie barked. "And this bastard is going to tell me how he does it."

"There's no reason—" Bob Robbins began.

"Seventy-two percent," Cherry said, interrupting him.

"What?" Fats growled. His face was almost purple, and he was gripping the gun so tightly his knuckles were white and bloodless. Cherry was as calm as a mortician.

"Seventy-two percent," Cherry repeated. "That's how much of the time I know what the cards are. It's always been that way, though I only started to gamble in the last few years."

Jackie Fats was baffled. "What are you saying?"

Cherry sighed a tired sigh. "You wanted to know how I do it, and I just told you."

"I don't get it."

"Okay, then try this. We sit down and somebody deals a hundred hands. In roughly seventy-two of them I'll know what everybody has."

"You mean you guess right almost three quarters of the time?" one of the other players asked.

Cherry shook his head firmly. "There's no guess to it. Some hands I don't have a clue, but most of the time I know. And I'm never wrong. I either know for sure or I don't know anything. It's either the whole hog or nothing with me. That's just the way it works, but I've got no idea why."

Sam was more alert than the others. "How did you get that precise figure?" he asked. "The seventy-two percent, I mean."

"I was tested in the Rhine experiments in ESP at Duke University."

"But that was . . ." Sam began, then tapered off in confusion.

"About fifty years ago, Sam."

"Damn! You can't be that old."

"Why can't I?" he asked. Then he turned and looked at

Sam, and his face was full of weariness. For a fleeting moment, Sam thought he saw something in Cherry Coke's eyes
that was deep and dark and ancient beyond knowing. Then
Cherry blinked and it was gone, and he was once again the
same bland, fortyish fellow Sam had known for a year, staring
back at him out of a face so plain and undistinguished that it
could hardly be remembered.

Cherry got leisurely to his feet and stood looking across
the table at Jackie Fats. "If you're going to shoot me, go ahead
and do it," he said.

Sam looked across at Jackie Fats. For some reason, all the
fight had gone out of him, and he wasn't in a shooting mood
anymore. His hand trembled a little as he slowly lowered the
gun. His gaze was riveted to Cherry's face, and his expression
was unreadable. Sam reached out and took the .357 gently from
Jackie's hand and tucked it in his belt. Cherry slowly and carefully stacked his winnings and slipped them into his inner jacket
pocket. Then he looked around the table and smiled. "It's been
a real pleasure," he said. "You were fine fellows to be with."

When Cherry walked out, Sam MacCord followed him.
The air was cold and bitter and full of a fine mist. In the parking lot Sam came abreast of Cherry and asked, "If what you
said in there about the Rhine experiments is true, then . . ."
Sam let his voice taper off.

Cherry didn't look at him. He just kept walking, but he
said, his voice resigned, "Then what?"

After a moment's thought, Sam decided not to push the
matter. "Nothing," he replied with a shake of his head.

When Cherry got to his car, he turned and stuck out his
hand. "I've enjoyed knowing you, Sam," he said. "I've always
liked having friends, but it's never paid me to try to hold on
to them too long."

A few seconds later the Marquis whisked softly off into the night. That was the last time Sam MacCord ever saw Cherry Coke, but he heard stories. About a year later, a couple of regulars at the Lufkin game took their wives out to Las Vegas on vacation. One evening they left the women parked at a show and took a cab over to sample the delights of the Mirage. That's where they saw Cherry at the five-dollar-minimum blackjack table, still clad in his dark pants and sand-colored sport coat. Whatever warm reunion they might have expected wasn't forthcoming. Cherry was civil but unsmiling and distant. After a couple of aborted attempts at reliving old times, they gave up and left him there amidst the clatter of chips and the whir of the slot machines, a loner in a lonely land. Six months after the game, Jackie Fats Reed was found sprawled on the living room floor of his Houston apartment with a .22-caliber bullet hole in the center of his forehead and an expression of pure amazement frozen on his ugly face. Speculation was that Cherry Coke had extracted his revenge for that dreadful night in Lufkin, but Sam MacCord knew better.

After he heard about Cherry turning up at the Mirage, Sam made a point of asking everybody he knew who went to Vegas about him. Word filtered back to Texas that the man had become a minor legend on the Strip, a sort of silent specter who never won heavily but who rarely lost, and who moved from casino to casino taking a thousand or so a week away from the tables—enough to live on reasonably well but never enough to annoy the Powers That Be. Then he vanished.

It was several months before Sam managed to shake loose from his affairs long enough to travel out to Nevada and try to run down the story. The trail led to an elderly Texas road gambler named Diamond Red Nash who now worked as a gaming consultant for one of the casinos. He and Sam had always liked one another, and their reunion was cordial. Sam quickly learned that Diamond Red had been Cherry's only real friend in Vegas. He also learned that Cherry had left town on his own.

"Didn't nobody run him off or do nothing to hurt him," Red said. "He just told me that he hadn't seen Europe in a long, long time, and then he was gone."

"Europe?" Sam asked in surprise. "Why there?"

"Well, he claimed he wanted to revisit some old memories. And he said he intended to try the baccarat at Monte Carlo."

Sam nodded and looked out the window into the desert air shimmering in the bright noonday sun and thought back to that cold, rainy night when he'd last seen Cherry. It seemed a whole world and a lifetime away, and for the first time he felt the full weight of his sixty years. "What was your estimate of him, Red?" he finally asked.

"I think he was the best blackjack player I ever laid my eyes on." Then he grinned. "And I believe he loved good pork sausage more than anybody I ever knew."

Sam smiled and nodded. "And . . . ?"

"I really liked the boy, Sam. I believe he'd do to ride the river with."

"I thought so too, Red. I thought so too . . ."

Sam shook the old man's hand and caught a late-night flight back to Dallas. The next day he called in a marker with a couple of local detectives who stayed a few hundred in debt to his book year-round. It wasn't long before one of them phoned to tell him that a Richard Coke had flown from Las Vegas to Atlanta and then on to Munich, where he had leased a brand-new BMW from a German agency. After that, there was no trace of him.

Sam decided to drop it. He considered Cherry a friend, and friends were entitled to their privacy. He also did his best to put the matter out of his mind. But from time to time, especially when he awoke in those lonely hours after midnight and sleep wouldn't return, he found himself thinking about Cherry Coke. He finally decided that besides being the best gambler he'd ever met, the man had been a consummate actor who could convince anybody of almost anything. That's what he believed because that's what he wanted to believe. The only other explanation that fit the facts led down a dark road that Sam MacCord did not want to travel.

PART III

BIG-CITY TEXAS

Lips so sweet and tender, like petals falling apart . . .
—Bob Wills and the Texas Playboys

MONTGOMERY CLIFT

BY SARAH CORTEZ

Houston

Every time I looked at him I saw Rosalie's first husband. The same thin shoulders. Pupils too dark to read their meaning. He felt me staring at him as I asked the same question every morning before I walked to work.

"What you doing today, son?"

"My lesson's at two."

Another one of Rosalie's dreams. That her son Monty would be a singer. She had found a man to tutor him at the small Catholic college in the neighborhood. Her son loved voice lessons and we found the money. Sometimes Nichols, the voice teacher, came into the hardware store I'd worked at since arriving to Houston in the late '40s after the war. I knew his face from a concert program Monty'd brought home and left in the kitchen. The man, about forty-five years old, was well fed, but only talked in a raspy whisper. The potential of his strong body was not borne out in his oily muttering.

I drained the last bit of coffee. "What else you doing today?"

Monty pulled his eyes up to meet my face for the first time that morning. "Practice. I have a piano studio reserved beginning at ten."

"Make sure you do your chores first." You'd think I wouldn't have to remind a boy fixing to begin college about his responsibilities. But this one—her son—had as much common sense as a domestic rabbit. All ears and big teeth. He was as useless as the movie star she'd named him after—that little shrimp, Montgomery Clift, with the dreamboat mug he sold for money so he'd never have to work a day in his life. Just pace around decked out in fancy suits and leather dress shoes while getting smooched by a beautiful actress. Montgomery, no kind of name for a man.

I glanced at the few keepsakes I displayed as decoration in my repair space at Southland's. A black-and-white photo of our squad before getting shipped out to the Pacific, all smiles and bravado. A keychain doodad of tubular, see-through plastic, about three inches long. Three red rings floated in the clear fluid. The game was to place all three thin rings onto a woman's lone leg extended in the liquid. Rosalie's gams had looked like that when I married her. The long line of perfect white skin extending up and up from her dainty knees. With her illness, the blood got throttled in her legs' thick blue veins and splotched her thin skin with a thousand red lines like smashed spiders. Just looking at them gave me the heebie-jeebies.

I had just put out the nut driver and wire cutters for the first job I had to tackle when Officer Linehan came in through the back entrance off the parking lot. His usual entrance for his usual coffee. Today, he was rushing.

"Morning, officer."

"Hey, Otto. I need some D-cell batteries. Five of them. Quick. They got a dead body under that railroad trestle on the bayou near the rice silos."

I handed him a pack. "Pay us tomorrow."

"Thanks. These damn runaways. You'd think they could get themselves killed somewhere else. You know, like Dallas. This girl's supposed to be young—maybe fifteen. They'll never find out who she is."

I watched him scuttle back to his patrol car. Not even eight a.m. and we were all sweating.

Later that day, Linehan shook his head back and forth. "That poor kid. She was as scrawny as a half-starved pullet. Whoever killed her did it good—back of the skull crushed."

"What did they use?" I asked, setting out a screwdriver to take apart a clock radio.

"Who knows? Who cares? Looks like she ran off to be a free-love hippie. Dripping with love beads and peace symbols. What a bunch of crap." He smiled into his afternoon coffee. "The only good thing about this flower-power B.S. is that none of them hippie chicks wear bras. Makes for some good visuals when they ain't dead."

My younger sister Lilly had run away to follow that handsome city dude. Before she left she had tried to confide in me. But I'd refused to listen, angry with her for always causing problems. Why couldn't she follow the rules of the household, like I did? I had enough problems of my own; I didn't want to listen to hers. She wasn't out of high school yet, although none of us were a book-learning family. It broke my momma's heart that we never knew for sure what Lilly did or where she went.

"Lost," Momma would murmur, eyes tearing. "My daughter's lost."

That evening when I got home from work, I went into Rosalie's bedroom first, as I always did. She lay under the faded yellow bedspread with pillows propping up her head.

Her dark eyes flickered open. "Hello, Otto."

"Hello, Rosalie. How you feeling today?"

"All right. Nothing better; nothing worse."

"I'll get your dinner after a while. Where's Monty?"

"Montgomery."

"Where's your son?"

"Practicing at St. Thomas."

"Okay." No point in continuing. The little strength she had, she used for her son—like all those phone calls to find a voice teacher, whose lessons I had to pay for. "Did he do his chores today?"

A small smile lit her thin lips. "I told him to go ahead on to practice. He couldn't wait to get out of the house."

I patted her hand and made sure my voice didn't show the anger I felt. "I guess I'll rustle up some dinner."

Monty came home after I'd fed Rosalie and me, washed dishes, and was sitting on the screened-in front porch waiting for the July evening to cool off.

He sidled in the screen door.

"You missed dinner."

"I . . . I ate already."

"Where?"

"At Mr. Nichols's house. He . . . he had extra and he invited me."

"You need permission to eat dinner elsewhere. You know that. Why didn't you call?"

"I forgot."

"Don't forget again."

He sucked in air through his wide-spaced front teeth, a childhood habit never broken, "Yes, sir."

The next day, Monty's voice teacher Nichols came into Southland's while I was waiting on customers up front. I knew who he was, but the man didn't know me from Adam and barely glanced in my direction as I asked him what he needed.

"Pipe wrench."

"For what size pipe?"

"Residential work. One-inch pipe."

"Follow me."

Walking down the aisles made me happy. Boxes neatly arranged on top of one another, edges as precise as finely honed knives. Nichols was whistling between his teeth, following me. When we got to the pipe wrenches, he picked a big one up and held it, balancing the weight in his hand. The clean angles of his blond crew cut meant he had a good barber. The hippie fever for girlie curls on men hadn't got ahold of him. But I'd bet those hands were soft on the palm side—not the hard-working hands of a real man.

A few weeks later, Linehan came in later than usual. I almost missed him because I was caught up on repairs and he was near the front register. He was angry at missing his early-morning coffee with us. "Man, we got another homicide last night. They sent me to hold the scene. White female, about sixteen, ice pick. She had more holes than a sponge. Homicide had better get busy and find the S.O.B."

That evening Monty came home late. I'd left him a Pyrex pie plate of food covered in tinfoil, warming in the oven.

"You're late, son."

"I lost track of the time."

"What were you doing?"

At that question, he raised his eyes just for a piece of a second. If he had said it was none of my business or even looked like he'd say it, I'd have backhanded him. But he didn't.

"I'm learning a new piece of music. I lost track of time."

"What's the phone number of that teacher of yours?"

His slouch turned into an alert posture. "Why?"

"I don't have a mind to keep wasting hard-earned money on someone who's late for dinner."

His dark eyes found me immediately and he almost wrung his pale hands. "Oh no, I got to keep going to voice lessons. They're . . . they're . . . the only thing I got."

This was the most he'd said to me at once in recent memory.

"I want to get my money's worth. Your mother's medicine costs plenty. I don't earn a lot of money."

He looked like he was going to cry—something no man should ever do. Hell, I'd made it through island after stinking island fighting Japs in the Pacific without crying, as my platoon was killed one by one. On some days, we were killed in vast numbers. None of us cried, not one single damn time. Not even the seventeen-year-olds who'd lied about their age to enlist. Or me, the oldest, balding even then and nicknamed "Pops."

Later that evening I sat on the front porch. The cicadas' late-summer droning had started this first week of August, like every other year.

I thought about that voice teacher. He made my skin crawl. What was it? His haircut was sharp. He had clean nails. Each time he was in the store, his shoes were fully shined, his jaw-line a little red from razor burn. All these should have added up to a regular Joe. But I didn't trust him. His slacks fresh from the cleaners, his dress shirts starched and new, long-sleeved even in Houston's humid heat. And the wicker picnic set the voice teacher had bought today? It carried an ice pick. Standard item, along with forks and knives.

Before I went to bed to sink into the deep sleep I'd been fortunate enough to have since childhood, I peeked in to see if Rosalie was awake. A board in the hallway must've creaked because she opened her eyes. I entered and sat on the bed.

"Good night, dear," she said, looking worn, as she always did.

"Listen, Rose, I've decided. Monty can't keep going to voice lessons."

"Montgomery."

"I've decided."

She lifted her pale hand to mine. "Dear, you have to let him. It's his biggest dream. Ever since he and I listened to the opera broadcasts on Saturday afternoons from the big radio in the hallway. You remember? For my sake . . . please." A tear trickled down from one eye.

I didn't want tears; I didn't want a scene. "That's it. I'll tell him tomorrow." She probably kept looking at me with those sad eyes as I left her room, but I didn't hear any more words from her.

In the morning Monty didn't come to breakfast. I knocked on his bedroom door and he yelled out that he felt sick. I left for work with my first headache in a long time.

Linehan didn't come in until around noon. "Hell. It's a Houston-humid version of hell—standing in a back alley in Montrose for six hours swatting at mosquitoes because some runaway gets herself bludgeoned over there off Avondale."

"Yeah?"

"Same old, same old. Back of the head. Only this time he left it behind. Looks brand new—except for the brains, bone, and blood. Twenty-four-inch pipe wrench."

I flashed back to the day voice teacher Nichols had bought his wrench. *Residential work*, he'd said. *One-inch pipe*. But the first one he'd picked up had a scratch in the handle's finish.

He'd picked out another one, saying he liked his tools *perfect*. What kind of man says something like that about household tools?

When I got home I went to my tool room in a sectioned-off part of the garage. All my tools were arranged on pegboard by type and size. Cleaned, oiled, ready to go. I picked up the hammer I'd tried to teach Monty how to use, the circular saw he couldn't control. He'd never been able to learn to rewire sockets or even a table lamp, what was positive and what was negative. How a ground worked. He hated it all.

At the breakfast table the next morning, Monty chewed slowly, his large Adam's apple bobbing an unreasonable amount. I couldn't put it off any longer. "Son, you're not going to voice lessons anymore."

"What??" His Adam's apple pumped furiously.

"That's *sir* to you."

"What did you say, sir?"

"I can't afford to pay for your lessons. Call that guy and tell him."

"But . . . but . . . I love my voice lessons. Dave—Mr. Nichols—says I have the voice of an angel. It's the only time . . ." his voice trailed off.

"The only time what?"

"Nothing. Nothing. I just . . . just . . ." The air whistled through his front teeth.

"Your mother isn't getting any better. I don't see you working to help support the family. By the time I was your age, I had me one job in town, and helped Dad with the farm before the sun was up, and I had to go to school."

He ran from the table, slamming the front door, then across the yard. I wondered where he'd go. Growing up, I'd had a place in the three-part junction of a huge oak tree's branches out by the slaughtering tables. It had been good to get away from everyone and look from afar on the dogs and cattle. I hadn't shown it to Lilly, who was too little to climb it by herself.

As I spread the white slices of bread with French's mustard to make my lunch for work, I dreaded the moment when Rosalie's door might open and I'd see the accusation in her sunken eyes. The slab of bologna smelled faintly in the early-morning heat. But her door didn't open, and I hoped she hadn't heard the jarring anger in Monty's slammed front door.

I waited all morning for Voice Teacher to show up, straining my ears for his girlie whisper. For the first time in my life, I hoped I was wrong.

Just before six, when we closed, he came in. I didn't wait on him; I disappeared to the back, so I wouldn't queer the deal. As soon as I saw his huge shoulders disappear into a sporty white Corvair, I asked the guy up front what he'd bought. *Pipe wrench, twenty-four-inch.* A strong man like him wouldn't need the leverage of the longest pipe wrench we carried. No, not a strong man like him.

That night Rosalie was up. To my surprise she had halfway cooked me dinner. She even sat at the kitchen table with me.

"Otto, Montgomery told me what you said."

I kept chewing on the fish sticks. There was no hurry. "I'm listening."

"He needs to sing. It's his only happiness."

"We can't afford it any longer."

"Why not to the end of summer? It's coming up soon. He'll start college. He'll meet young people his own age."

"There's plenty of young folks around Montrose. Look at all them hippies. Our neighborhood used to be respectable. Look at what it's become now. Love beads, hip-huggers. Long hair on girls and boys. You can't even tell for sure which is which most of the time. Rock concert posters glued to every storefront at night."

She sighed. "His only friend is Mr. Nichols. They have a lot in common."

"Like what?" I didn't like the suspicion suddenly forming in my mind.

"They both love music. They've learned some duets. Montgomery has something to be proud of—for the first time in years. He says their souls join when they sing together. He could be an opera singer. He's that good . . ."

"I'll think about it. That's all I can say for now, Rose."

She smiled her exhausted half-smile. "I promised him I'd ask you. You sleep so hard, Otto. He can't wake you to talk at night."

After dinner, I sat in the glider on the front porch as the evening darkened and I waited for Monty to get home. I searched my memory for what Linehan had said about the killings. All were teenage girls. All untraceable. No one cared if they disappeared. Linehan said no one at HPD was trying to solve the murders because no one cared about little whore-runaway hippie chicks. Was that why my sister Lilly never even sent a three-penny postcard? Had her body decomposed somewhere we'd never heard of, with no police officer caring enough to bring her killer to justice?

I must've fallen asleep sitting up because the noise of the screen door opening at Monty's touch woke me up from a bad dream of 1943 in the Pacific.

"What you doing coming home late, son?" I hadn't turned on the porch light earlier, so I could only see the outline of his head and the thin body that Rose called "elegant" against the screen.

He lifted his shoulders before replying, "I didn't know you were waiting up for me."

"Where you been?"

"Just walking."

"Didn't I tell you not to come home late again?"

"I needed to think."

I was beat, too beat to put up with someone living in my house and not paying me any mind. Before I even knew what I was doing, I backhanded him. Hard. He didn't stand up any straighter; he didn't move at all. He stood a hunched black silhouette against the humid glow from the streetlight half a block down. "Go to sleep," I told him, and he walked silently into the house.

I too finally walked into my bedroom, not even pulling down the bedspread. If I closed my eyes, the dream might return. The dream that had begun after that first time, and the pounding I'd given the nameless other Marine in late 1943. My unit was going island to island, taking them from the Japs one bloody inch at a time. We were on a nameless atoll, at night, after a day of fighting. The area secure and half of us cleared for shut-eye by the sergeant. Me, in a foxhole alone, sleeping. The dream was of the little honey I'd had back home. I felt her light touch on my crotch, and felt blood rushing to respond to her caress. Half-asleep, I drifted into the warm-blooded excitement of it. Suddenly, I remembered where I was and woke up. I saw his face close to mine. I pushed him away and went crazy. I pounded his face until it was a bloody pulp and hightailed it out of there, almost getting shot for a Jap by

Morrison over in another foxhole. Sometimes, like tonight, in a dream he comes for me again, with his soft touch and softer lips, and I awake sweaty but chilled, with an erection so hard I think I'll die, just like the one he coaxed out of me in my sleep. Sometimes, too, I thought that maybe I had those dreams because . . . well, Rosalie had been sick for so long. I couldn't ask her for what she couldn't give.

The forbidden images of the dream lingered the next morning as I drank coffee. Voice Teacher's face and clean, manicured hands flashed in my head. And I knew what had gotten under my skin about him all along. He was one of *them*. And he was after my son.

Linehan's uniform was already drenched with sweat when he came in for his early coffee. "How's the old man today?" he laughed, slapping me on the shoulder.

"Fair to middling." No point reminding him that I'd lost my hair but not too much else.

"Man, we got number four last night. This guy is bad news. I can't believe homicide hasn't found him."

"Where was this one?"

"At least it wasn't in Montrose. It was downtown near Allen's Landing. That place Love Street Light Circus. Used to be an old warehouse. The freaks pay to go in there, flop on cushions, and listen to music. I'd kill my daughter myself if she ever set foot in there."

"The weapon?"

"Baseball bat to the back of the head. Even left the bat, it's a good 'un."

"Any chance they'll find who did it?"

"Naw. There's no prints on any of the weapons he's left behind. With all the front-page ruckus in the papers, the whole department is catching grief because we haven't found the killer." He lowered his voice, "I'd like to find him myself," and I could see his large hand on the butt of his revolver. "All of night shift is itching to put him away."

Sure enough, Voice Teacher came into the store that afternoon. But he didn't come to buy a baseball bat. When I looked up from a repair, he was staring at the needle-nose pliers in my right hand. His posture was erect and the creases in his pale blue dress shirt were impeccable.

"I'm hoping you can repair this toaster," he said, removing the early-'50s stainless beauty from under his elbow.

"What's wrong with it?"

"The slide won't stay down. Can't toast the toast."

"Show me exactly what you do with it."

He gently rested a strong pink hand on the curving body of the toaster. Then he placed a powerful thumb from his other hand on the slide and pushed it down.

"You always do it like that?"

"Yes. I guess my thumb is too strong."

"No problem. I can replace the catch. Real simple, if you can spare it for a few days."

"Sure can."

I nodded and reached for the Sunbeam and placed it on a shelf behind me. When I turned back around, he was still standing at the counter.

"Do I need a claim ticket?"

"Nope. I'll remember you. I don't get too many vintage toasters in."

He looked like he wanted to argue, but changed his mind. He flipped out a card from a breast pocket and wrote something on it. "Here's my phone. Call me when it's done."

"Yessir. Be glad to."

* * *

That night Monty ate dinner with me, so I scrambled more eggs and set out two plates.

"What you do today, son?"

"Nothing much."

"Where'd you do nothing much?"

"I went to tell Mr. Nichols I had to stop lessons."

"What'd he say?"

"Nothing much." He darted his eyes back and forth across the faded green linoleum Rosalie was always too tired to mop.

"What else you do today?"

"I helped him run some errands. Just to sorta say goodbye."

"That was nice, son. I'm proud of you."

His eyes flashed upward to my face, and I saw something hard in them. Something that reminded me of the D.I.s in boot camp in the early '40s. The look of not giving a damn, not caring one measly iota. I got up from the table and walked to the refrigerator behind him to get the catsup.

"He took me to lunch afterward at one of those new restaurants in the 400 block of Westheimer. After that I helped him carry everything upstairs."

I sat back down and shook the catsup bottle, then poured. "He's a grown man, isn't he? Why didn't he carry them himself?"

Monty stared at the red layers on my eggs, then looked away.

"He's coaching the intramural program this year. He had to replace some equipment. You know, basketballs, baseballs, mitts, volleyballs."

I passed the bottle to Monty. "I bet it was hard carrying those long packages with the heavy baseball bats."

He shook his head before answering. "I was careful with them. He doesn't like his paint scratched."

I forked the hot eggs into my mouth before asking the last thing I needed to know. "I bet you were, son. Wasn't there anyone else to help y'all carry the stuff into his house?"

"Nope. He lives alone."

Working on Voice Teacher's toaster was easy—like I'd told him. I replaced the bimetallic catch, reconnected the wires, switched out the original plastic push-down knob with a metal replica I'd painted the same glossy black. I also disconnected the ground to the stainless housing. Everything would go smoothly. He would plug it in, insert the bread, adjust the small dial for darkness, place his left hand on the elegant metal body, then push the knob down and his heart would know what it was like to burn in hell. I put on my work gloves and wiped it real good with a rag. Put it in a box and set them on the counter ready for him. His influence over Rosalie and my son would evaporate as quickly as it had come—like a rainstorm through the Panhandle. Then the dreams of soft lips and caressing fingers would be washed away too. We could go back to the way things were before, all of us.

When he came for the toaster, I took his cash payment and didn't write out a receipt. He took it out of the box and left with it cradled under his pale pink starched shirtsleeve.

About five days later, I saw the obituary in the *Houston Post*. *Brilliant voice teacher, beloved professor of music. Graduate of the University of Indiana at Bloomington.*

Monty looked paler than I'd ever seen him. He stomped into his bedroom without speaking to me as he came through the front screen porch that evening.

I went into Rosalie's room after my dinner alone. I could hear the sounds of opera coming through the walls from Monty's room. He'd been playing the same record over and over for hours.

"Montgomery is devastated," she said.

"I noticed he looked peaked."

"His friend is dead."

"I saw the obituary."

"He was in the prime of his life. What a terrible accident."

"Monty'll get over it. He starts college in a couple more weeks."

"I don't know that he'll ever get over it."

"That guy was just his voice teacher. There's plenty more teachers around."

She looked at me all of a sudden, dark eyes focused and hard with emotion. "You don't have the slightest clue, do you? They were in love. Do you understand me? They had a passionate, wonderfully exciting life together, and now it's all over."

"Your son is a queer?"

"He's your son too."

"No, he's not. He's yours by your first husband, not by me. I haven't been able to touch you for years because of the illness. Besides, how much of a so-called life together could they have in a weekly voice lesson?"

She laughed, keeping her lips tight. "You sleep real heavy— remember? I let Montgomery meet Dave at night all the time. I wanted him to be happy and in love the way I was with his dad. His handsome, handsome dad." Her mouth settled into a thin, hard line. "They were made for each other."

I rose and walked out of the house into the August early-evening heat to get away from her gaunt face and accusing eyes. I walked for hours through the neighborhood, darkness finally coming around eight p.m. and sleep barely coming at all.

Going to work was a comfort the next day—just as it had been for the last twenty-odd years. The bins of nails reflecting the morning light cleanly, as if they'd never bite wood. The tree trimmer blades shining like crescent moons above the Pacific all those years back.

Linehan came in, but this morning he was excited and talking fast. "We got a great one last night. The body chopped up into so many pieces it looked like an explosion at a sausage factory."

My face went numb. It couldn't be. He was dead—I'd read it in the morning paper.

"The guy is one angry son of a bitch. He went to town—hacked off everything, even the nose."

I didn't want to ask it, but I'd asked every other time: "What kind of weapon?"

"Probably a hatchet, or a cleaver."

At lunch I walked home. Rosalie would be sleeping, but I didn't intend to talk to her or Monty. I pulled my key ring out of my pocket and unlocked the side door to the garage. I flipped the light on, and looked for the first time in many weeks at my beloved tools. On the pegboard, they rested on metal supports, just as I'd left them, except for one. Except for the one I figured would be missing—the hatchet.

A small sound behind me caught my attention. I turned and saw Monty, fresh from the shower, hair glistening wet as he stepped inside the narrow room.

He looked me directly in the eye. As always, his pupils were too dark to read meaning there. In his right hand, he carried my small hatchet.

"I've cleaned and oiled your hatchet, and I've brought it back." He lifted it to its resting place, the keen blade beautiful against the brown pegboard. "I told Dave he should take the toaster to Southland's because it's the best for repairs. You did your best on it, didn't you?"

His eyes never left my face and the small bit of stoniness I'd seen in them earlier this summer had taken over completely.

"You know, Dave taught me to appreciate tools. How to keep them perfect. How to use them and how to clean them. He taught me a lot, actually. Now, you're going to continue teaching me. Daddy, you know how."

"How did you get a key for my tool room?"

"Mom gave it to me. She knew I needed a particular kind of quiet place." He smiled with the hardness of a man who knows his business.

"What growed you up?"

"Mr. Nichols taught me how to follow them at night and pick one out. How to talk pretty. He'd offer them drugs, food—whatever they wanted. Then we got one who kept trying to unzip his trousers with her dirty little freckled hands. I couldn't let her do that, could I? It was so easy to do the rest, and even he couldn't stop me.

"Yes, you're going to teach me a lot now, Daddy. No more sneaking out at night. No more worries at all."

MORAL HAZARD

BY JESSE SUBLETT

Austin

The game warden, first through the door, threw up at the sight of it. The rookie deputy almost laughed, thinking it was a joke by neighborhood punks or looters scavenging the suburbs after the storm. The first thing that caught their eyes was the charred remains of a large chair with some junk piled in it. At the foot of the chair was a pair of latex zombie feet, like something from a costume shop. By some miracle, the only other thing seriously damaged in the room was the TV, blackened and half-melted, like the Salvador Dali painting of the clocks. The other strange part was how everything was coated with a nasty-looking pink dust. Plus the horrible smell. Hell of a weird joke.

Crossing the den, the rookie touched the door frame. The pink stuff had a greasy feel to it. He could see now that the burnt debris in the chair had once been a man, that the zombie feet weren't from a costume shop at all. As he stared, open-mouthed, at the blackened skull, one of the teeth dropped out.

The vomit appeared so suddenly it could've been the hand of God down his throat. Realizing that some kind of terrible miracle had taken place there, he ran out the front door, praising God and promising that he'd never again download pornography from the Internet or stare lustfully at the young blond clerk with the nose ring at the corner store.

Owned by a former state legislator turned lobbyist, the three-story brick home spread its bulk around a cul-de-sac in an upscale, unincorporated community called Wildcat Oaks just west of Austin. It was one of the areas that had suffered the most in the previous night's storms, yet the destruction seemed random. Two blocks away, an SUV had been blown apart by lightning, yet in the same driveway a child's bicycle leaned against a plastic wagon. On the cul-de-sac, a tornado had erased one home down to the foundation and bypassed another next door, zigzagged across the street to obliterate two more, hooked left to make a cloud of splinters of three in a row.

From the street, the brick home on the cul-de-sac appeared untouched, even serene. In the cobbled drive was a black Ford Excursion, its backside sporting two cheerful yellow *Support Our Troops* magnets. On the patio were painting supplies and a bright-orange extension ladder. The two men violently vomiting in the monkey grass made the only sound.

On this hectic day for police, cleanup crews, and the media, the TV news van arrived ahead of the sheriff's department and other officials. In the interim, the petite blond reporter interviewed the game warden, who explained how he came to discover the dead man's body.

The homeowner's wife, he said, was in Mexico, and because she knew the game warden from their Bible study class, the dead man's wife had phoned him at home that morning. She had seen footage of the destruction on CNN and was concerned about the condition of her home. Her husband, who traveled a good deal for business, had not answered her calls or e-mails for the past two days, and their only child, a student at the University of Texas, was "off the reservation," whatever that was supposed to mean. The game warden told the wife that he'd be happy to go by and check things out. In fact, he called her as soon as he arrived there and reported that everything seemed just fine, that she and her husband were very lucky.

The game warden had already given the reporter far more information than he would have liked. A month shy of his sixty-seventh birthday, the game warden was ready to retire next year and retreat to the two-bedroom cottage he shared with an aging, three-legged golden retriever.

He knew that fortune had not always smiled upon the owner of the giant brick home. Raised on a small egg farm on the other side of Dripping Springs. Both parents killed in a car wreck when he was twelve. Worked two jobs to pay his way through college and law school. Elected to the state senate in 1972 or somewhere around there, defeated for reelection. Went into the lobbying business and apparently did pretty well for himself. After all that time, most people still referred to him as "Senator." He traveled a lot, all over the world. Sometimes with the wife, but most times on business.

Approaching the property from the left side, the game warden told the reporter, he could see the collapsed back quarter of the home. Possibly caused by lightning strike. The heavy oak front door was unlocked, the huge brass knob warm to the touch. Going inside, he saw the thing in the den.

"But what would you say was the cause of death?" asked the reporter.

The game warden shook his head. He said he did not want to speculate.

The reporter was insistent. "Would you say it appears be a homicide?"

No comment. What he wanted to say was, *I'm not even sure that thing in there is human, but I guess it is. Fire can do some strange things to a body.*

When she came close enough to look inside, the smell was as revolting as what she saw. She wanted to describe the scene to her viewers as "what appears to be a savage and shocking crime," but she was a professional, so she carefully chose her words to convey a sense of that same conclusion, by stating questions she believed were surely on the mind of every viewer: "How could such a tragic death happen in this peaceful, picturesque neighborhood? And to a man like the victim, a friend of orphans and starving multitudes, whose brother was a prominent evangelical minister?" Of course, the reporter knew that the man was noted for his strident ultraconservative views on politics and society. There had also been rumors, watercooler talk, and political blogs about his lobbying firm's use of prostitutes, bribes, and strong-arm tactics—including blackmail and complex money laundering schemes—on behalf of its clients.

The dead man had a famous friend, a preacher known to his followers as "the Brother." The Brother was an evangelist from Houston whose Sunday services were attended by tens of thousands. A vast media empire delivered his thoughts to millions more. Years ago, the Brother and his religious retreat, called Revelation Gardens, had been ensnared in a financial scandal. He had founded the retreat on a 5,000-acre plot near Houston in the 1980s. During the chaos of an election year, when the dead man was expanding his client list through prayer groups which were attended mostly by drillers, speculators, and executives in the then-depressed oil and gas business, the charges had been quietly and mysteriously withdrawn. The retreat thrived and grew, doubling in size in the past fifteen years.

The reporter had seen secret video footage from Revelation Gardens showing the former state senator and the preacher cavorting in a golf cart like a pair of thirteen-year-olds. She had watched with a sickly fascination as the gray-haired men swilled vodka and raced the golf cart across the greens, tossing their empties on the ground, betting money on a pissing contest, giggling when they farted. After the video was over, the reporter felt a little sick to her stomach without knowing exactly why. Maybe it was a premonition.

But so what if the dead lobbyist and his preacher friend acted like adolescent assholes when they got drunk? The real question was, *What kind of person could tie someone to a chair and set him on fire? What kind of person could do that?*

He sat motionless on the edge of the steel cot, listening to the constant racket of the jail. He had the entire cell block to himself, as per orders from the top. The light was bright and he noticed that his body cast a narrow, crooked shadow on the wall. It resembled a letter of the alphabet, he thought, but couldn't decide which letter it would be.

Even now that he wasn't quite as thin as he once was, everyone still used the old nickname, Slim. He remembered what a bitter woman had once said about the name. "It makes sense," she said. "Because there's not enough of anything inside there to add up. You're slim on one side and hollow on the other."

He had a lean face and dark eyes. He might have had the chipped tooth in his smile fixed long ago except for the fact that it seemed to have a disarming effect on people. Accidents and tricks of nature now and then work in your favor.

When he thought back to the night of the storm, he remembered how the thunder rolled in before the rain and wind like a ham-fisted omen from a B movie. Sitting in his car on a steep hill above Austin, waiting for Teo and Ric to show up.

Nature was putting on quite a light show. The lightning would flash silver on the surface of the car and the trees and the ground, but the hillside below remained a pool of darkness, untouched. A few seconds later thunder would rattle the ground, as if the lightning had fallen down there and died.

Replaying the memory now, retracing his steps. Flash, boom, nothing. He didn't believe that before you die, your life flashes before your eyes. Whenever he'd been close to death, time went into fast-forward, not reverse, and he fought back, treaded water, or ran like hell, whatever it took.

Flash, boom, nothing. Thinking about the mountains in Mexico, where he and some drug-smuggling buddies used to fly across the border at Falcon Lake. Those mountains had claimed a lot more smugglers he knew than the DEA ever did. He didn't believe in hell or heaven.

Flash, boom, nothing. Teo and Ric never showed up. A total of four of them had been directly involved in the heist. Teo and Ric were with him when they pulled the job. Afterward, Teo took the briefcase to Tom, the money man, who knew the guy who would launder it for them.

But Tom got pinched on Tuesday, the day after the heist. They knew he'd already dropped the money off with the laundry. Question was, what did he tell the cops, if anything?

Maybe Teo and Ric got themselves tagged too, copped a plea and snitched on him. Can't fight human nature. That three musketeers crap was for fairy tales.

Any successful thief knows when it's time to split. Hang around too long anywhere, even when things are going great, and your luck runs out. His exit strategy: head to Houston, pick up his money stash and a new ID. He would contact no one, leave no tracks. Fade to black.

But instead of heading east to Houston, he drove west,

down the back roads on the edge of town, dodging the frightened deer and debris scattering ahead of the storms. Now and then the city would come into view, with the pink granite dome of the Capitol building, and behind it the UT tower, which Charles Whitman used as a sniper's perch on August 1, 1966, killing fourteen. As a UT student, Whitman had once gotten in trouble for gutting a poached deer in a shower stall in his dormitory.

Flash, boom, nothing. The lightning seemed to follow him as he pushed the coupe hard on the sharp curves. Lightning does strike twice in the same place, he knew that for a fact. Take the Kid, for example, he'd been struck three times in his life. He had to wonder if that had anything to do with the Kid's talent.

The Kid was a phenomenal guitar player. With the kind of talent he had, the Kid could've written his own ticket. He just needed a lucky break here and there, but now the Kid was dead.

According to the statement from the police department, being hit by a Taser during his arrest was only incidental to his death and the Kid suffered from a type of cardiac arrhythmia "typically found to be endemic in hard-core drug abusers." Never mind that the Kid wasn't a druggie, that he only got high on playing guitar.

The Kid was pulled over on a traffic violation when he supposedly "became violent." Extra units were called to the scene, and at some point a Taser was used to subdue him. EMS was called but he was DOA.

Slim had a guy inside the department, told him it was *four* Taser hits, not one. *All four were special order, paid for with cool, green, in-God-we-trust U.S. dollars.*

Rain fell. What was the last thing the guy said?

But I wouldn't trust anybody. Know what I mean?

Cell door clang, stench of vomit and disinfectant, darkness. When you came right down to it, Monday night's heist was a briefcase job: you got two guys—a guy with heavy government connections and a preacher—with a briefcase containing $300,000. Maybe they were barracudas in the suit-and-tie world, but they sure weren't streetwise. Taking the money away from these stiffs was a cakewalk.

But somewhere, the job had gone sour. Real sour, real fast.

Slim had already spoken with Tom's lawyer. No charges had been filed yet, but the feds might be involved. Forty-eight hours later, still no word. They can't hold you for longer than that without pressing charges. Except when Homeland Security is involved. Or just because they want to.

By Friday night, still nothing, no arraignment, no anything. Tom's in jail, the Kid is dead. Teo and Rick don't show up with the money.

Nothing. Zip.

The thieves assigned code names to the two guys with the briefcase. The preacher was Church, the lobbyist was State. Some of the info the thieves had on the stiffs was public record, the rest was thanks to the hacking expertise of Slim's friend, the Kid. State was the guy who had his tentacles inside the machinery of government. He had been inside, right at top of the food chain. He loved that power and the money that came with it. Ambition and vanity were Church's addictions. God was talking in his ear. That's what he said. Then, in the late 1990s, he found himself in the crosshairs of a grand jury, with Revelation Gardens on the verge of bankruptcy. He gave State a call asking for help. State flew to Houston to meet with Brother Church at Revelation Gardens. The place had a five-million-dollar chapel, where daily prayer meetings were led by the Brother himself, two four-star restaurants, three spas, a golf course, and other luxury amenities. State saw the place immediately for what it was: a great place to move money around, make it seem fresh and clean. "Think of it as salvation for dirty money," said State to Brother Church.

With his contacts in the oil industry and foreign governments, State was in a unique position to help Church. After 9/11, the federal government had begun distributing large amounts of aid to the rulers of impoverished populations in Muslim countries, basically paying people in foreign countries not to hate and resent Americans more than they already did. Representatives from oil companies and other industries with interests in the region said they wanted to help too. They knew State as a skilled facilitator in this area. State could coordinate not only the U.S. funds going overseas but the bribes coming in from his corporate contacts. With the help of State, Church opened a laundry. The laundered cash was then dispersed to the respective business lobbyists, as well as certain right-wing conservative causes, with a skim off the top split two ways between Church and State. A special allotment was set aside for Church to use on improvements to the resort, and if any was left over, he could tithe to a real charity, like the Salvation Army or something.

Slim laughed when he found out about the scam. He didn't give a shit what they did with the money. The world was corrupt and rotten and most people were thieves and liars at heart, even the amateurs. The pros just get paid more for it. He belonged to no political party, had never voted. In his profession, you couldn't afford to leave tracks like that. Even if he happened to give a fuck.

* * *

The Kid had dropped the whole job in Slim's lap. Besides being a virtuoso on the electric guitar, the Kid was a blazingly talented hacker. Using a hot-rodded laptop and a broadband connection, the Kid had hacked his way into Church and State's money laundering scheme. The beauty of the thing was that the four thieves would be stealing money that Church and State had stolen from the federal government.

By hacking his way into their accounting program, the Kid was even able to predict, within a day, when the skim had to be withdrawn from the money laundry, which meant that Church and State would meet and divide the money. Stealing it would be easy.

But that wasn't what the Kid wanted to do. He wasn't a crook. He was a do-gooder, an artist, an idealist. The Kid told Slim he wanted to stop these men, "to take these assholes down and expose them to the public."

Slim told him wait, he had a better way. He told the Kid to be cool. "Leave it alone for a while," he said. "These dudes are well connected, and they might fuck you up."

But the Kid kept hacking the system, building more of a case, finding more dirty secrets. He rarely slept.

Meanwhile, Slim got the crew together. Ric, Teo, and Tom were up for the takedown. The Kid told them the skim would be withdrawn Friday afternoon. Not because he wanted to help rob Church and State, but because it was a matter of pride. He was a hacker. He had to tell somebody.

The job was on. Teo and Ric kept a tail on Church, who rode in a black Lincoln Town Car. Slim followed State's black Ford Excursion.

The meeting happened on Monday at a restaurant in the suburbs. State lifted the briefcase from the trunk of the Town

Car in the parking lot. The two men froze when they saw the guys with guns. The thieves took the briefcase and split.

Nothing to it. Except for what came next.

It was a little over a week ago the last time Slim went to see the Kid play. The Kid was on fire. Making ungodly sounds with his guitar. Sometimes, facing the teeth-rattling wall of noise pouring out of the Kid's amp, time and space seemed to fall away like a broken curtain. Slim realized it was a kind of insanity to feel that way, but he didn't care.

He couldn't play a lick of music himself. He didn't buy many CDs and usually listened to whatever was on the radio or whatever came with the environment he happened to be in. But he supposed that the Kid was the main reason he had stuck around Austin longer than other places. Six months or so. He enjoyed the Kid's company. You could say they'd been friends.

The Kid, the idealist, had left a message on Slim's cell phone Saturday after midnight. "This will bring their whole fantasy kingdom tumbling down." Sounding nervous, as if he thought someone might be listening, the Kid spoke a sequence of three letters followed by a string of numbers. He repeated the sequence once more and added, "I'd say guard it with your life, but I know you don't value anything that highly." There was a laugh at the end.

Slim memorized the sequence and deleted the message. Obviously it was some kind of code or identification.

That was the last time he heard from the Kid.

"Some people here to see you," said the jailer. "Supposed to be your parents."

"Why not?" said Slim, his chipped tooth a hole in his smile.

A few minutes later, they were as close to him as a sheet of bulletproof glass. The man supposed to be his father said, "The D.A. seems very intent on the death penalty."

The woman supposed to be his mother kept staring at a spot in space just above and to the left of his head. "I want to pray with you," she said.

"Try it and I'll tell the guard you smuggled in plastic explosives by sticking them up your ass," he said.

That shut them up for a minute or so.

He couldn't remember just when, but at an early age he'd become convinced that these two people were not who they said they were. Fake parents, maybe even fake people. Or maybe he was the imposter. The physical resemblance was slight at best. He felt nothing for them.

The man supposed to be his father said he would like for him to consider donating his body to science. That way, he said, something positive might come out of this someday.

He told them he'd already put in a request to be torn apart by wild dogs.

The woman supposed to be his mother wanted to know how could anyone pour lighter fluid on another person and set him on fire? And just watch them burn alive? How could one human do that to another?

"Didn't you hear?" he said. "It was spontaneous human combustion. The guy was so rotten with corruption he just blew up."

Her upper lip twitched to the side, giving her the appearance of a cleft palate.

"The D.A. didn't like that story any more than I do," said the man supposed to be his father. After a long pause, he continued, "Wouldn't you like to know you did one good thing before you died?"

Slim laughed and for some reason felt obligated to explain. "That's the same thing the old fart said."

Twitching, the woman said, "You mean, the man you . . . ?"

The man tugged at her arm and said, "Let's go."

The rain was still heavy Friday night when Slim arrived on the cul-de-sac. He parked a block away and walked back. State had company. A little Saturn with Mardi Gras beads hanging from the rearview. The kitchen window proved to be the easiest way in. As he entered he could hear groans of faked ecstasy upstairs. Seventeen-years-old, with braces and fake boobs and a shaved package, Jennifer charged five hundred dollars an hour for house calls.

Slim had known her since she was twelve. There was no connection between her presence and his being here, just one of those coincidences that happen in a community of pirates and thieves. Small world. No telling how long he had to look around, so he got busy. Checked the garage first. A white Lexus, power tools, guns. A ladder, painting supplies, and other stray items were stored on the patio.

In a downstairs bedroom closet, he found some diamond rings, and in a locked hideaway drawer that took him all of two minutes to jimmy, he found a bag of stones, a few emeralds, some diamonds, and eighteen gold coins. He also found $800 in cash—about $250 in a money clip in a man's overcoat and the rest in one of the wife's designer purses.

Plus a safe-deposit box key.

There would be more loot upstairs. He settled into an overstuffed leather chair in a corner of the den and waited. They were still going at it, Jennifer shrieking every few seconds, followed by a low grunt like a dog barking. Sometimes the timing worked out so that Jennifer's shrieks followed a thunderclap. Flash, boom, shriek, bark. Flash, boom, shriek, bark.

And then it was over. It was quiet upstairs but the storm still raged outside. He settled into a comfortable chair and waited. The .380 automatic in his lap kept him company.

On the wall were signed photos of former U.S. presidents: Reagan, Bush, Bush. There were other photos on the mantel. In one of them, a man in a clergy collar, Church, stood in a dusty village surrounded by dark-skinned children staring up at him as though they thought he might be lost. A mangy-looking dog warily sniffed the man's pants leg. In another photo, State was shaking hands with an Arab man wearing an expensive suit and a headscarf. There was one photo of State with his wife and daughter. The daughter was good-looking in an anorexic way. A flap of skin on the wife's left eyelid was the only sign of relief on an otherwise hard, tight countenance. State was broad and jowly and tanned the color of roast ham.

On a side table next to the chair was a leather portfolio, and atop that, a hardcover novel in a red dust jacket. Keeping one eye on the staircase, he flipped open the portfolio and leafed through the contents. Corporate documents and memos, the jargon so dense and odd it could have been from an alternate universe. There was a handwritten note from someone named Eric. *Bob*, it said, *we need to run through all this with a fine-tooth comb. Need to check the precedents on moral hazard because it will probably come up.*

Leafing through the rest of the document, he found the words *moral hazard*, punctuated with a question mark, scribbled in the margins of almost every other page. The handwriting appeared to be the same as the guy who had scrawled the note.

He tossed the portfolio aside and picked up the novel in the red dust jacket. The title was *No Country for Old Men*. Post-it flags jutted out like yellow teeth. Flipping through, he saw that lengthy passages had been underscored with a red felt-tip pen. Weird.

A creak on the stairs. Jennifer, not exactly tiptoeing but carrying her high-heeled boots under her arm. Tucking some folded currency into her purse.

"Hey," she said.

He still hadn't replied when she reached the last step.

"Don't worry," she said. "He's out. He sleeps hard."

Slim nodded. "I'm not here."

A quick glance around the room, her eyes coming to rest on the .380. She swallowed hard. "Baby, I'm *so* not here, either."

"Right."

She paused to slip on the boots and zip them up, then left. He locked behind her.

He started for the stairs, then decided to give her more time to get down the road.

He went back to the chair and picked up the novel, using the gun barrel to hold it open. The book started out with a drug deal gone sour out in Big Bend. Bodies piled up quickly. The killer had some of the best lines, but the real pontificator was the old Texas sheriff. Gruff and as reactionary as the Old Testament, the old fart seemed to believe that all the violence and decay in the world today is our own fault, because we've been too liberal and permissive and have lost our faith in God. The passages expressing these sentiments were the most frequently bookmarked and underlined.

Almost half an hour passed before State came down. White-haired and wearing a sweat suit, as if he was going out for a jog. Smoking a cigarette.

The old man made a sour face when he saw the .380 automatic pointed at his midsection. "My God, what in hell do you want now?" he said, recognizing Slim from Monday night. "You're gonna be one sorry son of a bitch."

The thief smashed him in the face with the gun, then dragged him by his collar to the leather recliner and strapped him in tight with duct tape.

"You made a call about the Kid, right?"

The old man glared at him. Both the upper and lower lips were split, causing blood to cover his teeth and pool in the creases on either side of his mouth. "What do you think you're going to accomplish here? You want money?"

Usually, the person staring at the goodbye end of the gun did not ask questions that sounded like demands. Incontinence is common, along with profuse sweating and shaking. The old man displayed none of these symptoms.

"No," said Slim. "I want answers."

"You're a son of a bitch, coming in here like this."

"Yeah, I am. What's moral hazard?"

"Huh? What the fuck you want to talk about that for?"

"Moral hazard, you tub of lard. What is it?"

"It's a legal concept," he said, his face distorted by an ugly scowl. "It's a little fuzzy and subject to interpretation, but say you have a business where people end up taking advantage of you, cheating you out of money or breaking the law some other way. If your business is set up so that it tempts people to cheat or break the law, it's called a moral hazard and a court can hold you liable for it."

"Is that like saying the devil made you do it, or you did it because you ate too many Twinkies?"

The old man shrugged. "Well, like I say, it's kind of a fuzzy area."

The windows rattled as thunder rolled through. Rain peppered the roof.

"You're a corrupt piece of shit," said Slim, "but I don't care about that." He faltered for a moment, surprised at the sound of his own voice. "I came here because you and your people killed the Kid. You shouldn't have done that."

"He was a criminal just like you and the other three."

"You're a bigger criminal than me and my crew ever dreamed about being. And the Kid was no criminal, he was an idealist. Stealing the money, that was my idea."

"I'm sure these are all fine distinctions," said the old man, turning his head to spit blood. "I could use a cigarette, though. How about it?"

"Kill yourself on your own time, not mine."

"What the hell do you really want?"

Slim picked up the novel and thumbed it open. "You really believe the things this sheriff character says?"

"I surely do," he said. "That's a wise man wrote that book. He's one of us for sure. A true believer."

"*You can't go to war without God.* You put a big red star next to that line in the book. You believe that?"

"Absolutely."

"I guess that's why the war we got now is going so well."

"You've turned away from God's love," said the old man. "That's the one unforgivable sin, you know. God can't help you if you don't accept His grace."

"You hired some dirty cops to kill a twenty-six-year-old musician who had a naïve idea of saving the world from guys like you. And you're upstairs banging a seventeen-year-old girl. What's that shit?"

Color rose in the puffy folds of flesh in the old man's face as he grinned. "Let me ask you, son, have you ever committed a worthwhile deed in your whole, sorry life?"

"Not unless it was by accident."

"Look here, I can get you a half million and change. But you'd have to work with me on it."

"I'm listening."

"Tomorrow we'll go to a certain bank. You wait in the car or somewhere you can keep an eye on me because you could be recognized and arrested. You'll have to trust me, but I know you won't do that. I suppose you could hold someone hostage—"

"You mean like a family member?" Slim interrupted with a smile. "Like your wife or daughter? A preacher, like your brother?"

"I'd rather not go that route."

"But you didn't say absolutely not, no way. How about telling me the box number?"

"It would serve no purpose. You can't do anything without me."

"Let's see if I can trust you."

Reluctantly, State recited the number. It was the same sequence the Kid had left on his machine, except the last three digits were transposed.

"Try again," said the thief.

Color drained from the old man's face. He recited the number again. This time it was exactly the same as the message from the Kid.

"Good boy," he said.

"We have a deal?"

"So what's in the box besides cash?" asked the thief. "A little black book? Some disks with names and dates and figures showing how your scam works, and if you ever find yourself behind the eight ball, you can extort your way out?"

The old man wouldn't answer.

"But it would be trouble for you if the stuff came out now, without any control on your part, right?"

"You can't get in the box without me," said the old man. "You need me."

"Actually, I don't, I know a guy," he said, placing the muzzle of the .380 against the old fart's forehead and then watching him squirm as he wet his pants, like they always do.

You could be in the life a long time without ever having to kill anyone. Maybe there was nothing he'd ever wanted badly enough.

"You don't need to expose me," said the old man. "You'll have the money, there'd be no purpose in it. You say you don't give a hoot about morals and hypocrisy. If you've got a shred of humanity at all, you'll do me a favor and destroy those disks in that box. You'd just end up hurting a lot of innocent people."

Slim made no promises. What he did was loosen the tape binding the old man's right hand just enough to allow him to light a cigarette. He removed the pack from the old man's robe, grabbed a lighter from the side table, put both items in the old man's palm, and walked out the door.

He was halfway to his car when he visualized himself being pulled over, cuffed, jailed. Getting caught was always a possibility, but he hated the idea of it happening at this moment, the way things stood. The old man, sitting in his big fucking house, smoking his cigarettes. That superior look on his face.

The rain had let up but the wind stung his cheeks and there was a low howling coming from the east. Something in the tone of it made him think of one of the Kid's best songs, the one that seemed to turn time and space inside out.

He went back for one last thing.

* * *

Two months later, three young men were scarfing candy and energy drinks in the break room on the tenth floor of a high-rise overlooking Lake Austin. They'd been working overtime for several weeks processing insurance claims from the storm. All three looked haggard and stoned. Sometimes their topic of conversation was pornographic, more often it was a gruesome joke at the expense of a policyholder.

The rich old fart who burned alive in his recliner, for example.

"What do you think?" said Carney. "Coulda been lightning. The house did get hit, no doubt about that. We don't have a lot of 'Act of God' cases anyway. What'll the boss say?"

"Bullshit," said Willet. "I'd rather chalk it up to spontaneous human combustion. I'd love to see the look on old Rickstein's face when he reads that."

"Sorry, dude," Carney said. "People don't just up and bust into flames. I can't go for that."

"Too bad that guy got shivved to death in jail," said Lamont. "He could've told us how he did it."

"You mean the asshole they caught with booty from the old guy's house?" said Willet. "The murder charge against him was bullshit, purely circumstantial. I say the guy just exploded."

"Question is," Lamont said, "did the old bastard climb up on his roof and paint that message there before he exploded, or did somebody else do it?"

Lamont still had the aerial photo in his hands. His girlfriend, the television reporter, had given it to him. Taken by the pilot of a traffic helicopter, it showed a sea of ravaged roofs, uprooted trees, and crap blown all over hell. In the exact center was the old man's house. Someone had painted the words MORAL HAZARD in huge block letters on the roof, and below that, a sequence of letters and numbers. Lamont didn't know what they signified, but his girlfriend was working on it. A veteran investigative reporter from Fort Worth was helping her out. They were calling it "The Church and State Case."

"Fuck it," said Willet. "Wouldn't spontaneous human combustion be covered under the 'Act of God' clause?"

"Obviously you're joking, but it sure as hell isn't moral hazard, either," said Carney. "Who files for homeowner's damage and claims it was moral hazard? We didn't force them to take out a policy. I didn't shove an M-80 up that dude's ass. Maybe the wife did it."

"She was in Mexico," said Lamont. "And you're a little too stoned for this time of day."

"You're right," said Carney. "I need a couple weeks off. Somewhere good, where the sun shines all day and there's no thunderstorms or tornados. They say Bali is nice."

"Two words," said Willet. "Tidal waves."

"One word," said Lamont. "Suicide. Can you imagine a guy so full of self-hate and loathing that he'd douse himself with lighter fluid and torch himself? And why didn't anything else in the room burn? Why didn't his feet burn up?"

"Fuck, man, it's just the dynamics of fire," said Carney. "The body burns up like a candle because of the fat content. When the fire uses up all the oxygen in the room, it goes out. In this case, there was just enough for it to burn down to the feet. Air currents in the room cause the heat to rise to the ceiling and melt the TV. No mystery to it. What about Isla Mujeres?"

"My girlfriend and I went there," said Willet. "We loved the place. But you might as well forget all about it, Carney."

"Why?"

"Because with this kind of backlog and the hiring freeze, we're still gonna be wading through cases by the time hurricane season hits. We'll be working like dogs till we're wrinkled and gray, like old Rickstein."

"Frankly, Willet," said Carney, "I'd rather burst into flames."

They howled and giggled for several minutes. As they passed around the crime scene photos of the incinerated executive, their mirth gradually faded. Finally, Lamont put the photos back in the file and they quieted down and the color began to leave their inflamed cheeks and they went back to work.

They worked quietly and semidiligently until deep in the night. Even when Willet accidentally set the timer on the microwave oven for two extra minutes and the bag of popcorn burned until the stench stung their noses, no one said anything.

BOTTOMED OUT

BY DEAN JAMES

Dallas

Jared Lakewood opened the door to his new walk-in humidor and smiled. He had maxed out his last two credit cards and cratered his savings account to have it built and to stock it properly, but his holiday bonus would probably cover it all. Two months to sweat out the payments, and then he'd be clear.

He surveyed the shelves of cigars. Twelve hundred, numerous varieties, minus the five he had smoked over the past couple of days. At the rate he smoked—usually five a day—he would burn through them in less than a year. He would restock long before he reached that point though.

He selected one of his favorites, a La Gloria Cubana Serie R No. 7 Maduro, and took it with him back into the living room. He clipped and lighted the cigar before pouring a double shot of Talisker single malt. The contents of his liquor cabinet were another hefty expense, but worth it, he reflected as he sipped the Talisker and smoked his cigar.

Jared went to the window and gazed down Turtle Creek Boulevard at nighttime. He loved the view of Dallas from here, and he was only a few blocks from work.

He thought about his father. Today would have been the old man's sixty-fifth birthday. He had died seven years ago while Jared was in college, working two jobs to pay his own way through school.

Jared raised the glass of Scotch at the window. "Hope you're still roasting in hell, you bastard." He took another drink before drawing on his cigar. He watched smoke swirl into the air.

The old man would shit his pants if he could see his only son now. Andrew Lakewood had barely scratched out a living on his Georgia farm. His disowned faggot son brought down more money a year than Andrew probably had made in twenty years of backbreaking, soul-destroying labor.

Living well *was* the best revenge, Jared thought. If his dad were alive, he'd rub the asshole's face in it. Especially if the old man needed money. Jared could laugh at him and tell him to fuck off.

Thoughts of his father invariably brought back the memories he wished he could erase. The beatings started when he was seven. They didn't stop until Jared, at seventeen, told his father he was gay. After that Andrew wouldn't touch him, afraid of the blood.

He had no contact with his parents once he left for college in Houston. His father never wanted to see him again. His mother was too worn down to object.

Jared's head throbbed. The images burned into his brain, taunted him until he wanted to smash his hand through the glass of the window before him.

Instead he gulped down the rest of the Scotch in his glass and went back to the liquor cabinet for a refill.

Sometime later, thanks to the liquor and the cigar, Jared would feel calmer. Now, however, his thoughts turned to sex. He had no time for hookups during the week, but on Friday night he was more than ready to find a partner for the evening.

He changed into his leathers, feeling his adrenaline surge

a bit. Tall, muscular, handsome, he always had plenty of guys hitting on him. In the elevator, he frowned at a young couple who got on a couple of floors after him. They eyed his leathers and didn't look too thrilled to be cooped up with him.

Fuck you, he thought. He didn't apologize to anyone about being gay. Nor about liking his sex rough. Fuck them if they can't handle it.

Down in the garage he slid into his Porsche Boxster. Only ten payments to go, and it was all his. He guided the Boxster out of the garage and down the street. Destination: the Eagle, his favorite leather bar.

When he awoke around one on Saturday afternoon, Jared smiled. He felt great. Sessions like the five-hour one last night always put him in a good mood. The guy he brought home from the bar—Marcus? No, Martin, funny accent, maybe German?—had been an amazing bottom, willing to take all the pain Jared could inflict. He'd like to get his hands on Martin for another round, but the pig would need some time to heal before he could play like that again.

After some lunch he fired up a cigar, poured a little Scotch, and sat down to look over his bills. By the time he finished, he had a roaring headache. Dealing with his finances always affected him this way. In a couple more months, though, he could ease things up with his bonus. No sweat.

On Monday morning as Jared drove through the garage to the street exit, he glanced over at the elevator where a tall man was stepping out. The glimpse he had was only a brief one, but Jared could have sworn the guy was Martin, his trick from Friday night.

He had to be seeing things. He'd kept the guy blindfolded

on the drive home, until they were safely inside his apartment. Same procedure when he drove the guy back to the bar afterward. There was no way the trick could have figured out where he lived. Jared shrugged. Couldn't be the same guy.

He pulled into the street and drove the few blocks to work. He could have walked, but he took the car whenever he could.

He exited the elevator on his floor at work at eight-thirty. As he passed the break room on the way to his office, he glanced inside. Peter was there, chatting away with Amy Conover, executive assistant to the CEO.

Jared shook his head. He never had to indulge in gossip himself to find out what was going on in the firm. Peter always did it for him.

A few minutes later, Jared looked up from his computer to see Peter advancing with a cup of coffee. His assistant set it down on the desk in front of him before taking a seat nearby.

Jared sipped at the coffee while Peter launched into the day's schedule. Peter was efficient; Jared had to give him that. Hardworking too, though inclined to whine a bit when Jared asked him to do personal errands for him. But Peter didn't dare refuse outright. He knew Jared would find a way to make him pay for it if he did.

The schedule finished, Peter sat there staring at Jared, obviously bursting with gossip.

"Okay, what's the big news?" Jared leaned back in his chair and drank his coffee. If he didn't let Peter yammer away about whatever it was, he'd be sulky all day long.

"Some guy from the European division is here. Big corporate honcho, some kind of troubleshooter," Peter said, eyebrows arching. "They're saying that McCallister"—the CEO of the Dallas division of the energy company—"brought him in especially to shake things up. Amy says the board isn't happy with the Dallas office, and there are going to be some changes."

"Big whoop," Jared replied, unimpressed. "They're always complaining about something." He was one of the top performers in his division. And one of the youngest. They'd be making him an executive VP soon, he figured.

"I don't know," Peter said with the know-it-all grin that irritated the fuck out of Jared. "I wouldn't be too sure about that."

Jared stood to pull some keys from his pocket. He threw them across the desk at Peter, who caught them deftly. "Sometime this morning I need you to pick up my dry cleaning. You can drop it off at my place on the way back."

Peter rolled his eyes, and Jared ignored him. Jingling the keys for a moment, Peter sat there. Abruptly, he stood. "I wouldn't get too complacent if I were you, Mr. Lakewood, sir. After all, your numbers have been down for two quarters now."

With that he flounced out of Jared's office.

"Bitch." Jared flung the word after his assistant, but Peter didn't respond. The door shut firmly behind him.

Jared turned back to his computer. He tried to shrug off Peter's barb, but it had found its target. His numbers had been down, despite his best efforts, and for a moment he felt uneasy. But then his usual confidence reasserted itself, and he dismissed the thought. Peter was needling him because Jared was making him pick up his clothes.

Jared focused on his work. He had a meeting at ten he needed to be ready for. That was far more important than his prissy queen of an assistant.

Peter lingered over lunch at his favorite restaurant a few

blocks from work. If the arrogant prick sent him on personal errands, then he shouldn't complain if his assistant spent over an hour to eat his midday meal. Besides, Peter enjoyed the growing anticipation. He grinned as he walked to his car. Now he couldn't wait to get to Jared's apartment.

Picking up the dry cleaning didn't take long. Peter parked on the street in front of Jared's building and lugged the clothes to the elevator. He should handle them more carefully—he was probably toting about fifteen thousand dollars' worth of suits. How on earth did the jerk afford them? Peter knew his boss's salary, and he was pretty sure Jared spent every dime he made, and more.

Inside the apartment Peter stowed his burden carefully in the master bedroom closet. Then he took a stroll around, ending up in the bedroom that Jared had turned into a sexual playground. He examined the new humidor in the closet, trying to add up the cost. He was tempted to help himself to a couple of the cigars, but Jared probably counted them every day and would figure out who swiped them.

He slowly closed the door to the humidor behind him and leaned against it. Jared had that look about him this morning when he walked into the office—the look that told Peter he had scored in a big way over the weekend. Peter couldn't wait to see the video.

Two weeks ago, with Jared safely in the Big Easy, Peter installed a video camera in the playroom. He congratulated himself on his clever work in placing it so that Jared would have a hard time ever spotting it. He mounted it under one of the shelves of sex toys, figuring that in the dim lighting of the playroom Jared would easily overlook it. He had reset it Thursday morning when he had to retrieve some papers Jared left at home that morning.

He detached the camera, an expensive device that fit in the palm of his hand. He figured the investment was worth it though. He'd soon give the asshole a taste of his own medicine *and* get a better job out of it at the same time.

Back in his car again, he turned on the camera to watch some of the video. There were some scenes of Jared going into the humidor for cigars. Peter fast-forwarded to get to the good stuff.

A few minutes later, Peter knew he had hit the jackpot big time. Jared had royally fucked himself with his choice of sex partner. When Jared found out about the tape, Peter would enjoy every second of it.

Jared frowned at the clock. It was nearly a quarter past two. Where the hell was Peter? He should have been back by now. He buzzed again.

"You rang, boss?" Peter stuck his head in.

"Where the fuck have you been all this time?" Jared stood. "I expected you back by one-thirty at the latest. I need you to finish putting together that report for the three o'clock meeting."

Peter rolled his eyes. "Had to wait in line at the cleaners. Relax. The report's almost done. It won't take me ten minutes to finish it." He stepped back and shut the door.

If Peter wasn't so good at his job, Jared reflected, he'd have already fired his tight little ass. He was a pushy bottom, no doubt about that. Jared grinned, thinking of the couple of times he had Peter in his playroom—*before* he hired him as his assistant, of course. It didn't pay to fuck around with coworkers.

Ten minutes later Jared walked out of his office to Peter's desk. Peter looked up with an I-told-you-so grin.

"All done. Just sent the job to the big printer, and it'll be ready in a few minutes."

"I'll go." Jared headed down the hall to the printer and copy room. He needed to stretch his legs anyway, work off a little tension before the meeting.

As he neared the printer room, he glimpsed a tall blond man entering an office at the end of the corridor. Jared paused, frowning. There was something familiar about that head and back.

He was waiting for the collated and stapled copies of the report to spit out when it hit him. That back and head belonged to Martin, the guy he had tricked with on Friday.

Fuck it, this was getting nuts. Was he on some kind of weird trip? Was he really seeing this guy?

First at his high-rise, now at work.

What the hell was he doing *here*?

The report forgotten for the moment, Jared walked back to his office. Peter was on the phone, big surprise. He hung up as Jared approached.

"Not finished yet," Jared said, stopping by Peter's desk and looking down at his assistant.

Peter shrugged. "Shouldn't take that long, unless someone else is running a big job."

"Go check on it for me." Jared turned away to step into his office, but turned back as if an afterthought had struck him. "By the way, I spotted a really tall blond guy going into Treadwell's office. Somebody I haven't seen around before. You have any idea who he is?"

Peter coughed suddenly and put his hand over his mouth. It took him a moment to speak. "Oh, it's probably the hatchet man from London. You know—the one I told you about this morning."

Jared frowned, his unease growing. "What's his name?"

"He's German. Name is Martin Leitner." Peter raised an eyebrow. "Supposed to be hard as nails, especially when it comes to firing people. Or so Amy says." He stood. "Well, I'd better go check that report, boss. Back in a few." He scurried down the hall, coughing again.

Jared barely heard him as he went into his office and shut the door.

Shit, shit, shit. For a moment, that was the only word he could form in his mind. *Shit, shit, shit.*

He had really screwed himself this time. The man he tricked with Friday night—the man whose back and ass he had practically beaten until they were bloody—had it in his power to fire him.

He began to sweat.

Jared spent the week terrified. He had yet to encounter Martin Leitner face-to-face in the office. What the hell should he do when he finally met the man? Pretend the weekend never happened? Or give him a knowing glance and be cool about their shared sexual tastes?

If Leitner tried to fire him, Jared could threaten him with the details of their time together.

Then he realized the stupidity of that. Exposing Leitner would screw his chances even further. He would definitely get fired then.

The axe fell on Friday morning. Around noon, a security guard showed up with a pink slip. He gave Jared an hour to box up any personal stuff and then escorted him out of the building. Peter had disappeared, and other coworkers looked away as Jared walked past their desks on the way to the elevator.

Lunch that day consisted of two-thirds of a bottle of

Talisker and a couple of cigars. When Jared awoke from a Scotch-induced nap, it was nearly five. Though his tongue felt furry and his head ached, he finished the bottle of Scotch and smoked another cigar. All he could think about was paying Leitner back for firing him.

But how?

When the doorbell rang around five-thirty Jared stumbled to the door. He peered out the peephole and couldn't believe it. Martin Leitner was standing there.

What the fuck?

His head suddenly clearer, Jared opened the door and stepped back. Leitner walked into the room and turned, waiting for Jared to shut the door.

"Good evening, sir," Leitner said, staring down at his feet. "I trust you will overlook this intrusion, sir, but I think we must talk."

"You're damn right we should talk, you fucking German pig." Jared felt his blood pressure rising.

"Yes, sir," Leitner said, his head still down. "I understand your anger, sir, but I will do my best to explain."

Jared walked into the living room to his leather armchair. He pointed to the sofa as he sat. "You can sit there, pig."

"Thank you, sir." Leitner sat. For the first time he raised his eyes to meet Jared's.

Jared tried to read the man's expression but failed. His words were submissive, but something about that gaze wasn't.

A memory from earlier in the week surfaced. "I saw you in the garage here on Monday morning. What were you doing here?"

"I have rented a flat in this building, sir. Before we met on Friday, of course. I did not know you lived here too, sir, until today." Leitner smiled. "Purely a coincidence—but perhaps a convenient one."

Convenient for me to beat the hell out of your ass again, Jared thought.

"Why the fuck did you fire me?" Jared had to keep control, show the German who was master here.

"I regret, sir, I had no choice." Leitner regarded his host coolly.

"What does that mean? You fired me because we had sex."

Leitner shrugged. "In a way, yes, sir. But it is more complicated than that."

"How so?" How could it be more complicated? "Explain it to me, asswipe."

"Yes, sir, I will. Your assistant, Peter, he has betrayed you, but I am sure you were not aware of this."

"That little cock-sucking queen." Jared thought for a moment the top of his head would come off. Then he realized he still didn't quite understand. "Betrayed me? How?"

"He has a video of the two of us and the time we spent together last weekend."

"So he hid a camera in the playroom." Jared felt stupid. He never should have trusted Peter, let him come into the apartment on his own. "I fucked myself."

The German nodded. "It was all rather easy, I gather, sir. He came to me on Thursday with the video. He said he is prepared to send it to the entire board of directors and the CEOs of all the divisional offices."

"He wants my job, doesn't he?" Jared stared hard at his guest.

"I suppose so, sir. His main intention seemed to be to make you lose your job. He hates you, sir." Leitner regarded him, his expression blank.

"He'll hate me even more when I get through with him," Jared said.

"Just so. Sir." Leitner smiled, and Jared felt a chill along his spine. "I have arranged for Peter to arrive here in about thirty minutes. He thinks that he is going to help me over-power you so that we can take you into your playroom and treat you the way you treat your bottoms. He is quite excited by the thought of this."

"But that's not going to happen." Jared was going to beat Peter raw and bloody.

"No, sir, it is not." Leitner gave that cold smile again. "Peter is the one who will suffer." He pulled a palm-sized camera from one of his pockets. "I will record it all, and Peter will be neutralized."

"Why are you willing to go along with this?"

"I will submit to men such as you. It is my choice, and I would do it again. But no one blackmails me." The flat tone was menacing.

"You think there's any chance of me getting my job back after all this?" Jared didn't dare hope, but perhaps Leitner could make it happen with Peter out of the way.

"We shall see, sir." Leitner rubbed his crotch while staring right into Jared's eyes. Jared could see the outline of the German's cock through his tight jeans. "I am sure you can convince me somehow."

Did Leitner expect him to be the bottom next time?

Fuck that.

Jared had two more shots of Scotch. Leitner turned down any offer of drink. Jared left him alone in the living room for a few minutes while he changed into his leather gear.

By the time a smirking Peter arrived shortly after six, Jared felt like he was vibrating with rage. The moment Peter was inside the apartment, Jared grabbed him around the neck and twisted his right arm behind his back. Peter squealed loudly. Then he yelled at Leitner to help him.

Leitner didn't respond.

Jared picked Peter up and carried him, kicking and protesting, into the playroom. Leitner followed.

Inside the playroom Jared threw Peter on the floor and kicked him twice in the side. Peter screamed and appealed again to Leitner for help.

Leitner stood over Peter. "You are getting what you deserve, you fucking little cunt." He reached down and slapped Peter hard across the face.

Peter stopped making noise. He lay mute, terrified.

Jared, with Leitner's help, stripped a now-docile Peter and put him in the sling. They slid restraints on his wrists and ankles, and Jared forced a ball gag into his mouth. A big one that would make it difficult for Peter to do more than grunt. Leitner suggested a hood. Jared found a latex one with holes only for the nostrils. He forced Peter's head into it.

Jared stood back and gloated at the sight of his former assistant, now completely helpless. This was going to be one fucking awesome scene. By the time he and Leitner finished with Peter, the little bitch would be lucky if he could crawl out of Jared's apartment.

"Be right back," Jared said in a low voice to Leitner.

The German nodded. He was doing something with his camera, and Jared left him to it.

Jared opened a new bottle of Scotch and took it back to the playroom. He also helped himself to a fresh cigar. After three swigs of Scotch, he set the bottle out of the way. He was ready.

Exhaling smoke, he set to work. Soon he was flying high.

The more Peter writhed in pain, grunting like the pig he was, the harder Jared played him.

Jared was dimly aware that Leitner was always nearby, moving around the room as he filmed. But little else intruded into his concentration on Peter.

Finally Jared had to take a break. He needed a fresh cigar, for one thing, and water. He had sweat so much he was dehydrated.

"Back in a minute."

Peter lay mute in the sling, one leg twitching a little. Faint moans came through the latex hood.

Jared stumbled into the kitchen as he came down from the extended high. His hand trembled while he filled a glass with water. He gulped down two of them and felt a little better.

Back in the playroom he decided he wasn't ready for another cigar yet. His mouth tasted like ash. Feeling his energy coming back, he wanted to go another round with Peter. He had more to do to him. A lot more.

But first he wanted another Scotch. Might as well finish off the bottle. Leitner stood by, camera poised and ready.

Jared grabbed the bottle, about a third full, and chugged it down.

Tastes a bit odd, he thought. *I've been smoking too much.*

He dropped the empty bottle on the floor and moved back to the sling. Glancing down at Peter, he realized something was wrong.

The latex hood was twisted. The holes for the nostrils were in the wrong place. Peter's nose was completely covered.

His hands shaking now, Jared adjusted the hood, moving the holes back to their proper place.

Jared shook Peter's leg. "Peter. Wake up. Peter."

There was no response.

Jared shook the whole sling. Peter's body bounced around, but it lay still when Jared let go of the sling.

"Fuck, fuck, fuck." Jared turned to find Leitner regarding him, that cold smile back on his face. "I think he's dead."

"I believe you are correct. Sir." Leitner laughed.

Jared glanced at the German's hands.

Why was Leitner wearing latex gloves? He hadn't been wearing them before.

Had he?

Jared shook his head. He was having difficulty remembering. Thinking.

Getting a little hard to breathe.

He reached out toward Leitner.

Stumbled to his knees.

Stared up at the German.

Leitner smiled down at him. "It will end soon. You will go to sleep. Sir." He held something out to Jared. A bottle.

Though his hand and arm felt too heavy to lift, Jared grasped the bottle.

What was happening to him?

"Thank you. I needed your fingerprints on the pill bottle. You Texans are arrogant, yet you are most helpful. It is quite an amusing paradox." Leitner laughed, and the sound made Jared want to cry.

Leitner walked away.

Jared tried to crawl after him, but his limbs were too heavy. He passed out on the floor, the bottle still in his hand.

CRANK

Ito Romo

San Antonio

He was fucking scared. No shit. Really scared. Although he was in his mid-thirties, he'd never done such a thing before—picked up a woman at a bar, driven her crosstown to the west side to buy cocaine. Never. Never even done coke himself. But he did what she wanted him to. He was horny. Hadn't had a girlfriend for over a year now, and had been with the last one for twelve years. And he wasn't lucky with the ladies, always told his friends, "No, you don't understand, I have to chat them up first. I have to charm them."

But that night he didn't have much of a choice; testosterone had taken over, and although there were slim pickins, he made his move to the end of the bar where she was standing. She had a thumb hooked into the pocket of her jeans, and in her other hand she held a cigarette over the ashtray on the bar. It was late, closing time. The barkeep announced last call. And rather quickly—it had been easier than he'd thought it would be—they left the bar together, and he found himself driving his truck farther and farther away from familiar territory. She asked him to get money for the dope. He drove to the closest bank and withdrew forty bucks, guaranteeing, he thought, he'd get laid.

"Lights off," she said softly. "Turn your lights off and pull over. Yeah, right there, man. I see him. Ahí esta. Good. We lucked out."

He coasted to a stop. "Where?"

"Over there. Shhh . . . I'll be right back."

She opened the door, slipped out, then closed it really carefully and walked over to a car parked on the other side of the street, a little behind where they had rolled to a stop. Through the rearview mirror, he saw the car's door open slowly. A man stepped out, a gun stuck into his pants right above a big silver belt buckle, like a rodeo champion. The revolver sparkled in what little light shone from the moon shrouded in silvery clouds.

The windows fogged up quickly, the air hot with alcohol and adrenaline. Inside the cab of the truck, it smelled like a bedroom after two very drunk people had sex.

He was scared. "And all for pussy, all for pussy," he whispered, eyes darting from the rearview to the mirror on the driver's-side door, then ahead of him.

Suddenly she tapped at the window as he zoned, drunk, focusing on what he thought was someone inside a car two vehicles ahead. He twitched, then adjusted his vision, squinted to make out her face through the clouded window, had to double-check; the streetlamp had been shot out. Her earring clinked against the glass.

He rolled down the window. Even in this dark craziness, she looked beautiful, like a movie star, like a young Sophia Loren. Thumb hooked into her jeans pocket again. She had sad eyes, he thought, pleading and lost.

"Give me the money, man."

"What? How much, how much?"

"Twenty, thirty, whatever. C'mon, man. He's waiting."

"Well, I'm a little uncomfortable—"

"Shhh . . . just gimme the money, man, come on." She

placed her hand on his mouth, pressed down hard like she meant business. It hurt a little. "Shhh . . . just gimme the money, man. He's waiting. I gotta give him some money now or he's gonna get mad at the *both* of us. C'mon."

Her teeth clenched tight.

The urgency in her voice scared him. He fumbled through his shirt pocket, into which he had shoved the bills, and pulled out the two twenties, crisp, folded in half, fresh out of the ATM.

I'm gonna die. Dear Jesus, I'm gonna die, he thought, his upper jaw still smarting from her forceful grip.

She quickly counted the money he gave her and went back to the car across the street.

"Thank you, God. Gracias, Jesus Christo Redentor." She was jonesing, jonesing really bad.

"Here, babe, two big rocks. Smoke 'em, man. Break 'em up a little, then smoke 'em. You'll get the most mileage that way. It's good stuff. Promise. Good stuff."

"Thanks, Johnny Boy. You're my man. You always got my back. Thanks, man."

"Hey, Sonia, do me a favor. Don't bring that dude back here no more."

"No, Johnny Boy. He's cool. Promise. He's cool. He's all square, man. He works at a bank. Don't worry."

"Don't bring 'im here no more. Okay, mi morenita?"

"Okay, papacito. Love you, man."

She put two fingers to her lips to flick him a kiss and went back to the truck. He would've hurt her if she had come here with no money—not badly, but he would have slapped her a couple of times. She knew it. She'd seen him do it.

But she was beautiful, and this had always helped her.

He acts all nice and all, but he'd hurt me, just like that, she thought as she walked back to the truck.

In one hand she held the dope in a tight fist—tight, tight fist; the thumb of her other hand was hooked into her jeans pocket.

"Thank you, Jesus." She made the sign of the cross, and at the end, right at the end of the sign of the cross, right when she usually kissed her thumb as if holding the cross hanging at the end of a rosary, just as her mother had taught her to do, she kissed the sweet little plastic pouch and jumped back into the truck.

Once in, she put her face to her shoulder, sniffed her underarm. "Damn, I still smell like fish," she said. "I gotta quit that job, I swear. Let's get the hell outta here." She leaned over, kissed him, slipped him some tongue, let him know she was grateful for the money, for the ride, for bringing her all the way across town, and sat back. The dope was in her hands. She could feel it there. It reassured her. Made her happy.

He put the truck in gear and drove off slowly, didn't turn the lights on until the end of the block. He'd gotten the picture. He wasn't stupid.

She checked her underarm again. "Do I smell like fish? You know, fried fish. You know, like my work. Do I smell like Long John Silver's?"

He wrung the steering wheel. "No, you don't smell like fish."

"I told you I work at Long John Silver's, right?"

He nodded yes, kept his eyes on the road, afraid to get stopped. He thought, Not only am I drunk, but there's speed in the car now too. Fuck.

He had just wanted to loosen her up. Never thought it would be this dangerous. He could've gotten held up, hurt, the truck stolen. But no, had to go along with it, didn't I? he thought. I gotta get home. Gotta get home. Gotta get home. Gotta get home.

"I have a degree, you know. Aha, an associate's degree in food management. That's right, from City College on the east side. You know, right? You know St. Philip's, right?"

"Yes."

"I graduated in May. My grades weren't so hot. But I finished, didn't I?"

"Yes."

"What bank you work at?"

He thought up a lie, afraid now of the guy back there in the car, of her ilk.

"I work in real estate at the bank. Don't really have anything to do with money."

"Ooh, good. Yeah, me, I'm a home owner. That's what you mean by real estate, right?"

She pulled a cigarette out of her bag and lit up.

She didn't even ask me, he thought. He wanted to tell her not to smoke in his truck. Decided not to.

Be careful. Slow down, he thought. They got to a busy intersection. Slow down, slow down, he kept thinking.

"Take 35. Take the expressway," she said. "I really gotta pee."

"I can't get on the expressway right now, like this. I'm drunk. Too many cops. Can you hold it for ten minutes? We'll be at my house in ten minutes."

"Can't you pull over and let me pee? Just over there. Look, it's dark. Pull over, man. I gotta pee."

"I promise. We're five minutes from my house now. Okay? You okay with that?"

"Okay. Okay."

She really didn't have to pee, just wanted to get to his house and smoke the crank. He knew it and started getting angry, feeling upset, used. But just then, just as he turned the corner, her purse rolled over and popped open. He saw it in there, clear as day, a knife, a big one, a switchblade. So he shut up.

She looked at him as she grabbed her purse, put it back in order. Leered at him. Hated him for not pulling over. For such a smart man, banker, real-estater, whatever, he's a fucking idiot, she thought. Look at him, such a sissy, all scared and all. I ain't gonna hurt you, honey. I just wanna smoke a little of this shit, man. I just wanna get out and smoke a little of this shit. Fuck him. Like he can't pull over for just a minute? How much longer? How much longer?

"Hey, how much longer?"

"See that white house over there . . . on the right? That's my house." They pulled into the driveway. "Relax, we're here, we're here."

Yeah, shit, you relax with these little candies in your hand, motherfucker, she thought, you fucking relax. She was turning into a fiend, a monster, someone he had not recognized in that dark bar.

She jumped out of the truck and waited for him at the door. "Come on, man, I gotta pee, please hurry."

"I'm coming, I'm coming. Don't make so much noise. It's late. The neighbors—"

"You wanna fucking commotion? You wanna see what a commotion really is?" she said loudly.

He got the picture, hurried and unlocked the door, switched on the light.

She slipped in. "Where's your toilet?"

"Straight ahead, straight ahead. You'll see the door."

Just take the damn stuff and then I'm going to get you out of here, he thought. I promise, Jesus, get me out of this one and I'll never do it again, never, promise.

She came out of the bathroom rather quickly. He didn't even hear the toilet flush. "Do you have foil? Tin foil? I need some foil."

"What for?"

"To smoke this stuff. Come on. Get the foil."

"You smoke it? I thought you were supposed to snort that stuff?"

"Can you get the foil, please?"

He went to the kitchen. He wanted to find it, was desperate to find it, take it back to her, let her smoke her damn stuff, then get her the hell out of the house. He grabbed the box of foil and rushed back to the dining room where she was sitting at the table.

"Hey, get me a little plate, okay, like a coffee plate, you know, like for under a cup of coffee."

He ran back to the kitchen, pulled a saucer out of the dishwasher, ran back to the dining room.

She opened her hand. The little plastic baggie was stuck to her palm. She peeled it off, struggled with the tiny seal, finally opened it, and carefully poured the two crystals onto the plate.

"Give me the foil."

He handed her the box.

She reached for her purse, which she had set on the chair next to the one she was sitting in. Pulled out the switchblade.

He jumped back.

She giggled. "Hey, man, don't worry. I'm just gonna break this shit up, man. What'd you think? I was gonna slice you up, man? C'mon, man. You're silly, silly, real silly." She stared at him, pressed the button, and the blade switched open. She broke one of the crystals in two—*clink*.

"Fuck the foil," she said, and went back into her purse for

her pack of cigarettes. She pushed the little piece of crystal that looked like rock salt into the tip of the cigarette. Lit up. Her eyes rolled back into her head. They were solid white for a while, almost pearlescent, almost beautiful.

"Take a hit," she said. "Let me load it for you. Here. Look . . ."

"No, not really. Don't do that. Thanks. You do it all."

She pressed hard on the second piece to break it up into smaller bits, the blade flat on it this time, and when she did so, a few grains spilled off the plate onto the floor.

"Oh my God! What did I do? How much fell?" She pushed off the table and fell immediately to her hands and knees, touching the ground as if blind. Then she looked up at him suddenly, crazed, and asked, "Is somebody back there? Are the cops back there?"

Damnit, she's wigging out, he thought. "No, there's nobody back there. Promise."

"Let's go see."

"Okay." He took her to the back of the house, past the bathroom. Pulled her into both bedrooms. Showed her the closets. Pulled up the dust ruffle from around each bed. Made her look underneath. "See, no one's in here. I promise. No one's in here."

"What about outside? They're waiting outside, aren't they, the police?"

"No," he said loudly, almost yelling, exasperated. "Come and see for yourself." He pulled the curtain aside, yanked up the blind. Nothing there. She saw. Just a backyard. Plain backyard. Not even a dog.

Then she looked at him, dazed, stoned, and slurred, "I thought your house was bigger, you know, being a banker and all."

She turned away from him and started walking, slowly,

headed back to the dining room, almost as if she were floating, sat down at the table, but in the chair opposite the one she'd been sitting in.

"So I can look back there," she said, pointing to the back of the house. "Wanna make sure no one's back there. You sure no one's back there?"

He stared at her. Started hating her.

She smoked the rest of the crank. With every hit, her eyes rolled back into her head. Smoked it all except for two crystals still on the saucer.

He started wondering if she'd been casing the house, acting wasted, paranoid, looking for vulnerable places, entries, windows her gun-toting friend could break in through in the middle of the night, kill him. For what? he thought, my TV, my VCR, my computer, my DVD player, my poor, dead mother's silver? He thought Johnny Boy might even be on his way over already, right now. He trembled, barely, but visibly now, visibly, at least to him—angry, truly afraid for his life. She puffed away.

"Positive," he said. "You saw yourself. No one's back there."

He was now beginning to think that she was going to overdose. She'd smoked so much. It seemed too much. He'd never done it, but he knew what speed could do to a person. He'd seen the movies. Seen the special report on *Nightline*, "The Meth Crisis." He imagined her heart pumping faster and faster, harder and harder, then stopping. Just like that. He closed his eyes. Should I call an ambulance? What'll I do if she ODs? How do I explain it to the police? Jesus, help me, he thought.

"Haven't you smoked enough of that stuff?"

She looked at him, one eye closed. "What? You pay for this

shit?" Then she giggled, remembering that he had. "Just kidding, amigo, just kidding. Sit down with me." Stoned. Wasted. Gone. Here. Come. "Sit right here, my sweet papaya. Close to me." She patted her hand on the seat of the chair next to hers, then pulled another cigarette from her purse, pushed the last two pieces of rock into the tip.

He sat down.

She caressed the inside of his thigh, made her way up to his crotch. Smiled sweetly. Lit up.

"Oh, sweet little jewel," she said.

"Why are you so quiet?" she asked him, coming out of her stupor, as she had done a few times during the ride to get her home, enough to let him know where to take her. Back to the same neighborhood they'd been the night before. He thought about dropping her off at a bus stop, dumping her. It would've been easy enough, she seemed so lifeless, wasted. But he couldn't do it. He'd take her home even if it meant going back to that part of town. He'd take her home. Get rid of her. Anything to get rid of her.

"I'm tired, that's all," he answered. No interest in talking with her, angry, really angry now that the sun was out, now that it was light, now that he felt safe.

"Hey, don't worry. I know lots of guys who can't get it up sometimes. No big deal. Get some Viagra," she said to him rather lucidly, giggling. This made him even angrier.

He pulled down the visor—the strong, early morning, South Texas sun blinding him. He could barely see where he was going. Even now, still a little drunk. In shock. Still nervous. Edgy. Knew he wouldn't be all right until she was out of the truck. Away from him. His life. His home.

She nodded off again.

"Hey, wake up," he said to her a few blocks later, shaking her rather severely, a little too hard. "You have to tell me where we're going. Wake up. Don't fall asleep."

She opened her eyes slightly, dazed. "Where are we? Oh, yeah, up there. I see. Up there. Take a left on Zarzamora. Just up there. Yeah, right up there. Up there," she repeated, pointing in no particular direction. "Yeah, one more block. Right here. Turn. Right there. Yeah, just right there on the left. Yeah, drop me off right there. That's my momma's house. She's dead now. Dead. She left it to me. The house, that house, the white one with the red roof. Que pretty, right? Yeah, that one. Right here."

She leaned over, tried to kiss him. He turned away. She laughed, got out slowly, slammed the door shut.

THE DEAD MAN'S WIFE

BY BOBBY BYRD

El Paso

Alex opened his eyes. The sunlight was creeping from around the heavy motel curtains. He shut his eyes and opened them again. Same thing. He was on the edge of a king-sized bed. He was naked and uncovered. Curled up like a dead baby. He could feel her warmth pushing up against him. He stuck a thumb in his eye and rubbed. Six hours before, the two of them had begun their postorgasm journey on the other side of the bed next to the night table, she asleep in his sweaty arms. But during the night they had migrated eight feet, him inching away from her, her tracking his warmth. A long nighttime journey.

As if, Alex thought, *she was stalking me in her sleep.*

But he didn't feel happy with himself. He wasn't even satisfied, whatever that meant. Maybe Alex considered satisfaction some form of forgiveness. Some form of hope.

He pushed himself up and sat on the edge of the bed, elbows on his knees. He cradled his head in his hands like it was a foreign thing—an egg in the wrong nest. Or the bloody head of Danton harvested from the basket behind the guillotine. Poor Danton. Robespierre was such an asshole. These were his strange thoughts. He stood up in the semidarkness and walked the narrow path to the bathroom. He grabbed his black boxer shorts. He didn't shut the door. He used his left hand to pee. The right hand scratched his chest.

Twice during the night he had gotten up to pee, and each time upon his return the woman had pulled him back again in her arms. Alex had drunk a lot of beer. They had gone to sleep around two and now it was seven or eight. So getting up twice to pee wasn't bad.

There were two plastic liters of water next to the sink. He took one and went to the table and sat down next to the window. The table was round with two uncomfortable chairs. Mexican chairs were always uncomfortable. He peeked around the curtain and looked at the morning. The desert sunlight made him shut his eyes. A few women walked with their children toward a church that must have been hiding behind storefronts—pottery, bathroom fixtures, tile, a bar named Café Soul. The street was filthy with Saturday-night garbage. There was a drunk asleep on the ragged grass in the median. Cars came and went in the freedom that Sunday morning brings. He was the dead man again. He wished he were north of the river. He wished he were home on his front porch drinking coffee.

But he wasn't. He had come across last night because it was the time of the month to get fucked. It was his ritual. The third Thursday of every month, nine p.m. Six months after his wife died, he started coming across. First, it was every few months. But after a while he made it a monthly ritual. A *ceremony of my confusion*, he called it. He knew two cab drivers. He was their friend. Or, more aptly, their "business acquaintance." He had met them through a friend of a friend. He wanted to be safe on the other side. And he had been hearing about the women disappearing. They were raped and killed and dumped in the desert or in vacant lots. No one was ever arrested. Sometimes the police didn't even find out who the woman was and where she came from. Nobody seemed to care. The victims were forgotten. Alex didn't want to think about those women. He wanted to come across and conduct his personal ceremony. He wanted to resolve this thing he called *confusion* in his body. So, thanks to the friend of the friend, he had searched out the two cab drivers. One was named Tony and the other was named Pete, and they were partners. Together they owned a beat-up green cab. A Plymouth four-door. Tony or Pete, one or the other, would be sitting in the No. 107 cab when Alex walked across the bridge. They would smile at each other and shake hands. Alex would get in the front seat and they'd go shopping. Alex was a two-hundred-dollar man, so Tony or Pete would take him to a two-hundred-dollar club and together they would choose a two-hundred-dollar whore and Tony or Pete would negotiate while Alex listened and then Tony or Pete would take Alex and his two-hundred-dollar whore to the Best Western on the Avenida de las Americas. The whole night would cost Alex maybe four hundred dollars. It was in his monthly budget. It was part of his life.

The two-hundred-dollar whore on the bed was Arcia, and she was feeling around in the dark for the man she had stalked in her sleep. She groaned. The man was no longer there. She didn't understand that the man was dead and that the dead man was sitting on a chair looking at her. She was naked and lying on her belly like she was swimming. She pushed herself high enough up to look around, her eyes blinking. She saw Alex and sighed, then fell facedown into the sheets again. Alex watched her turn over to look at him but he wasn't thinking about her.

He was thinking about a night ten years before. Maybe it was fifteen years before. He didn't care which. His wife was still alive, and they were holding hands. They were driving home on the old road between Las Cruces and El Paso. They had been to a dance party. They never went to dance parties. But this had been a special occasion. Some sort of fundraiser with an old-time C&W band. They had promised themselves that they would dance, and they had wandered around the floor with their stiff-legged waltz and clumsy two-step like they were driving bumper cars. The band had a very fat guy yodeling funky old songs. The fat man sat on the stool and sang with a wonderful tenor voice. The flaps under his chin trembled. The whole night the fat man never got up to pee. Alex and his wife loved the fat guy. On the way home they laughed and made up stories about the fat guy who had sung "Danny Boy" like he was Pavarotti. Alex had wanted to cry.

His wife said: "Let's take the old road. The freeway puts me to sleep." She usually wanted to get straight home.

"Sure," Alex said.

It was a beautiful black night with stars flickering. The old road was a two-lane blacktop that followed along the banks of the Rio Grande and swung back and forth through little farming towns. They came to the place where the road enters a huge pecan grove that stretches for miles. It was early summer, so the trees were fully clothed with leaves. The starry sky disappeared and they were driving through a cool and damp cavern. Alex slowed down to forty and rolled down his window. His wife did the same thing. They were quiet.

Halfway through the grove Alex pulled the car over to the gravelly shoulder and drove until he found a dirt road that ducked even deeper into the canopy of trees. He turned into the road. He turned off his headlights, but kept the parking lights on.

She said, "What are you doing?"

"I need to pee," he said.

"You and the fat guy," she said.

They laughed together, and he said: "Yeah, me and the fat guy."

He was quiet for a few seconds while he navigated the darkness. The road was mostly dry, but the groves where the trees stood were wet from irrigation a few days before.

He said: "Besides, it looks like a good place to pee." Alex was the kind of guy who took pride in pissing outdoors.

"Sure," she said.

He stopped the car and turned off the lights and the engine. He opened his door and got out and went searching for a good tree to lean against. He found one that seemed perfect to him. In the dark night it had a thick fleshy trunk and a bowl of dark leaves where the pecans and the stars hid themselves. While he listened to the sound of the pee falling into the dirt, he looked around. There was not much to see, just more darkness and the apparitions of rows and rows of pecan trees going about their business growing pecans. He felt like he was in a church. He was zipping back up when he heard her door open and shut.

She said: "Where are you?"

"Right here," he said.

Both of them were almost whispering. He could hardly see her. Her face and neck and the half-moon of her shoulders were riding above her black dress. They met halfway between the car and the perfect tree. They wrapped their arms around each other.

She asked him: "Was it nice?"

"Very nice."

She said: "I took my shoes off. The ground is wonderful. Here, let me take off yours."

And she kneeled down in the mud and pulled off one shoe

and sock and then the other shoe and sock. He put his hand on her head for balance. Yes, she was right—the muddy earth felt wonderful to his feet. She stood up and kissed him. He loved the taste of her lipstick. They walked down the corridor between two rows of trees. They held hands, they kissed each other, they stopped, and he felt her breasts. She had already taken off her bra and panties. She must have left them in the car. Standing up against the rough bark of a pecan tree, they made love in the pecan grove.

The drive home was quiet. They each had their own thoughts. As they turned up their street for the last few blocks before home, she reached over and grabbed his hand. She asked him: "When a man has an orgasm, where does that man go? It's like he's dead and somebody else takes his place. Sooner or later the dead man reappears, and he says hello to me. I see the dead man, and I'm glad he's come home."

That seemed like so long ago, and now Arcia, who was a young girl, probably younger than his very own daughter, was asking him: "¿Prenda las luces?"

"Por supuesto." And he asked her, "¿Como amaneciste?" His Spanish was formal and clumsy.

"Bien, bien," she said.

He reached over and flicked on the light on the table. It was a sixty-watt bulb, but it sprayed off enough light so that her nakedness embarrassed her. She reached up and covered her breasts with her small hands. But then she realized that her crotch with its finely trimmed tuft of hair was also uncovered. She sat up with a start and thrashed around for the sheets. She found them and pulled them up to her chin.

Alex smiled at her confusion. She was like a little girl. She was little girl. He said: "¿Cuantos años tienes?"

"None of tu beezness!" she said.

"¿Veinte? ¿Dieciocho?"

"Bah! None of tu beezness!" She pulled the sheets over her head.

"¿Tienes hijos?"

"No, no, no, no!" She threw a pillow at him and he ducked, laughing.

She was laughing now too. She said: "¡Cierra tus ojos!"

He grinned at his bashful prostitute and pretended to shut his eyes. But he didn't. He watched her jump out of bed and scurry around picking up articles of clothing and her purse. Her blouse was on a chair, her bra and black skirt were on the floor, her panties and stockings and shoes were under the bed. Everything was black. She had to get down on her hands and knees to look under the bed. Her buttocks bobbed up and down. He had enjoyed Arcia. They had talked for a while afterward. She told him not to ask her if she was in school. She said that all gringos asked her if she was in school. So they talked about her family. About her mother who worked as a maid on the other side. She didn't know her father. He went away to Gringolandia and he never came back. Then she had gone to sleep. Or maybe it was he who had fallen asleep. He couldn't remember.

After she had collected her possessions, she disappeared into the bathroom. He heard the bathtub filling up. He heard the toilet flush. He listened to her bathing herself. She was singing a song in Spanish. She was a little girl. She was his two-hundred-dollar whore. He pulled the drawstring on the curtains, and the sunlight poured into the room. He felt old and mean.

Once, after they had made love, this time in their bedroom, his wife had said to him: "I want to see the face of God." She had a warm washcloth in her hand and she was cleaning their crotches—first his, then hers. Back and forth. Her green eyes were ecstatic.

"The face of God?" He had reached up and touched her breast. Then he said: "Where is the face of God?"

"I don't know," his wife said. "But I think the face of God is right here in this room. I think we're staring at the face of God."

"How can that be?" he said.

"I don't know," she said, and she continued cleaning his genitalia with the damp, warm cloth.

The bathroom door opened, and Arcia stood there staring at him. She was barefooted. She was wearing only her bra and slip. Her hair was wet and her face was scrubbed clean. She let him look at her but she didn't say a word. She simply turned and faced the mirror. She studied herself and Alex watched her from his chair across the room. He knew Arcia also wore the face of God. This is what his wife would have understood. His wife had always been wiser than him. Arcia bent down over the hot running water and scrubbed her face some more with a scrub brush that magically appeared. Then she went to work with powder and mascara and eye shadow and lipstick. She carried all of the required tools and ingredients in her large leather purse. He picked up his chair and moved closer to her so that he could watch. She ignored him, but that was okay by him. He just wanted to watch. She worked for twenty minutes crafting her face.

When she was done, she turned and looked at him. She looked ten years older, she looked like a veterana. Her lips twisted into a smile. Or maybe it was a sneer.

She said: "¿Quieres más?"

"No," he said. He was lying. He could feel warmth in his face and he knew he was blushing. She was beautiful. But she was not the young girl he watched wake up in the darkness only an hour or so ago. "Maybe next month. En el mes que viene. The dead man is dead. You killed him last night. Remember? Pero estás muy guapa. Muy beautiful."

She screwed up her face. She knew what the word "dead" meant. This worried her. She didn't want him to be one of the strange men. She knew the stories about the dead women. But she knew he had more money. She always needed more money. She stepped into her black skirt and pulled it over her hips. She watched him while she did this. It was her performance. Then she put on her black blouse. She left all the buttons except one undone.

He looked at her. He could feel his sex moving inside him. And he felt ashamed.

He said: "Hay que tener cuidado. You must be careful."

"¿Cuidado?" she asked. She was sneering at him. "Soy cuidado. Todo el tiempo." And she shut the door in his face. He could hear her pissing into the toilet. It flushed, and she washed her hands. She was very careful. She opened the door. She was ready to go. The night was over.

He said: "¿Tienes hambre? ¿Quieres algo para comer?"

"¿Porque no?" she said with a little laugh. "Pero no estas listo. Ponga tu ropa, viejo." He still had on only his boxer shorts. His stomach was hanging over his legs. The hair on his chest was gray.

He said: "Okay. Okay. Dame un momento."

He started searching around for his clothes. She opened the door, and let the heat and light fill the room. He looked out the door and he wanted to go home. A man his own age with a belly protruding over his belt walked slowly past the window and by the door. He was wearing a cowboy hat and boots and a clean white shirt with gold cuff links. He looked at Arcia who was leaning against the doorjamb in her black clothes and high heels. The man peered inside the room like he was looking inside a refrigerator. He saw Alex in his boxers. The man turned back for his wife who followed behind him. At least Alex assumed it was his wife. She was wearing slacks and a shirt. A straw hat was perched on her head to protect her from the sun.

The man in the cowboy hat said: "Come on, honey. Hurry yourself along." He grabbed the woman's hand. The two women looked at each other, they were looking across a distance they couldn't comprehend, and then the man pulled his wife away.

Alex said: "Go on downstairs. Wait for me outside. Baja. Baja. El taxi está in the parking lot." He had lost all of his words and his jaw hurt. He was tired. Arcia glanced at him over her shoulder and moved outside to the railing of the concrete overhang. He pulled on his pants. He walked out the door where she was standing. He was barefooted and with only his pants on. He was very white. His hair was gray. The green taxi was downstairs in the parking lot. Number 107. Pete waved at him, and Alex waved back. He had known either Pete or Tony would be there because he owed them fifty dollars. That was part of the deal. Arcia saw the taxi too. She hung her purse on her shoulder and walked toward the stairs, her hips casually moving back and forth. She was very young and very beautiful in the desert's morning light.

ABOUT THE CONTRIBUTORS

Stephen Fisch

MILTON T. BURTON is a fifth-generation Texan, born in Jacksonville, Cherokee County. He has been variously a cattleman, college history teacher, political consultant, and an assistant to the dean of the Texas House of Representatives. His third crime novel is *Nights of the Red Moon*.

BOBBY BYRD—publisher, poet, and essayist—is the copublisher of Cinco Puntos Press in El Paso. Byrd is the recipient of the Lannan Fellowship for Cultural Freedom, an NEA Fellowship, the D.H. Lawrence Fellowship awarded by the University of New Mexico, and an International Residency Fellowship (NEA/Instituto de Belles Artes de México). He is also the coeditor of the nonfiction anthology *Puro Border: Dispatches, Snapshots, & Graffiti from La Frontera*.

JOHNNY BYRD is copublisher of Cinco Puntos Press in El Paso, and the coeditor of the anthology *Puro Border: Dispatches, Snapshots, & Graffiti from La Frontera*. As a Spanish-to-English translator, he translated the novel *Out of Their Minds: The Incredible and (Sometimes) Sad Story of Ramon and Cornelio* by Luis Humberto Crosthwaite. Byrd is also a freelance essayist, writing articles for online publications about culture and music.

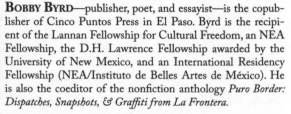

Pat Mazzara

DAVID CORBETT is the author of four acclaimed novels: *The Devil's Redhead*, *Done for a Dime* (a *New York Times* Notable Book), *Blood of Paradise* (nominated for an Edgar Award, named a Top 10 Mystery & Thriller of 2007 by the *Washington Post*; and a *San Francisco Chronicle* Notable Book), and *Do They Know I'm Running?* Corbett's story "Pretty Little Parasite" (from *Las Vegas Noir*) was published in *Best American Mystery Stories 2009*.

Gabino Cortez

SARAH CORTEZ was born and lives in Houston, where she is a police officer. Of Mexican, French, Comanche, and Spanish descent, her roots inform her poetry, fiction, and essays. Edward Hirsch described her award-winning collection *How to Undress a Cop* as "nervy, quick-hitting, street-smart, sexual." She is the editor of *Windows into My World: Latino Youth Write Their Lives*, *Hit List: The Best of Latino Mystery*, and *Indian Country Noir*.

Michael Gallacher

JAMES CRUMLEY (1939–2008) has been described as "one of modern crime writing's best practitioners" and "a patron saint of the post-Vietnam private eye novel." His characters Milo Milodragovitch and C.W. Sughrue have become part of the pantheon of the hard-boiled heroes of the noir genre. Do yourself a favor and read *The Last Good Kiss*, one of "the most influential crime novels of the last 50 years."

DEAN JAMES, a Mississippian long transplanted to Texas, has published numerous mystery short stories and has coauthored a number of award-winning works of mystery nonfiction. Writing under his own name and three pseudonyms—Miranda James, Jimmie Ruth Evans, and Honor Hartman—he has published fifteen mystery novels. He's earned a PhD in medieval history and an MS in library science. He currently works as a librarian in the Texas Medical Center in Houston.

Alex McVey

JOE R. LANSDALE is the author of thirty novels and twenty short story collections, and has won an Edgar Award, seven Bram Stoker Awards, the British Fantasy Award, and the Grinzoni Cavour Prize for Literature. His novella *Bubba Ho-Tep* has been made into a cult movie directed by Don Coscrelli. His latest novel is *Vanilla Ride*.

JESSICA POWERS is the author of *The Confessional*, a murder mystery set on the U.S.-Mexico border which "morphs silkily into a clever noir adaptation" (*Library Journal*). She grew up in El Paso, Texas, and currently lives in California.

Ricardo Gutierrez

ITO ROMO was born on the border in Laredo, Texas, in 1961. His recent work, dubbed "Chicano Gothic," shows the dark and gritty life along Interstate 35 through South Texas, where the road finally ends at the international bridge. Romo, a writer, painter, sculptor, and teacher, holds a PhD from Texas Tech University and is an associate professor of English at Northwest Vista College in San Antonio, Texas. He is the author of a novel, *El Puente/The Bridge*.

LISA SANDLIN was born in Beaumont, Texas, and grew up in that bayou refinery town near the Louisiana border. *The Famous Thing About Death* and *Message to the Nurse of Dreams*, both published by Cinco Puntos Press, reflect her background. Her book *In the River Province* (Southern Methodist University Press) is set in New Mexico, where she went to live after college. She teaches at the University of Nebraska at Omaha.

CLAUDIA SMITH grew up in Houston and spent many childhood summers in Galveston. Her collection *The Sky Is a Well and Other Shorts* won Rose Metal Press's short-short competition. Her second collection, *Put Your Head in My Lap*, is available from Future Tense Books. Her short-shorts and stories have been published in numerous places, including *New Sudden Fiction: Short-Short Stories from America and Beyond*. She now lives and writes in Hattiesburg, Mississippi.

JESSE SUBLETT, a native Texan, is a novelist and musician living in Austin. His Martin Fender detective novels are set in that city, and his band the Skunks is credited with helping put Austin on the international rock and roll map. Sublett has also written for film and television. James Ellroy described his memoir *Never the Same Again: A Rock 'n' Roll Gothic* as "a harrowing, wrenching, spellbinding work of great candor and soul."

Karen Arneson

TIM TINGLE, a member of the Choctaw Nation of Oklahoma, is a storyteller and writer. His collection of short stories *Walking the Choctaw Road* traces the history of the Choctaw Nation from the "Trail of Tears" until now. His illustrated book *Crossing the Bok Chitto: A Choctaw Tale of Friendship and Freedom* won numerous national awards, among them the 2008 American Indian Library Association Award for Best Picture Book. Tingle grew up in Pasadena, Texas.

Nina Subin

LUIS ALBERTO URREA has written many books, including the national best-sellers *The Hummingbird's Daughter* and *The Devil's Highway* (a 2005 Pulitzer Prize finalist). He has also won the Kiriyama Prize for fiction, a Lannan Literary Award, an American Book Award, a Christopher Award, and a Western States Book Award. Urrea lives with his family in the Chicago area, where he teaches creative writing at the University of Illinois, Chicago.

Dani Bezden

GEORGE WIER works and lives in Austin, Texas, with his wife Sallie. He is a writer, researcher, historian, and speaker in the narrow yet rich field of Texas crime history, as well as an up-and-coming author of crime and adventure novels.

Also available from the Akashic Noir Series

LOS ANGELES NOIR
edited by Denise Hamilton
360 pages, trade paperback original, $15.95
*A *Los Angeles Times* best seller and winner of an Edgar Award.

Brand-new stories by: Michael Connelly, Janet Fitch, Susan Straight, Patt Morrison, Emory Holmes II, Robert Ferrigno, Gary Phillips, Naomi Hirahara, Jim Pascoe, Héctor Tobar, Diana Wagman, and others.

"Akashic is making an argument about the universality of noir, it's sort of flattering, really, and *Los Angeles Noir*, arriving at last, is a kaleidoscopic collection filled with the ethos of noir pioneers Raymond Chandler and James M. Cain." —*Los Angeles Times Book Review*

BROOKLYN NOIR
edited by Tim McLoughlin
350 pages, trade paperback original, $15.95
*Winner of Shamus Award, Anthony Award, Robert L. Fish Memorial Award; finalist for Edgar Award, Pushcart Prize.

Brand-new stories by: Pete Hamill, Sidney Offit, Arthur Nersesian, Ellen Miller, Maggie Estep, Adam Mansbach, Nelson George, Chris Niles, Pearl Abraham, Norman Kelley, Nicole Blackman, and others.

"Brooklyn Noir is such a stunningly perfect combination that you can't believe you haven't read an anthology like this before. But trust me—you haven't. Story after story is a revelation, filled with the requisite sense of place, but also the perfect twists that crime stories demand. The writing is flat-out superb, filled with lines that will sing in your head for a long time to come."
—Laura Lippman, winner of the Edgar, Shamus and Agatha awards

INDIAN COUNTRY NOIR
edited by Sarah Cortez & Liz Martínez
288 pages, trade paperback original, $15.95

Brand-new stories by: Joseph Bruchac, Kimberly Roppolo, Jean Rae Baxter, David Cole, Lawrence Block, A.A. HedgeCoke, O'Neil De Noux, Mistina Bates, Melissa Yi, R. Narvaez, and others.

"In what comes as a pleasant surprise, most of the tales selected by [the] editors take place in a broader conception of America as Indian country—the entire northern continent, in fact . . ."
—La Bloga

BOSTON NOIR
edited by Dennis Lehane
240 pages, trade paperback original, $15.95
*Finalist for Edgar, Anthony, and Macavity awards.

Brand-new stories by: Dennis Lehane, Stewart O'Nan, Patricia Powell,
John Dufresne, Lynne Heitman, Don Lee, Russ Aborn, J. Itabari Njeri,
Jim Fusilli, Brendan DuBois, and Dana Cameron.

"In the best of the 11 stories in this outstanding entry in Akashic's
noir series, characters, plot and setting feed off each other like flames
and an arsonist's accelerant . . . [T]his anthology shows that noir can
thrive where Raymond Chandler has never set foot."
—*Publishers Weekly* (starred review)

CHICAGO NOIR
edited by Neal Pollack
260 pages, trade paperback original, $14.95

Brand-new stories by: Alexai Galaviz-Budziszewski, Achy Obejas, Joe
Meno, Amy Sayre-Roberts, Adam Langer, Peter Orner, Kevin Guilfoile,
Bayo Ojikutu, Claire Zulkey, Andrew Ervin, Todd Dills, and others.

"*Chicago Noir* is a legitimate heir to the noble literary tradition of the
greatest city in America. Nelson Algren and James Farrell would be
proud." —Stephen Elliott, author of *The Adderall Diaries*

LAS VEGAS NOIR
edited by Jarret Keene & Todd James Pierce
320 pages, trade paperback original, $15.95

Brand-new stories by: John O'Brien, David Corbett, Scott Phillips,
Nora Pierce, Tod Goldberg, Bliss Esposito, Felicia Campbell, Pablo
Medina, Lori Kozlowski, Preston L. Allen, Janet Berliner, and others.

"Just because mystery fans will be unfamiliar with many of the 16
contributors to Akashic's latest entry in its acclaimed noir series
doesn't mean the quality isn't up to volumes boasting bigger names
. . . This anthology does a fine job of illuminating the dark underbelly
of Sin City." —*Publishers Weekly*